THE NAKED
PHILOSOPHER

PAUL MARGOLIS

ARDEN
HOUSE
PUBLISHING

978-0-9967892-0-2 (paperback)
978-0-9967892-1-9 (eBook)
Library of Congress Control Number: 2015914760

Arden House Publishing
Los Angeles, California
ArdenHousePublishing@gmail.com

Cover Design: Virtually Possible Designs

For Becky—
Adored wife, best friend, pain in the ass
Forever and always, my inspiration

ACKNOWLEDGMENTS

S o many friends, old and new, helped make this book possible. I am tremendously grateful to each and every one, and hope they all will forgive me for not naming them here. However, there is one person I would like to single out for thanks, my father Joseph Margolis.

Like the character he inspired in the book, my dad is a well-known philosopher with a ferocious devotion to his work. (At 91, he is still teaching, writing and accepting speaking invitations all over the world, with no signs of letting up.) But that's where the similarity ends. With the exception of my father's intriguing philosophy, which I tried to thread into the mystery without detracting from it, everything in *The Naked Philosopher* is pure fiction.

So thank you, Dad, for letting me borrow your views on life, death and the human condition. Also, for sharing why they are so important to you—and should be to the rest of us. It took me a while to understand but I think I'm finally getting it.

+
PROLOGUE

Salazar walked into Terminal 5 at LAX clutching a small white teddy bear with a big red bow around its neck. The place was busy as usual: friends and family waiting to meet loved ones, tourists puzzling over guide books, limo drivers holding up signs, trying to match faces with names. This being Los Angeles, there were people of every color, class and ethnic background, a wonderful chaos of peaceful coexistence, the kind that might give one hope about the future of humanity—if one didn't know better.

With studied casualness, Salazar weaved his way over to the monitors showing the status of arriving flights. He took a few moments to look at the board without focusing on details. None of them mattered. All he cared about was giving the appearance, for the sake of the security cameras covering the hall, of being an Hispanic gardener or day laborer there to pick up his young son or daughter. Who would suspect a devoted father with a present for his kid? Salazar had learned the value of theatrical props during his four and a half years in Puente Grande Federal Prison near Guadalajara. Choosing the right ones helped him smuggle in the weasel dust and hydrocodone pills that kept him sane during his incarceration, as well as the crucifix shiv he used to cut the throats of two guards during his escape. Of course it didn't hurt that Salazar was also intimately familiar with police and surveillance procedures, having begun his crime career as an officer in the elite anti-kidnapping unit of the Mexican PF, the *Policia Federales*.

Confident he had blended in, Salazar wandered over to a corner and took in a full view of the Arrivals greeting area. He considered a pair of college-aged girls strolling by with heavy backpacks. Their Nordic features and carefree gait suggested European students on holiday, an excellent target. In another direction a man with a fake tan, loud shirt and Testoni loafers without socks made his way toward a rent-a-car counter. Gays with money were also good prey. A few other potential marks flashed across Salazar's radar.

Then Salazar saw what he was looking for.

To the untrained eye she was unexceptional: a brunette in her late twenties, attractive in a librarian sort of way, sporting a ponytail and glasses. Salazar discerned a stylish modesty in the young woman's sleeveless white tee and dressed-down khakis, purchased from somewhere like Banana Republic rather than higher end stores. Yet one detail about her stood out, assuming one had knowledge of such things. And

Salazar did. It was what made him so very good at his job. What distinguished the young woman was a folded magazine protruding from the red leather tote slung over her shoulder. It was a luxury lifestyle magazine called *Departures*, published by American Express for its most valued members, those who carried platinum and black Centurion cards.

The young woman appeared to be waiting for an arriving passenger. As she checked each one walking out of the security doors on the way to Baggage Claim, Salazar observed her body language, another skill picked up in prison. He noted the way she kept tucking her hair behind her ear while craning forward and biting her lip. Even a blind man could see she was waiting for someone she was involved with romantically, a romance with problems.

Seconds later the young woman straightened up. She stepped forward to embrace someone emerging from the Arrival doors, a distinguished-looking man in his early sixties carrying a worn leather satchel. The man appeared surprised to see her. At the same instant, the young woman realized the man was with another male passenger and converted her embrace to a handshake.

Salazar's soft, brown cow eyes continued to take it all in.

The distinguished-looking man betrayed a hint of coolness toward the young woman as he introduced her to his travelling companion, a pear-shaped colleague who fumbled with his carry-on bag to shake hands. Then the young woman led the two men away.

Salazar inhaled deeply, savoring the moment. This was the part of the job he most enjoyed, a guilty pleasure: watching people go about their business as usual, unaware that everything was about to change in a way that would shatter lives, sometimes end them.

Salazar headed for the exit, still no more than a face in the crowd. Not until he was outside the terminal, well past range of the security cameras, did he dump the teddy bear in the trash.

PART ONE

1

JACK

Jack killed the radio playing *A Whiter Shade of Pale* and pulled up to the Commerce Casino, the center of the poker universe just south of downtown Los Angeles. A medallion of St. Michael, the one Jack used to tuck into a pocket of his bullet proof vest, dangled from the dashboard as a female parking attendant breezed over with white and pink valet tickets. The pink ones were for high-end cars to be parked out front, less for added protection than for bragging rights. The valet took one look at Jack's '92 Jeep Wagoneer with the taped-together side mirror and handed him a white ticket.

"Good luck, sir."

Moments later Jack was seated in his 'office', a hundred dollar no-limit Texas Hold-Em table, with a fresh stack of chips and his usual breakfast: coffee, cheeseburger, side of pancakes. For the past three years Jack had come here five days a week to grind out a living. A grinder, that's what he was. Sometimes it took minutes to make his quota, sometimes hours, but as soon as he did he was out of there. No exceptions. That was his rule. He learned the hard way that higher-stakes games and dreams of the Big Score could get him into a pack of trouble.

Jack folded his first twelve hands including several he would have played back in the days when gambling was still about the thrill, a deluded test of self-worth. His mind returned to *A Whiter Shade of Pale* and its iconic opening line. *Skip a light fandango.* For the longest time, longer than he cared to admit, Jack thought it went *Skip the life and dangle.* That pretty much expressed the way he felt growing up. It also described what was going on in his life at the moment. Hell, for the last three years. Ever since being kicked off the force.

When a seat at the table opened up, it was filled by an unshaved grandpa with a walker, who was helped into the chair by his female caregiver who looked more like a hooker than nurse. The old man played like a drunk—chasing bad hands, exposing his cards, bleeding money—until Jack found himself pitted against him head-to-head, everyone else having folded.

"Raise!" Grandpa slurred.

Jack tapped the crooked slope of his aquiline nose, the brunt of endless jokes as a kid until he grew into it, and squeezed his cards to reveal a pair of queens, his favorite drawing hand.

"Call," he said.

The dealer burned a down card and dealt the flop. Then the turn. Then the river. Having checked every round, Grandpa stared at his hole cards in disgust, as if they would change.

"Check," he snapped.

With another queen on board for trip ladies, Jack was pretty confident he had a lock. Enough money in the pot to reach his quit number. His play was textbook.

"All in," he said.

"Call!"

Even before Jack reached for his chips, Grandpa turned over his hole cards to reveal a gutshot straight.

"Gotcha, donkey! Read 'em and weep!"

Jack could feel the blood rush to his face. The old boozer had chased with one of the worst hands in poker and caught a Hail Mary on the river. There was no justice in it. But, as often happened, injustice had won.

With a stoic shrug, Jack wrapped his half-eaten burger in a napkin for his freeloading roommate and drove home in silence. Once upon a time, Jack could pick up on tells no one else could. It made him a better-than-average card player and, before everything went bad, a damn good cop. But in poker, as in life, there was always the risk of over-thinking, of getting stuck on some wrong angle, especially in situations where emotions came into play.

Maybe someday he would learn, Jack thought.

He cruised north, through L.A.'s vibrant city center, then east into Chinatown where he parked and walked toward his place. Along the way Jack thought about hitting Eagle Nest "D" at the Angeles Shooting Ranges and killing a few paper bad guys. Later he might grab some broccoli spaghetti at Cynthia's Revels, a favorite food truck that frequented the area, then go out to one of those clubs in Hollywood where they still allowed smoking and lose himself in some local rock band that would never make it.

Jack reached the red door to his loft, wedged between a Laundromat and a souvenir shop that had gone out of business. As he pulled out his keys, a voice assaulted him from behind.

"Hey, shithead."

Jack turned. Crossing the street was a big ape of a guy in a biker jacket with a beard that looked like a squirrel clinging to a branch. It wasn't until the guy was right in his face, shaking his hand, that Jack recognized him.

"Franco?"

"How quickly they forget."

Detective Francis Russo, Franco to his friends, struck a mock pose with his arms spread wide.

"My home-grown terrorist look. You like? Kate says if I'm not off this case soon, she's taking the kids and leaving."

Jack grinned.

"Long time."

"Too long," Franco said. "Was hoping to run into you at Mike's barbeque but I guess you were busy, huh?"

"I was out of town last week."

"It was a month ago."

"I doubt I was missed."

"Becky was there."

Jack's grin faded.

"So what brings you down here, Franco? No Panda Express in your 'hood?"

Franco knocked a fist against his head.

"Remember those migraines I used to get? Been coming back lately. My chiro suggested some Chinese herbal thing."

Franco visit a chiropractor? No way, Jack thought, until Franco pulled out a doctor's prescription.

"Any idea where I can get this stuff?"

"Sure," Jack said. "C'mon."

Jack led Franco down the street to a Chinese pharmacy where the herbalist knew Jack and filled the order quickly. As they walked out, Franco, a bloodhound in another life, sniffed the contents of the pharmacy bag and made a face.

"So your poker thing. How's that working out?"

"Fine," Jack said. "Great."

"Still going to meetings?"

Jack nodded. A lie.

"What about you?" Jack said. "The new partner?"

"Not new. Three years now."

"Good fit?"

"What can I say? He's not you."

Franco glanced at Jack nonchalantly as they kept walking.

"So I was working this case last week and an opportunity came up. Thought you might be interested."

Here it comes, Jack thought. Migraines my ass.

"Maybe you forgot. I don't carry a shield anymore."

"Naw, hell, nothing like that," Franco said. "I was gonna say there's this gentleman's club that got robbed. The owner owes me a favor and, well, long story short they're looking for an assistant manager."

Jack frowned.

"Gentleman's club?"

"Okay, strip joint. But not the sleazy type. Obviously they're impressed by your background. Don't worry, it wouldn't be a glorified security guard thing. Steady paycheck, maybe benefits. Maybe a free lap dance. Hey, I'm kidding."

All Jack could do was shake his head.

"So it's come to this," he said.

"No pressure. Check it out is all I'm saying."

"You must think I'm desperate."

"Naw," Franco said. "I just think you're stuck."

Jack felt a nerve being hit.

"Franco, I appreciate the offer—"

"But what? Too busy atoning? Still laying low in case anyone thinks those freakin' lies about you were true? Wake up and smell the coffee, Jack. Stop waiting for some come-to-Jesus moment. Close the door and move on before you dig yourself a hole you can't get out of."

Jack didn't answer. Having opened the floodgates, Franco got ready to give him another piece of his mind. But something—maybe the look in Jack's eyes or maybe that Franco didn't believe what he was saying, that he still had questions about what went down three years ago, questions he had never asked Jack—made him stop himself.

"Okay, Jack. I tried."

The two men walked on in silence. It was the same overwrought hush Jack remembered from their under-cover days, when they would take position before raid-ing a crack house or meth lab. By the time they got back to Jack's place and he fumbled out his keys, the silence was deafening.

"Good seeing you, Franco."

"You too, Jack."

"Give Kate a hug for me."

"Hey buddy—"

Franco waited for Jack to look at him.

"Promise if you need anything—"

"I'll call."

"Call anyway."

They locked eyes, both knowing it would be a long time, if ever, before they saw each other again. Then Franco broke his gaze, bumped fists with Jack and walked away.

Jack winced at the keys in his hand. He knew he had come across cold but it was better that way. The last thing he wanted was for Franco to worry about him anymore. Of all people, the one who stuck by him in his darkest hour, even when Jack had given up on himself. Hadn't he put his ex-partner through enough? Better to let Franco think he was shut down, had stopped caring, than for him to know how deep the hurt ran. Still. The hurt caused by what happened in that house of horrors three years ago.

Involving that innocent child.

A terrible mistake.

Jack's mistake.

The thought of the firing range came back. Jack needed to take out his anger on something for how badly the day had gone so far. How much worse could it get?

As fate would have it, he was about to find out.

2

JOSEPH PEARL

The clinking of glasses and boisterous socializing filled the chancellor's residence at UCLA. A cocktail party was in full swing to kick off the third annual Interdisciplinary Conference of Philosophical Thought being hosted by the university. In attendance were professors from around the country, the elite of the American philosophy world, along with job-hunting PhD candidates and invited scholars in related fields: linguistics, history of science, even art criticism and theology. Trays of hors d'oeuvres were wolfed down as quickly as they circulated. At a makeshift bar, cans of non-alcoholic beverages remained untouched as student bartenders poured liquor with both hands, struggling to keep up with the demand for refills.

Claire Evans, the modest but attractive brunette who had been watched by Salazar at the airport, ordered a dirty martini. She surveyed the room. It was a little known fact that philosophers were among the most shameless and energetic party animals on the planet, in stark contrast to their physical appearance which ranged from bookish to downright slovenly. And yet, while looks might be important in other circles, what mattered most here was the allure of ideas. To these intellectual heavyweights and their devoted followers, an audacious new slant on logical positivism or a fresh twist on hermeneutics could be as seductive as sex, and often led to it.

Claire removed her glasses and checked her reflection in a mirror: hazel eyes and high cheekbones courtesy of her mother's Mediterranean genes, full lips and caramel skin from her African American father. Taking a nervous breath, she cut through the crowd to join three philosophers engaged in a spirited debate.

"Hi," Claire said. "What did I miss?"

The three men looked up. Tom Gottlieb, bow-tied dean of the philosophy department at Yale, greeted Claire with a paternal smile.

"Hello, my dear. We were having a little fun discussing the allegory of the Cave."

"Plato?"

"Professor Singh here was conjecturing whether Plato's assertions would hold up if the shadow watchers were naked."

Deepak Singh gave Claire a cursory nod, wearing his usual lemon-sucking expression. He looked too young to be a Princeton professor and dressed like an undertaker.

Claire tossed off a shrug.

"Obviously it would make no difference at all."

Singh raised his unibrow.

"Oh?" he said. "And how is that?"

Claire avoided eye contact with the third philosopher standing there, the distinguished-looking man she had surprised at the airport. It was enough to know she had his attention.

"Well," Claire said, "In the allegory Plato imagines a group of people imprisoned in a cave all their lives, their only sense of reality being the shadows they see on the walls. It's basically a metaphor for the state of human existence, how we tend to focus on the reflection of things, our interpretation of reality, rather than looking past those shadows to see what's making them: the truth itself. As a philosopher would."

"Yes, yes, we know all that," Singh said. "However, it still doesn't address—"

"Being stripped bare of our illusions and the comfort they bring. By naked, Professor, I assumed you meant something of that sort."

Claire's eloquence, together with her disarming sincerity, rendered Singh speechless. Gottlieb made a proud gesture to her.

"My favorite graduate student. You can see why."

The distinguished-looking man also appeared impressed, as Claire had hoped. Singh mumbled something about needing another drink and beat an escape to the bar.

"Oh now, forgive me," Gottlieb said. "You two haven't been properly introduced. Claire Evans, this is—"

"Joseph Pearl, from Harvard," Claire said, already shaking the hand of the distinguished philosopher. "I'm a *huge* fan. In fact, I happen to be reading your latest book. It's sitting by the bed in my hotel room. Perhaps you'd be kind enough to autograph it."

She squeezed his hand, no longer shaking it but not letting go. A trace of color came to Pearl. To his relief Gottlieb didn't notice, having spotted someone in the crowd.

"Well, well," Gottlieb said. "Speak of the devil."

Both Pearl and Claire followed the dean's gaze to see a long-haired man in his late forties holding court across the room, slashing the air to make a point like a conductor powering through a Schoenberg symphony. It was impossible not to notice Arthur Constantius with his 'unmade bed' look. Like Pearl, he was a rock star in the profession. Among those surrounding the Berkeley logician were a disproportionate number of beautiful women.

"Your old nemesis, Joe," Gottlieb said to Pearl. "I understand you and Constantius will be debating on Saturday. Sure to be the highlight of the conference."

Claire raised her martini.

"Here's to no ears being bitten off."

As they all clinked, Claire turned back to Pearl.

"Excuse me, Professor, I wonder if I could steal you away for a moment?"

Before Pearl could answer, Claire hooked her arm in his and coaxed him away through the crowd to a corner for privacy.

"What are you doing, Claire?"

"Trying to get your attention."

"This isn't the place."

"Why haven't you returned my calls? Hey, I've got a great idea. Why don't I take you back to my hotel? Then after you give me that autograph—"

"Claire, it's over."

Claire stared, thrown.

"No," she said. "Don't say that."

"We talked about this. I thought we agreed."

"Why, Joe? I'm not smart enough, is that it?"

"Claire, please."

"Or pretty enough? Any other man here would be flattered to have a woman half his age practically throwing herself—"

Others nearby began to notice their drama, looking up from erudite conversations. With a polite nod, Pearl deflected the curious glances. He continued to speak to Claire with the same calm, reasoned tone that made him such a force of nature in his profession.

"Claire, I'm sorry. I think you know I mean that. I don't want to be unkind but I'm afraid there's nothing I can offer that will make you feel any better."

Tears pooled in Claire's eyes.

"Then I can't be responsible for what I might do."

Her desperate tone drew a look from Pearl.

13

"If you're suggesting, Claire, that you might try to hurt yourself again...."

"Would you even care? Of course not. To you, I'm just another groupie, a deleted footnote. And the sickest part? The irony? Here you are, the famous philosopher who's spent his entire life figuring out how people should live. But it's all bullshit because even with your fancy theories and rhetoric, you have no idea how to live, how to feel, how to connect with people. And you never will."

Overcome, Claire hurried from the room.

Pearl stared after her. Though never quite comfortable with Claire's feelings for him, he felt he had handled the matter with her best interests in mind. Furthermore, he was confident that she would be fine despite her threat, even considering the near-overdose of Ambien she had taken after his first attempt to break things off at another conference in Chicago a few weeks ago. Yet Claire's words nagged at Pearl. There might be a grain of truth to what she said. Perhaps more than a grain.

3

JACK

Jack got sidetracked. Instead of hitting the firing range, he ended up shooting hoops with some ball rats in Compton, getting his 31-year-old ass seriously kicked. Instead of Cynthia's Revels, he settled for a stale pre-packaged sandwich from 7-Eleven. Instead of going to a club for soul-healing rock music, he found himself driving to a quiet residential street in Santa Monica where he sat in his car for a while and stared at the lights burning in a second-floor apartment. The whole day seemed random and spontaneous until he was back on the road heading home and the common thread hit him. Everything he'd done since his surprise run-in with Franco was stuff he used to do three years ago. Could have been torn from the 'before' page in his life. Except for that apartment. Three years ago, Jack would have been inside the place, not out, fighting with Becky as usual—she would be throwing things, he would be calling her names—until they would hear themselves and crack up and wind up in bed.

Safe to say, it was the most maddening, dysfunctional and happy relationship Jack had ever known.

The Spartan gloom of the loft was comforting to Jack as he walked in and threw his keys by the chessboard where he always had a game going. Boxes of books sat in a corner, Jack's half of the ones he and Becky had acquired while living together. The walls were bare and the fold-out couch was unmade, but Jack didn't care. Neither did his roommate. They were both loners, which is why they got along so well. Besides the plumber who came with depressing regularity to fix the kitchen sink, visitors were few and far between.

On a cinderblock shelf, gathering dust, lay a manila envelope containing a copy of the Internal Affairs transcript from three years ago, which Franco had pulled strings to get for Jack after he was dismissed in disgrace from the LAPD. Despite his hope at the time that something in the record might vindicate him, Jack had never been able to bring himself to break the seal on the envelope.

Jack glanced around the loft.

"Trouser?"

From a dark corner came the noisy yawn of Jack's roommate waking up, then out trotted a chocolate Lab with his tail wagging excitedly. Trouser jumped up and covered Jack's face with slobbery licks as if he were still the homeless puppy that Jack had found scratching at his door a few weeks after his last day as a detective.

Jack always suspected that his down-the-hall neighbor Mrs. Woo had left the dog there as a present, to lift his spirits, although the kindly woman denied it. Whoever was responsible, Jack appreciated that someone had faith that he could take care of such a helpless creature, though it soon became clear to Jack that he was the helpless one and Trouser was taking care of him.

"Okay, goofball," Jack laughed. "I surrender!"

Jack noticed the leash he had left on the kitchen counter was now on the hook by the door, which meant Mrs. Woo had taken Trouser for a walk, as she often did with her beloved Yorkies, Muffin and Fu. From his jacket, Jack pulled out the half-eaten cheeseburger from the casino and held it out.

"Who's a good boy?"

Trouser woofed and whined.

"What? Too rare for you?"

Trouser pawed Jack's leg.

"Okay, if that's how you roll..."

As Jack looked away in pretend disappointment, Trouser nudged the burger out of his hand and gobbled it up. With a chuckle, Jack gave Trouser a good belly rub, then stepped over to his land line to check voice-mails. There was one new message, one more than he usually got, from a Filipino street urchin named Lim who Jack had agreed to sponsor in exchange for the kid doing reduced time in juvie. Lim's drunken stutter left no doubt that he had fallen back into his old ways. Again.

"Jack, w-where are you when I need you? No, I'm serious, man. For real this time. Call. P-please. Soon as you get this."

Jack clicked off, shaking his head. He was still pondering how to deal with Lim when the phone rang in his hand. He punched the talk button and dragged the handset to his ear.

"Okay," Jack said. "Slow down and tell me what happened."

"Jack, is that you?"

It was a male voice but not Lim's. A voice deepened by age and refinement.

"I got you," the voice said. "How nice. The old number I had for you didn't work so I tried information."

A passing siren made it hard to hear.

"I'm sorry," Jack said. "Who is this?"

A soft laugh came over the phone line, humbled but not offended.

"Fair enough. I suppose I deserve that. Am I calling at a bad time?"

As the siren faded, Jack froze with recognition. The voice belonged to a famous philosopher named Joseph Pearl. A stranger Jack knew by a different name.

"Dad?"

"You sound well, Jack. It's good to hear you. Tell me, how have you been?"

"Fine, great."

Jack cringed. Could he have made it sound any less sincere?

"Uh, sorry," he said. "Guess I'm a little surprised."

"Yes, of course. It's been awhile, hasn't it?"

"Try years."

"How many?"

"I don't know," Jack said. "I kinda lost track."

He tried to make it sound as if it was no big deal but it came out the opposite.

There was no change in Pearl's tone. If he had picked up on his son's lack of warmth, he was too gracious to let on.

"You're probably wondering why I called."

Understatement of the century, Jack thought.

"I'm in Los Angeles for a conference. A few days, that's all. As long as I'm here I thought it might be nice to meet."

Jack was tongue-tied. His first thought was to change the subject by asking his father about his work. He was sure his old man would be happy to fill him in on his latest accomplishments: the international speaking invitations, the arcane theories he was tackling at the moment, the latest book he was banging out on his manual Olympia typewriter. As he had all his life, Jack would throw in a "Really?" or "That's interesting", not so much meaning it or caring as wanting to please his father in hopes of getting what he had never managed to as a kid. Attention. His. A feeling that his dad actually gave a shit. Dare he say it? Love. What made their relationship even more frustrating was that Joseph Pearl was a good man, albeit one who was more interested in his life's work, philosophy, than being a parent. And he made no bones about it. In fact, Jack knew, his dad would be the first to admit it, a humbling self-honesty and sense of purpose that were conspicuously missing in his son's messed-up life.

"Jack? Are you still there?"

Jack had lied to his father. He knew damn well how long it had been since their last meaningful conversation. It was ten years ago, the night his mother surrendered to drink and depression and drove her car off an embankment, while his dad was out of town, as he often was, at some philosophy conference. Jack had called him from Mass General, white-knuckling the note that had been found in his mother's pocket—"I'm sorry" was all it said—and had screamed himself hoarse as he blamed his father for her death. By the time the philosopher had caught a flight back to Boston, Jack was gone.

Ten long years. Almost to the day.

In all that time, they had never talked about it.

"Perhaps lunch tomorrow, Jack. How does that sound? That is, if it's not too complicated and you can spare the time. I realize you're busy with your police work."

Jack felt his jaw clench. That was how long it had been. How well his old man knew him. Not at all.

"So what do you say? Shall we?"

Jack didn't hesitate.

"I don't think so," he said.

Pearl's voice registered surprise.

"Are you sure?"

"Positive."

"Very well. But in case you change your mind—"

"I won't."

"I'm staying at the W Hotel. Room eight-eleven. I imagine they have a nice restaurant here."

"I gotta go," Jack said.

"I'll make a reservation for noon."

"Good luck with your conference."

Jack hung up without even saying goodbye. It was the most satisfying and painful thing he had done in a very long time. Painful because he had to do it sober.

4

SALAZAR

A thousand cars a minute, the blood that coursed through the veins of the City of Angels, rocketed past the tri-level overpass southeast of downtown. Below, in a graffiti-scarred no man's land between gang territories, a silver Cadillac Escalade waited with its lights off, motor running.

Salazar sat at attention behind the wheel. His soft brown eyes raked the darkness with the same patient intensity he had displayed while watching Claire at the airport. On the Escalade's sound system, a Caribbean hip hop artist known as Manifest sang about pain and redemption. The music was turned up, loud enough to drown out the terrified whimpers of a teenage girl coming from the floorboards of the back seat.

Up ahead, headlights appeared.

As Salazar killed the music a blue Ford pickup swung into view and stopped ten yards away. Out of habit, Salazar touched the Kimber Super Carry .45

under his jacket. He opened his door and climbed out. So did the occupants of the pickup, two men and a woman, all Hispanic. The driver, a young gangbanger named Reaper with prison tats on his neck and the lean hungry slouch of a hyena, gave Salazar an all-cool nod. The other man, older and damp with worry, wore an expensive gray suit and carried a rolled-up grocery bag in his hand. He hung back with the woman who clung to his arm like a frightened bird.

Salazar sized up the woman.

"And who, may I ask, is this?"

"Chill, man," Reaper said. "The kid's auntie, is all."

"Did I not say her father was to come alone?"

The man in the gray suit held out his bag.

"Please, senor, I have the money."

Salazar gestured for Reaper to check it. As Reaper ripped open the bag and counted the stacks of hundreds inside, Salazar scanned the area. One couldn't be too careful in this line of work. That was why he had taken on Reaper, despite the kid's shortcomings. No one knew the mazelike backstreets of the city better than Reaper for losing the heat, or was more skilled at sniffing out tracking devices or marked money. From his years in Guadalajara and later in Phoenix where there were more abductions for ransom than anywhere outside Mexico, Salazar knew these were the careless oversights that got most kidnappers caught.

"All here," Reaper said. "All clean."

Salazar turned his attention back to the woman, in time to see her sneak a glance at the Escalade's license plate.

"The car is stolen," Salazar said. "Also the pickup. So I'm afraid tracing the tags won't do you police any good."

The woman looked confused. Salazar stepped close to her. He withdrew his Kimber and kissed it, one of the many superstitions he shared with other officers of the Mexican Federal Police. Then Salazar calmly pointed the gun at the woman's face.

"Take the barrel," he said. "And put it in your mouth."

Terror flooded the woman's eyes.

"Please do as I ask or I'll make you watch me kill the girl in the car, in a way you've never seen someone die before."

There was no threat in Salazar's tone, merely politeness. Both the man in the gray suit and Reaper stared in shock, neither daring to move, as the woman reached out with trembling fingers and guided the cold, blued steel into her mouth.

Salazar tightened his finger around the trigger.

"Now look in my eyes," he said. "And tell me you're a cop."

As the woman gagged on the barrel and whimpered for mercy, Salazar saw what he was looking for. Even in the face of certain death, she couldn't say it. It meant she was clean.

He withdrew the gun.

The woman fell to her knees, sobbing.

Salazar nodded to Reaper who opened the back door of the Escalade. Out staggered a 14-year-old girl, dazed and in shock, her wrists bound with electrical wire. As Reaper jumped behind the wheel with the bag of money, Salazar turned back to watch the man in the gray suit embrace his daughter. The sight touched him. It also reminded Salazar of a painful chapter in his past, the tragedy involving his brother Ignacio. He shook it off and slipped into the Escalade and it roared away.

Within seconds the silver car had ramped onto the freeway and was swallowed up in traffic.

Reaper threw Salazar a look.

"Ain't no way she was a cop."

"Family," Salazar said. "Family is everything."

They took the Vernon Street exit and sped south along the Los Angeles River toward the rail yards, an area between police radio districts they knew was rarely patrolled.

"We should ditch the wheels," Reaper said.

"As usual."

"And lay low for awhile."

"No."

Dark thoughts, carefully laid plans, played out in Salazar's mind but he gave away nothing.

"The next one," he said. "Already have it lined up."

Reaper's hyena features tightened with interest.

"Another dealer? Coyote?"

Salazar shook his head.

"Something special. Not the usual low hanging fruit. A consignment arranged through my personal connections. You will see."

"When?"

Salazar punched the sound system to hear Manifest again. The blur of passing lights danced in his eyes.

"Tomorrow," he said.

5

JOSEPH PEARL

"The tradition of Western philosophy begins in a kind of confidence that there is a changeless truth underlying all conjectures about the changing world."

The main lecture auditorium in Dodd Hall at UCLA was filled to capacity, a mid-morning plenary session of the conference. All eyes were riveted on the featured speaker, Joseph Pearl.

"That concept is associated with Parmenides, the first clearly identifiable Greek philosopher. As you know, Parmenides made a fantastic pronouncement in a famous poem he wrote. We only have part of it, but that pronouncement is the following: What is *is*, and what is not *is not*."

An amused murmur rippled through the crowd. Pearl paced and gestured as he continued to speak.

"If you knew that, you were oriented to whatever could be discovered in the world. All you had to do was know that what you are talking about is related to what is or what is not in a certain way. But Parmenides failed to address the concept of *change*, which means you couldn't talk about science or the human world in any intelligible way."

In the audience Arthur Constantius listened with his entourage, a scowl of disapproval on his ugly-hand-some face—in contrast to Milton McGurk, the rotund professor that Pearl had introduced to Claire at the air-port, who sat across the aisle eating coffee cake and appeared enrapt.

"Enter Aristotle who answers this brilliantly," Pearl said. "It's one of his master strokes. Aristotle's solution? That we have to distinguish between what is *not*, and what is not *this* but *something else*. In other words, he made a distinction between what we call not being anything at all and non-being. That is, being something which is not this or that, but something else, which is change."

Also present was Deepak Singh, seated halfway between Constantius and McGurk, dressed in fune-real black as usual. He jotted down thoughts on bright orange Post-It notes organized in neat little columns as if playing solitaire.

"In my view," Pearl said, "To agree that the world is continually changing, that change is the defining feature of our world, is easier to defend than the changeless—"

Constantius shook his head.

McGurk nodded in agreement.

Singh rearranged his Post-Its.

"—And from that point of view, starting from the idea that the world is in constant flux, inherently changing, then all notions of regularity or of stability or of constancy or of fixity or of necessity or anything of that kind—all of these are provisional posits relative to what is changing."

Pearl pressed his hands together as if in prayer.

"You see the humor of the argument," he said. "And its power. It frees you from being doctrinally committed to any fixed position that you are never going to be willing to give up. It's reassuring. But a lot of people find it terribly disturbing."

As Pearl continued to enthrall the crowd, Claire watched from the back of the hall with conflicting emotions: admiration, self-pity, love, hatred. The more Pearl talked about change, the more painful it became. Unable to take anymore, Claire left.

An hour later Pearl ended his talk to thunderous applause. As he slipped his lecture notes into his worn leather satchel, McGurk bounded down to the podium to shake his hand.

"Bravo, Joe! Bravo!"

McGurk brushed cake crumbs from his crimson Harvard sweater vest and pointed out Constantius skulking away with his posse.

"Off to sharpen his axe, no doubt," McGurk chortled. "For your big debate this weekend."

"I'm afraid it will take more than that to save him."

There was a flatness to Pearl's voice, as if weighed down by a secret, but McGurk was too busy thumbing through his conference program to pick up on it.

"Let's see what's next on the menu," McGurk said. "*Interpretation, Relativism and the Metaphysics of Culture*. Or a critique of Foucault's *Madness and Civilization*. Which sounds more appetizing to you, Joe?"

Pearl shook his head.

"Regrettably, I will have to miss both."

"Oh?"

"I have an appointment that was arranged for me earlier. To view some art pieces. Then lunch."

McGurk's jowls sagged with envy.

"Lunch with someone important?"

A pensive smile came to Pearl.

"As a matter of fact, yes," he said.

6

JACK

Jack walked into the Commerce Club to find it buzzing with activity. While less than half the tables were in use this early in the day, all the going games were filled including his preferred one hundred no-limit. It meant Jack had to give his initials to the floor man and hang around until a seat opened up.

While he did, Jack took in the scene: the incessant jangle of chips, the long line at the ATM, the circles of lotus eaters hunched over thin rectangles emblazoned with numbers and symbols. All for what? Not for fun or excitement or even to win, Jack was sure, but rather in some attempt to control the risk and chance of life. As if that were possible.

Jack's thoughts drifted to the dream he had last night, a memory from childhood. He was six years old and standing by the stairs in the old brownstone in Boston where he grew up. Down the hall he could see his mother in the kitchen, dressed in her Sunday best, obsessively cleaning and polishing as she always did. In the dream, Jack's younger self listened for the faint sound of the typewriter coming from the study in the attic, but the house was silent which meant his father was gone, no doubt teaching one of his classes at the university. On tiptoes, young Jack snuck upstairs and peeked into the room he had been told to stay away from. What he saw made his eyes widen with delight. The place looked as if a tornado had hit it, books and papers everywhere. And there, in the middle of the wonderful disarray, was the mysterious black machine that occupied so much of his father's time. Jack meandered over and dared himself to press one of its gleaming brass keys. Then several. Soon he was typing as fast as he could, the way he had seen his dad do it, until the keys jammed. He tried to bang them unstuck but it only made things worse. It was then that he heard a sound behind him and whirled to see his father standing in the doorway. There was no anger in his dad's face. He didn't say a word. Jack wished he cared enough that he had. All the philosopher did was give his son a wince of disappointment that made young Jack tear from the room—and wake up in a cold, adult sweat.

"J.P. One hundred no-limit. J.P.!"

Jack snapped out of his trance to see the floor man waving him to a seat being vacated by some poor fish who had lost all his chips. On his way to the table, Jack checked the time on his cell phone. Exactly twelve noon. It made Jack stop and wrestle with himself. No, he thought. Forget it. Bad idea.

The floor man waved to him again.

"J.P., you want this seat or not?"

Jack did a gut check. Something made him shake his head. As the floor man called the next victim, Jack headed for the exit.

He got a break with traffic and pulled up to the W at ten minutes before one. The valet examined the Wagoneer's damaged side mirror and marked it on the claim ticket before Jack walked into the cool, trendy hotel. One glance around told him it must have been chosen by the conference organizers, not his father. Ascetic was more Joseph Pearl's style. As long as his old man had his books and papers with him, he would be happy at a Motel 6.

Across the lobby Jack spotted a posh cafe where people were lunching. On his way over, he caught his reflection in a mirrored wall and was surprised to see how nervous he appeared—not because he was looking forward to a reunion with his long-lost dad but because finally the two of them were going to have that talk, the one they should have had a decade ago. And his father, it seemed, was ready for it as well. Why else would he have called his estranged son out of the blue?

A hostess with an acting-class smile looked up from sorting menus as Jack walked over.

"Hi," she said. "Do you have a reservation?"

"For noon. I'm late. I believe it's under Pearl."

As the hostess checked her book, Jack scanned the room but there was no sign of his father.

"Here it is," the hostess said. "For two. Looks like you're the first to arrive."

Jack frowned. Joseph Pearl, he knew, could be absent-minded, especially when working on his philosophy, but he was always punctual to a fault.

"Are you sure?" Jack said. "Maybe he came and left. A man about sixty, tall, professor type? I think he's staying here."

The hostess shook her head, not recognizing the description.

"If he's a hotel guest, might check with reception."

"Good idea. Thanks."

Jack doubled back to the lobby and asked a front desk clerk to ring Joseph Pearl's room. He waited. The clerk hung up with a shrug.

"Sorry, sir, no answer. Care to leave a message?"

"No, that's okay."

Jack felt a prickle of embarrassment. He was that kid again, the one who kept holding out hope that his dad would show up. First to piano recitals and little league games. Then later, when he was stealing cars and flunking out of college. And most indelibly ten years ago when Jack learned he wasn't the only family member who had suffered because of Joseph Pearl's love affair with philosophy. And now here he was again to find that nothing had changed. Or maybe he was folding his hand too fast, Jack thought. Maybe it was up to him, not his old man, to reshuffle the deck.

Jack turned back to the clerk.

"On second thought, maybe I will leave a message."
He wrote one down and slid it across the counter:

IMPORTANT WE TALK
LET'S RESCHEDULE
JACK

7

JACK

I f there was one thing Jack hated it was falling behind. As a kid it was what made him set his alarm clock twelve minutes fast. In his marathon days it was the reason he never missed a training run, even when injured. Today it was poker. Thanks to a lucky drunk and that unexpected call from his father, he was two days behind in his gambling quota. So Jack did what any self-respecting obsessive compulsive would do. He went straight back to the Commerce.

It took a few hands to get his groove back but soon he was winning. Or, rather, he couldn't lose. Sometimes luck came in such tidal waves it could only be described as shameful and while Jack wanted to take all the credit, he knew full well it wasn't deserved. The best he could do was ride the wild monkey for all it was worth, then have the brains and discipline to get out before it turned against him. As it always did.

By the time he walked out into the warm summer night, Jack had pocketed enough to cover his nut for the next couple weeks. Sure, he had broken his cardinal hit-it-and-quit-it rule but he was feeling too good to sweat technicalities. When the female valet brought his car around Jack tipped her an extra twenty. The look she gave him, while flirtatious, made it clear he still wasn't going to score a pink ticket anytime soon.

Jack treated himself to a blood rare filet at Cut in Beverly Hills, then drove across town to a little-known cigar club in Silver Lake where the Cuban Cohibas were as sublime as the jazz. Like most gamblers, Jack felt the need to indulge after a big win. The only thing missing was someone to share it with.

He got back to his loft around midnight. Trouser was passed out on the couch, one of his hind legs twitching from a dream. Through the open windows the sounds and smells of Chinatown wafted in. The ceiling fan rotated in the dark, its whir creating a mismatched heartbeat with the flashes from a neon sign across the street. Jack left the lights off and tossed his keys by the chessboard. As his gaze fell on the phone gleaming in the dark he remembered the note he had left at the W.

He checked voicemail. There were two new messages. At least one Jack expected to be from his father but both turned out to be from Lim—furious stuttering rants, half in Tagalog, about how Jack had blown him off in a time of need and that Lim would never trust him again.

Jack hung up, ashamed for letting Lim down. He was about to call the kid back when something made him stop and think.

Joseph Pearl made a reservation but didn't show.

Jack left a message but his father didn't call back.

Neither one by itself seemed odd. Together they felt wrong somehow. Especially in light of his old man being the one who had initiated contact. Especially after so many years.

Was he making a big deal out of nothing? Easy way to find out. He called the W and asked to be connected to Joseph Pearl's room. The phone rang several times before switching to an automated message system. Jack called the W again. This time he asked if the note he had left earlier had been picked up. The clerk checked. No, he said. With a bit more probing Jack learned that several phone messages had also been left for Joseph Pearl since that morning. They too had not been retrieved.

Jack hung up.

That 'off' feeling wouldn't go away.

Trust your gut, Jack thought, the first thing every cop learns. Second, never let your emotions get in the way of taking action. As his father's son, Jack didn't want to get involved. But as a former undercover detective, albeit a fallen one, Jack knew he had to check it out. Before he could change his mind, he grabbed his keys and headed back out the door.

8

JACK

Jack parked a block away from the W—undercover habits die hard—and walked into the lobby. Most hotels would have been quiet after midnight but this one was a scene. The same cafe where people were having power lunches when Jack had been there earlier was now a bar with a deejay jammed with the young, beautiful, too-cool-for-school set, most of them spending more time texting and tweeting on their smart phones than paying attention to each other.

Jack considered his options. He could go to the front desk, explain his concern and have someone escort him to Joseph Pearl's room. But he didn't want anyone else involved until he knew more. Besides, raising a red flag might limit or prevent his ability to search the room if necessary. For now, Jack decided, it was better if he controlled all the variables, even if it meant bending the rules a bit.

Across the bustling lobby he spotted a house phone. He strolled over and picked it up. When the hotel operator answered he asked to be connected with housekeeping. Soon a pleasant female voice came on the line.

"This is Rosa. How may I help you?"

"Hi, Rosa," Jack said. "This is Mr. Pearl in—"

He remembered the room number his father had given him.

"—In eight eleven. I stepped out for a moment but I wonder if I could trouble you to bring up some fresh towels please."

"Of course, sir. Right away."

"Thank you."

Jack hung up and turned his attention to the elevators. A uniformed employee was stationed there checking key cards of guests going up to their rooms. Not uncommon in upscale hotels. As luck would have it, the employee was young, bored and not very diligent in his checks.

Jack waited for his opportunity which didn't take long. While the security guy was busy dealing with a couple of girls from the bar, he fell in behind a middle-aged man headed for the elevator. The man flashed his key card. The security guy glanced up. Jack gave his best I'm-with-him nod. Next thing he knew, he was on his way up to the eighth floor.

Room 811 was on the left, halfway down the hall. As Jack had hoped, the door was propped open which meant someone from housekeeping was already there.

Jack paced himself and arrived as a maid was coming out with an armful of used towels.

"Oh, excuse me, sir," she said.

Jack recognized her voice.

"You must be Rosa. I'm Mr. Pearl. Boy, that was fast!"

Nothing like a little flattery to distract someone.

"Oh, and sorry about the mess in there," Jack said. "Don't tell anyone, okay?"

Or a little humor, even if unfunny. Jack pressed a twenty into the woman's hand.

"Don't worry, sir," she grinned. "Your secret is safe with me."

With no reason to believe he didn't belong there, the maid headed away. As she did, Jack snuck a glance at the towels she was carrying, looking for anything suspicious like blood. Once a cop, always a cop, Jack thought. To his relief there was nothing.

Jack slipped into the room and the door clicked shut behind him. He glanced around. Everything appeared normal. There were two queen-sized beds, both made. Draped across one was a white dress shirt, wrinkled from being worn. It suggested that Joseph Pearl had been there after the room was serviced. Taken together with the missed lunch reservation, it gave Jack a rough time line to work with.

He began searching. There were philosophy books strewn about. Some lay open with his father's distinctive backwards check marks in the margins, identical to those in the thousands of books that filled the Boston house growing up. In the inside pocket of a worsted tweed jacket, Jack found an envelope covered with his old man's indecipherable chicken scratches—whether some insight or a grocery list, it was impossible to tell. All Jack could make out was one line in red ink, rather than black like the rest of the scribbles, which was circled several times:

NO 2 OC

Jack continued his search. Wallet, keys and any day planner his father may have used were all missing from the room. So were laptop, cell phone, electronics of any kind. But that hardly surprised Jack. Like the worn shaving brush and straight razor he found in the bathroom, it confirmed that his dad was the same set-in-his-ways dinosaur Jack had known as a kid.

His scrutiny shifted to the blinking light on the phone. He stepped over and punched up messages. There were three, each one time coded. A robotic voice prompt announced they were new which confirmed that his dad hadn't checked them yet.

The first was from someone who identified himself as Milton, expressing friendly concern that Joseph had not showed up for a panel he was scheduled to chair that afternoon.

The next was from a man with an Indian accent who sounded agitated, some matter evidently pressing on his mind. The man said he would call back but left no name or number.

The last message was from another anonymous male with a deep, imperious voice. While he complimented Pearl on his morning lecture, there was something disingenuous in his tone.

To be thorough Jack checked the in-box for any messages his dad might have saved. Sure enough, there was one. It was a female voice, full of violent longing and on the verge of tears.

"It's me, Claire," the voice said. "In case you forgot already. I know you're not there but...I didn't mean to put you through all this, for it to turn out this way."

The voice stumbled on, fragile and slurring as if stoned.

"I hate you for letting me in and I hate myself for caring so much. I'm sorry, I'm sorry, I'm sorry. That's all I wanted to say...and that I still love you."

Hurt bled from every word, trailing off into a breathless whisper. Then the message ended.

Jack stood there riveted by what he had heard. A woman, fairly young judging by her voice, expressing soul-crushing despair over a passionate affair with Joseph Pearl, which the philosopher had broken off from the sound of it. For Jack, it was hard to reconcile with the man who had been so distant growing up, and brought into sharp relief how poorly Jack knew his father.

Could this woman explain his dad's disappearance? Was it possible he was with her right now, perhaps to make up or console her? Jack doubted it. Even assuming his father had somehow forgotten about their lunch, there was no way he would have missed a professional obligation, let alone one he was expected to chair, as the voicemail from 'Milton' had indicated.

However little Jack knew his old man, that much he was sure of. It gave Jack more reason to be troubled and made him wonder if the young woman on the message might know something.

She called herself Claire.

Jack scoured the room in hopes of finding out more about her, but came up empty. Then he noticed a pale green leaflet lying nearby and picked it up. It was a program for the philosophy conference, covering four days of events. Halfway down the second page Jack noticed the name CLAIRE EVANS, listed as a PhD candidate from Yale University. According to the program, she was scheduled to present a paper entitled *Peirce's True Debt To Royce* in Room 127 of Dodd Hall, at nine o'clock tomorrow morning.

Jack checked for contact information on Claire Evans. There was none. He rang the hotel operator on the chance she was also staying at the W. No one was registered under that name. He pulled out his cell phone to call Yale. It wouldn't be hard, Jack thought, to get campus security to give him an emergency number for this woman or at least an e-mail. However, if he reached her at this hour he would have to explain more than he wanted to. That was assuming the Claire from the program was the same one who had left the phone message. And even if so, what was to say she knew anything about his father's whereabouts?

Impatient as he was for answers, Jack realized, he would have to wait.

As he returned his cell phone to his pocket, his eye caught a slip of paper sticking out of one of the philosophy books. Jack opened the book to find numbers scrawled on the paper. Though in his father's illegible hand, Jack realized it was his own phone number, the one his old man had called information for. Jack took a moment to consider the book cover which featured a prancing stallion with its head held high, an ancient terra cotta artifact of some kind, dramatically backlit against a black background. Above the clay horse was the book title, *Pragmatism: A Yard of History, An Ounce of Prophesy,* and below it the name of the author, Joseph Pearl.

Jack frowned. His old man had cranked out dozens of works in the course of his career, all with unfathomable titles. From the time Jack had first cracked one open as a kid he had never been able to understand a single word of any of them. Not that he hadn't kept trying over the years. In bookstores it was the reason he would sometimes find himself drifting over to the philosophy section. But this book looked new, set apart from the others. If not for vanity, why would his father have carried it with him all the way from Boston?

Curious, Jack thumbed open the book again. What he found on the title page stopped him in his tracks. It was an inscription, unquestionably written by Joseph Pearl though not in his usual illegible hand. An inscription penned with care to ensure it could be read:

FOR JACK, LOVE DAD

9

JOSEPH PEARL

Pearl's eyes blinked open to nothingness. Even before his mind could make sense of it, his body flooded with adrenaline. Then came the pain, like none he had ever experienced before, a throbbing supernova radiating from the back of his head to every fiber of his being.

I'm dead, thought Pearl.

An avalanche of fractured thoughts assaulted him.

Wittgenstein's *Tractatus*: "Death is not an event in life. We do not live to experience death."

Dylan Thomas: "Rage, rage against the dying of the light!"

Pearl's eyes strained for meaning. Pinpricks of detail emerged from the darkness. As the fog of unconsciousness began to lift, Pearl realized he was wedged into some kind of tomblike space. With no light or room to move, all he could do was feel the gash on his head and the handcuffs cutting into his wrists.

One by one, his other senses awoke. He could hear the echo of water dripping somewhere. He could smell oil, decay, rat droppings. He could taste blood in his mouth. Together they triggered a memory flash:

A pawn shop.

A pre-Columbian figurine.

A doorbell jingling.

Another image came to Pearl: standing in a lecture hall at Harvard, passing out his final exam to students, the one he was renowned for, a blank sheet of paper with a one-word essay question at the top: "Why?" Whatever godforsaken hell he was in right now, Pearl burned to know the answer to that question. And, for once, not for philosophical reasons. Not in reference to the logical scrutiny of Frege or Russell or Quine, nor the deconstructions of Derrida, nor Spinoza's notions about the nature of God. For Pearl there was but one relevant point of reference that mattered at this moment.

Survival.

His mind told him to cry out for help. He tried. All that came out was a pained whisper. He tried again. It was no use. He was too weak. Then from out of the darkness Pearl heard a new sound, the mournful wail of a train horn coming on fast.

As the train thundered past, its lights strobed through the edges of a boarded-up window, illuminating the space where Pearl lay. The bursts of light lasted long enough for him to see that he was lodged behind a tangle of steam pipes in some kind of long-abandoned, hangar-sized factory containing rows of junked, rusted industrial equipment.

With jarring suddenness the train roared off into the night and everything went black again.

How had he gotten here? Pearl had no recollection. Yet he had one advantage over others who might find themselves in the same nightmare. He was a philosopher. As a philosopher, he was someone who had devoted his life to tackling problems, the kind most people would find too difficult. He was trained to regulate his actions and judgments by the light of reason. He was able to remain rational and composed when put to the test. As a philosopher, Pearl was capable of directing his mind away from the horrific nature of his circumstances to the eternal questions they posed.

What is fear?

Is thought real?

Are free will and determinism compatible?

Is consciousness a physical or mental phenomenon?

What happens at death?

The more Pearl diverted his focus to the questions in the darkness of the abandoned factory, the more exhausted he became. In time his thoughts became dreams and he slipped back into unconsciousness.

10

JACK

As long as it was still the middle of the night, Jack decided the best plan was to stay put in his father's hotel room. The poker player in him wanted to believe there was still a chance his old man might come walking through the door. The ex-cop in him knew it was never going to happen. As Franco was fond of saying to bad guys who swore they were innocent, "And in that world where rhinoceroses fly, they speak *what* language?"

The thought of going to the police crossed Jack's mind but he quickly dismissed it. From his years on the force, he knew that filing a missing person report without proof of foul play would be a waste of time. Besides, Jack had another, darker reason for not getting his former brethren involved. It had to do with the contents of that sealed I.A. envelope in his loft.

Jack pulled out his cell phone and began making unpleasant but necessary calls. The first was to the county morgue. Of the seven John Does who had been brought in within the last twenty-four hours, none matched his father's description. Jack then called every emergency room in a twenty mile radius. Despite the ambivalence he felt toward his dad, Jack was relieved there were no unidentified patients who sounded like him.

Next, Jack considered accessing his dad's cell and e-mail, but given the philosopher's aversion to all things modern Jack was pretty sure he didn't use either. Nevertheless, any calls Joseph Pearl had made from the phone in the hotel room might yield some leads. The one person who could help Jack retrieve those calls, a tech wiz named Gary, kept his phone off at night because of his wife's insomnia. He wouldn't be reachable until morning.

Jack combed the room once more, breaking it down into quadrants as he would a crime scene. When he was satisfied there was nothing he could have missed, he returned to the table where he had found his father's book.

He picked it up again and reread the inscription, then turned the page to find a printed dedication:

For dolphins, falcons, brothers of the Sahel,
los desaparecidos, the jailors and the jailed
Of every apartheid,
marshes, rain forests, the very air,
lucky lucky Fool
however diminished within all this sweet space

What the hell, Jack thought. Yet, oddly, it made sense. That was his father in a nutshell: someone who would dedicate a book to an idea rather than a person, the kind of man who could express deep sympathy for the world at large yet would forget to hug his own kid. Or am I feeling sorry for myself, Jack thought. Was he a "lucky lucky Fool" looking for someone to blame for failing to get his own life together?

Fatigue hit him. It had been a long day, in more ways than one. Jack lay down on the bed next to his father's white dress shirt, promising himself it would only be for a minute.

11

JACK

J
ack dreamt he was sitting in the café at the W and realized he had been stood up. But not by his dad. By Becky. He stormed out and suddenly found himself in Becky's law office. The dream version looked different than her actual office in Century City, larger with big 'name partner' windows, but Jack knew it was hers by the faux Franz Kline on the wall, the one they had drunkenly painted together back when they were still in their honeymoon phase. It was the same painting that Becky later destroyed with a steak knife right in front of Jack, to let him know it was over between them. As Jack stood there pleased to see the canvas in one piece again, Becky walked in—that Modigliani face and neck he had fallen for—looking stunning as ever. Her tailored black skirt and crisp white blouse were a perfect counterpoint to the black and white slashes on the Kline. Jack started in about

her leaving him stranded at the restaurant but Becky cut him off.

"You're missing the point," she said.

"And what is the point?"

"It's not your father you're looking for. It's you."

Jack bolted awake, disoriented, to find morning light filtering through the hotel room drapes. His eyes shot to the clock radio which read 7:45 A.M. It took a few seconds for his head to clear but then he remembered why he was there.

He shot to his feet and grabbed the book inscribed to him along with the envelope with his dad's writing on it. Near the TV he found a check-in folio with a spare key card inside, which he slipped into his pocket. Before walking out, Jack picked up his father's wrinkled white shirt and buried his nose in it. It smelled of starch and perspiration, scents he recognized from childhood, and one he didn't: ever-so-faint hints of vanilla and leather from an expensive woman's perfume.

UCLA was a stone's throw from the W. In need of caffeine first, Jack sidetracked to a Starbucks in Westwood Village and called Mrs. Woo to ask if she would take care of Trouser in his absence. Dog lover that she was, the Chinese woman was happy to oblige but scolded Jack for wasting his life on poker instead of getting a real job. As soon as he hung up, Jack put in a call to Gary. Their paths had crossed many years ago when Jack and Franco had busted an Oscar-winning actor for possession of heroin. A search of the star's home turned up a bug planted in the bedroom phone which they traced to Gary who worked as a repairman for AT&T. Seemed Gary had a lucrative side business going, using his high-tech wizardry to record the private conversations of famous people and sell them to the tabloids. In exchange for not being shut down, Gary agreed to provide off-the-record tech support to Jack and Franco, usually in situations where they were unable to acquire a warrant for a legal wiretap.

When Gary answered his phone Jack explained what he needed. Gary knew Jack was no longer a cop but didn't ask questions. He told Jack to hang tight, then rang back ten minutes later with three outside numbers that had been made from Joseph Pearl's hotel room.

One was to 411, directory information.

One was to Jack.

One was to a number with a 657 area code which meant it was in Orange County—"the O.C." to locals—a patchwork of beach cities and upscale enclaves directly south of L.A. Whoever the number belonged to had probably moved there recently since the area code was an overlay to 714 which had only gone into service in the last couple years.

Jack tried the number on his cell. It rang a couple times before a female voice picked up: refined, sensual, French accent.

"Hello, bonjour."

"Hi," Jack said, "This is—"

"Please do leave a message and I shall be delighted to return your call."

Jack sighed to himself and waited for the beep, then gave his first name and number. All he said was it concerned Joseph Pearl, something important, and to please call back right away.

As Jack punched off the phone, his thoughts returned to Becky's words in the dream. *It's not your father you're looking for, it's you.* Three years ago, Jack had also been searching for someone, a ghost who left a trail of death behind him and vanished with a ton of drug money. Ten million in cash. In his obsession to bring down the elusive killer, Jack walked into a trap, a crack house littered with dead bodies, staged to look as if Jack had committed the murders. It was then, in his compromised state, that Jack heard a sound and fired his service revolver without thinking. Only later, too late, did he discover he had killed the lone survivor of the massacre who had managed to escape the fate of the others by hiding behind the body of one of the victims.

A six-year-old-boy.

A horrible mistake that couldn't be undone.

Jack's mistake.

Something in Jack died that night along with the kid. Since then, not a day went by when Jack didn't replay the scene in his mind. And now here he was trying to find someone again. His father this time. Could it be, Jack wondered, that all this was really about the failed detective in him wanting, *needing*, another chance to make things right?

Jack drained his coffee and realized it was already half past eight. If he was going to talk to Claire Evans before her lecture, he had better get moving.

The Wagoneer's broken mirror rattled like chips on a poker table as, a short time later, Jack pulled into Lot Two on the northeast corner of UCLA. From there it was a quick walk past the sculpture garden to Dodd Hall, a three-story brick building with a corner clock tower.

Jack strode in. The corridors were teeming with students and professors heading for classrooms where conference lectures were about to begin. Jack found his way to Room 127. People were wandering in, others loitering near the open door. Among them Jack noticed a brunette in a ponytail and glasses conferring with a cocky-looking guy sporting a T-shirt that read "QUESTION EVERYTHING." The brunette gestured toward the classroom and pressed a manila folder into the guy's hands.

Jack entered the room where the audience was settling in and buzzing in philosophy-speak. A podium and microphone had been set up for the lecture but no one was there. Jack checked his watch. It was already nine.

Where was Claire Evans?

All of a sudden Jack remembered the brunette and the way she had motioned toward the room before handing over the folder. Containing lecture notes perhaps? Could it have been Claire?

Jack bolted back out into the hall. There was no sign of the brunette but the guy she had talked to was bent over a water fountain, still clutching the folder. Jack charged over and spun him around, the name JULIAN WADE on his conference badge.

"That girl," Jack said. "The one you were talking to. Was that Claire Evans?"

Wade glowered back, wiping water from his chin.

"Hey," he said. "Do you mind?"

"Where is she? Where did she go?"

Jack's intensity unnerved Wade who pointed down the hall.

"She said an emergency came up. I was only trying to help."

Wade prattled on about how Claire had talked him into presenting her paper, but Jack wasn't listening. He tore down the hall and out of the building.

There was no sign of Claire.

While Jack scanned the area he reminded himself that there was nothing but her name connecting this woman to his father. For all Jack knew, she might not even know Joseph Pearl, let alone his whereabouts. Then again, it beat the hell out of Jack's backup plan, considering he didn't have one.

He was about to turn back when he spotted Claire on the far side of the sculpture garden. She was behind the wheel of a red Mustang convertible pulling up to the pay booth of Lot Two, the same structure Jack had parked in. Jack rushed toward her while waving and yelling to get her attention but Claire either didn't notice or deliberately ignored him and exited the lot, making a swift right onto Westholme Avenue. Jack's last glimpse of the Mustang was of its taillight blinking to signal an upcoming left turn.

Anyone else would have let it go. Jack couldn't. He sprinted back to his Wagoneer. Seconds later he tore out of the lot.

That blinking taillight, Jack realized, meant Claire intended to make a left on Hilgard Avenue which T-boned at Sunset Boulevard a few blocks up. But which way Claire had gone on Sunset, east or west, was anyone's guess.

Jack roared up Hilgard. The light at Sunset was green, giving him only a split second to decide. As in a dead-even percentage play in poker, Jack knew, the difference between winning and losing all came down to intuition and attention to detail. The way Jack read it, there was only a single variable that favored one direction over the other: the only freeway in the area, the 405, was to the left.

He hung a sharp left turn.

The distance to the 405 was about two and a half miles. That meant more variables for Jack to consider: one, that Claire was actually headed that way and, two, that he could catch her before she got on the freeway. If not, Jack knew the odds of finding her would be reduced to virtually zero, about the same as drawing a royal flush. A quick calculation put Claire about a mile ahead of him and traveling at average speed. That meant Jack would have to go fast to catch her, way faster than the posted speed limit, along one of the curviest stretches of road in the city.

Jack floored it.

For the next two miles he sheered around corners and threaded the needle through traffic to a rage of horns. As he finally came within sight of the freeway he spotted the red Mustang convertible up ahead nearing the entrance ramp. To his surprise it cruised on past, continuing west on Sunset. Only when Jack got close enough to make out Claire behind the wheel, shaking out her ponytail to let her hair flow in the wind, did he ease his foot off the accelerator.

So much for his brilliant powers of deduction, Jack thought. It was sheer, dumb luck that he had made the correct turn back at Sunset and managed to catch up to Claire. But where was she headed? More to the point, was this all a fool's errand or could it help him find his father?

Having come this far, Jack continued to follow the red Mustang—past Brentwood, through The Palisades, all the way to the ocean where Sunset ended at Pacific Coast Highway. At P.C.H., the Mustang turned right and headed north along the coast toward Malibu. Jack kept following. Along the way he happened to spot some dolphins unusually close to shore and took his eye off the road to admire them. When he looked back he had to slam on his brakes to avoid hitting cars in front of him that had stopped for a red light.

Jack fired a look at the Mustang. It had already cleared the intersection and was driving away.

As Jack was forced to wait for the light, he swore and banged the wheel, to the amusement of some beachgoers using the crosswalk. The instant the light turned green, Jack took off again, tires smoking. But the Mustang was already long gone.

He had come this far, Jack thought, he wasn't about to give up now. Mile after mile, he checked every red vehicle, convertible or otherwise, on both sides of the ocean highway.

Nothing.

He drove past Malibu, past Zuma, continuing to search in vain. Then north of Trancas he caught a glint of something red out of the corner of his eye and turned in time to see a car parked off a beach access road on the other side of P.C.H., partially hidden behind some azalea bushes.

It was the Mustang.

Jack pulled a U-turn and swung up behind the convertible. Even before climbing from his Wagoneer, he could see there was no one in the car. He walked over and peered inside. Keys were dangled from the ignition, a yellow Hertz tag attached. On the passenger seat lay a purse that had been rifled open. Beside it was an orange plastic prescription bottle with its cap off.

The bottle was empty.

A bad feeling came over Jack.

He raced all-out down the beach road. A hidden cove came into view, deserted except for a lone figure wading into the crashing surf. It was Claire. She was already waist deep. A wave swelled and she let go, allowing it to take her under.

Jack charged into the ocean. By the time he reached Claire she was lifeless. Through pounding waves he half-dragged, half-carried her back to the beach where he gave her C.P.R. She coughed up sea water. Her eyes shot open and flooded with drug-glazed terror. As she tried to bat Jack away, he yanked her up like a rag doll, locked his arms around her from behind and gave her a sharp Heimlich thrust.

Again.

Again.

Finally Claire puked her guts out and collapsed on the sand.

12

JOSEPH PEARL

In the boarded-up netherworld of the abandoned factory, a rat the size of a small dog sniffed for food. It scurried under and around equipment until suddenly it froze, coming face to face with Pearl handcuffed to a steam pipe.

The philosopher stared back, heart in his throat.

Spooked, the rat darted away.

It took several moments for Pearl to recover his breath. He had woken at first light, thankful to be able to see where he was. Ironically, it was a theme he had explored many times in his work, the need to establish a frame of reference before tackling a philosophical problem. Yet the full depth of its importance had never been apparent to Pearl until now.

For hours, he didn't know how many, Pearl had been forced to lie there in the same cramped position. Having gained back some strength, he had yelled for help until he could yell no more. He had tried every way he could think of to break or twist out of his restraints. He had held his bladder as long as possible before letting go. Every human emotion, from despair to boredom to morbid fascination, had gripped him. But the one that kept him alert was dread. It was the certainty that whoever had done this to him would be returning sooner or later.

To assuage his fear, Pearl directed his thoughts back to the rat. It brought to mind Darwin's *Origin of the Species* and the seismic impact of that seminal work on philosophy as well as on science, reminding Pearl of questions about culture, language and the distinction between the human animal and the concept of a person that went to the very heart of philosophical understanding. In turn, it caused Pearl to think about the grand unifying theory he had been working on, the one he hoped would bring together his own bold notions of constructivism with the entire history of philosophy. To his knowledge no one had ever attempted anything quite so ambitious or, some might say, so foolish.

For several stolen moments Pearl forgot where he was as he tackled a few of the thornier abstractions he had been grappling with. Then a sound reverberated across the cavernous factory, the faraway bang of a door slamming shut. It jarred Pearl back to earth. The bang had come from somewhere below. It was disorienting and made Pearl realize for the first time that he was on the second floor of the abandoned building, not the ground floor.

Another sound echoed, behind Pearl this time and growing louder: the rhythmic clang of steel-tipped boots trudging up a flight of metal stairs. As the boots approached, Pearl twisted and turned, straining to see, but his chains made it impossible. Nonetheless, the philosopher in him was relieved. Come what may, there would be clarity.

Finally a shadow fell over Pearl.

"Well, well," a raspy voice cackled. "If it ain't the golden goose."

It was Reaper. The young gangbanger snickered to himself and circled behind Pearl, taunting him by remaining hidden in the gloom.

"Goes to show," Reaper said, "Never can tell about people. Reckon if I saw you on the street, no way would I figure you'd be worth shit."

Pearl struggled to remain calm.

"I'm sorry, I can't see you," he said. "Would you please come around?"

Reaper howled.

"Now that's a new one. That's good! Usually the first thing you hear is 'Where am I?' or 'What the fuck's goin' on?'"

"I'm sure you'll share that all in good time."

The polite intelligence of the philosopher unsettled Reaper. As he slouched into view, Pearl noticed the colorful tattoo on Reaper's neck, illustrated in intricate loving detail: a pretty Latina holding a cherubic infant.

"How's that suit you?" Reaper asked. "Better?"

"Thank you."

"Any more special requests?"

"When you're ready," Pearl said, "I'm listening."

"Oh, is that right?"

"With all due respect."

"Man, I don't think you get it yet. See, you do not wanna fuck with me."

Without warning Reaper kicked Pearl in the face. The blow sent him slamming backwards against the pipes, roaring in agony.

"Listening ain't what you need," Reaper said. "What you need is to pray. Pray to God or Whoever the fuck's up there that your peeps think you're worth more breathing than not. So's we can get rid of you and I won't have to look at your *mas feo que Picio* face no more."

Reaper reddened with anger, causing the mother and child in his tattoo to appear bathed in blood. From his back pocket Reaper pulled out a white plastic trash bag. The sight of it made Pearl recoil.

"What is that for?"

"You'll see."

Reaper shook out the bag as if to slip it over Pearl's head. When Pearl struggled, Reaper slammed him against the pipes with even more savagery than before.

The sickening crack echoed through the factory.

Pearl tried to raise his head but was unable to. The clarity he had sought had come, but it was not the clarity he hoped for. Beneath the fog of blood and pain, he realized he had been stripped of his only defense, his power of reason. Nothing he could summon from the fine-tuned instrument of his mind was strong enough to help him now.

13

JACK

ack found an old canvas jacket in the trunk of his car and wrapped it around Claire. As they sped back toward Malibu, she threw him a woozy look.

"Where are we going?"

"The nearest hospital," Jack said. "To get you help."

"No, please, I'm fine..."

Claire swiveled to face him, trying to sell it with a forced smile. That's when she noticed something over Jack's shoulder that made her eyes go wide.

"Wait," she said. "*Who are you?*"

Jack adjusted his rear view mirror to see what she was staring at: his father's book lying on the back seat, the one he had taken from the hotel room, which he had tossed there and forgotten about. In the same instant, Claire flung open her passenger door to escape the moving car.

"Claire, no!"

Lunging, Jack barely grabbed her wrist in time while slamming on the brakes. As he managed to swerve to the shoulder without causing an accident, Claire fought him to break free.

"Let go!"

"Easy," Jack said. "I can explain."

"How do you know my name? And why do you have that book?"

"Joseph Pearl," Jack said.

"I know who wrote it."

"I'm his son."

Claire blinked, thrown. Her look of confusion and distrust made Jack pull out his wallet and show her his driver's license. Claire traced Jack's surname with a shaky finger, then turned a bright shade of red.

"Did Joe tell you to follow me?"

"No."

"Then why...how...never mind, I don't want to know."

Jack was relieved that he didn't have to explain. But he could also see that Claire was in no condition to answer the questions he had chased her all the way out there to ask. And while getting her medical attention was the right thing to do, it wouldn't prevent Claire from hurting herself if she really wanted to. The only choice, Jack realized, was to leave her in the care of someone she knew.

The passenger door was still open.

Jack reached past Claire and yanked it shut.

For an awkward few minutes they sat there in silence as traffic whizzed by. Then Jack asked Claire about friends or relatives she could contact. Claire shook her head. She had few of either, she said, and none who lived in California. As for people at the conference, she was worried about any of them seeing her this way, the potential damage to her reputation, which was why she refused to go back to her hotel where many of her colleagues were staying. There was only one person she felt she could trust in such circumstances, who wouldn't ask her to explain. The irony wasn't lost on Jack: it was the same person who had dropped out of sight twenty-four hours ago, a certain famous philosopher who Jack had been trying to find despite the long-unresolved feelings it was dredging up.

Jack considered his options, none of them good, and roared off again. A few miles down the road, he pulled up to the drive-thru window of a McDonald's and ordered two Big Macs and a large coffee. When they came, Jack handed them to Claire who looked as if she was going to be sick all over again.

"I don't drink caffeine," she said.

"You do now."

"And I don't eat junk food."

"It'll soak up what's left of the pills you took."

Claire realized it was an order, not a request. As Jack drove off once more, Claire studied him between queasy sips and bites.

"You have the same nose. I thought Joe broke his."

Jack shook his head.

"About the only thing we have in common. Unfortunately his brains didn't come with it."

"He never mentioned he had a son," Claire said.

"Why am I not surprised?"

"But he must have told you about me."

"Not exactly."

"Then how did you find me?"

Served him right, Jack thought, for not keeping his mouth shut. On a positive note, Claire was starting to come around. Now was as good a time as any to find out what she knew.

"That isn't important," Jack said. "What matters is my father is missing."

Claire stopped eating. She looked baffled.

"Since yesterday," Jack said. "I was hoping you might know something about it."

"Missing? Why would Joe be missing?"

It sounded strange to Jack's ear, hearing his father referred to by his first name. Especially by a woman who knew him intimately. Jack wasn't sure whether to be repulsed or fascinated.

"Tell me the last time you saw him," Jack said.

Claire shook her head, trying to remember and also forget.

"Couple days ago," she said. "We had a fight."

"What about?"

"It's...complicated."

"Your relationship?"

Claire pretended not to be surprised that Jack knew, but it brought added sadness to her face.

"More like the end of it," she said.

"So you have no idea where he could be?"

Claire shook her head, fighting back tears.

"When you see him, please don't tell him what I tried to do. Please, I beg you..."

Claire brought her knees to her chest and pulled the jacket tighter around her. Then she leaned her head against the passenger door and closed her eyes.

They continued south on P.C.H. When they reached Santa Monica, the scenic ocean-view highway looped through a tunnel and became the un-scenic I-10 heading east toward downtown. Jack turned on the radio and caught *Strange Days* by the Doors. *Strange days have found us, Strange days have tracked us down.*

Perfect, Jack thought.

By the time he ramped off at his exit, Claire was slumped asleep hugging her seatbelt.

14

JACK

The Wagoneer cruised through the dragon gates of Chinatown. Jack parked in a red zone in front of his building and carried Claire, still sleeping, up the two flights to his loft. Trouser met them at the door, his ears perked up with curiosity.

"I know, boy," Jack said. "Long time since we've had someone over."

The Lab appeared to smile, wagging his tail so hard that his whole body quivered.

"Hey, none of that, knucklehead. Don't even go there."

As Trouser licked Claire's dangling hand, Jack gently lowered her onto the couch. He could smell the sea on her along with faint traces of vomit and perfume, that leathery vanilla scent he had caught on his father's white shirt. Without her glasses which had been lost in the waves, Claire looked softer, more radiant, even with all she had been through. Jack let his eyes wander down the curve of her neck to her blouse. The top button had broken off, revealing a hint of cleavage. For a moment Jack watched the rise and fall of her breath until the ring of his cell phone made him catch himself.

He pulled out the phone and checked the screen. It was that 657 number Gary had retrieved from the hotel room phone, the one belonging to the French woman on whose voicemail Jack had left a message. Jack ducked into the kitchen to answer the call.

"Hello," he said.

"Professor Pearl?"

Instead of the refined, sensual female voice Jack expected, it was some guy with the flat, laid-back tone of a native Californian.

"Not quite," Jack said. "Who's calling?"

"Sorry, must have the wrong number."

"Wait, I'm Pearl's son," Jack said. "I'm the one who left that message about him."

The guy on the line clicked his tongue.

"Son? Oops. My bad. I told Esma the message was from Pearl himself."

Jack frowned.

"Esma?"

"I'm her assistant," the guy said. "She asked me to ring back to say she hoped her idea helped."

"What idea? Helped with what?"

"That's all she said. Her exact words were: tell Joseph I trust my suggestion was helpful and that all went smoothly."

"Well, maybe I could speak to Esma," Jack said.

"You just missed her."

"Is there another number where she can be reached?"

"Afraid I'm not at liberty to give that out."

"It's important. When do you expect her back?"

"Couple hours. But she has plans later. Your best bet? Call tomorrow when she's not so busy."

Jack rolled his eyes. If he changed *important* to *urgent*, he might get the guy to put him through. On the other hand, if this Esma had information about some matter his father had pursued at her suggestion, there might be value in hearing it face to face.

"Okay," Jack said, "I'll try back tomorrow. By the way, Esma's last name is spelled..."

"Same as it sounds. K-A-Y-A."

"Yeah, that's what I thought. Thanks."

Jack hung up and glanced through the kitchen doorway to see Claire still sleeping soundly. Trouser now lay by her feet with his paws crossed as if to protect her. With a tap of the browser icon on his phone, Jack ran an internet search on Esma Kaya. It turned out she was a respected historian of architecture as well as a tireless patron of the arts, once married to a wealthy American businessman, who divided her time between homes in Orange County and the south of France. Photos revealed her to be one of those natural beauties, even in middle age, whose attention and energy could get fellow philanthropists to write large checks. As he continued to search, Jack stumbled on an image of Esma with none other than Joseph Pearl, taken at an aesthetics conference in Istanbul over a decade ago. They were standing close and smiling in that wooden way people do when trying to hide the attraction between them.

It was the second time in twenty-four hours that Jack had learned of an amorous side to his father. But this time he was more uneasy than surprised as he realized that the date of the Istanbul photo was uncomfortably close to that of his mother's suicide ten years ago. Could it be, Jack wondered, that his mother had learned of the affair and that was the reason, not her husband's commitment to philosophy at the expense of all else, that caused her to take her own life? The disturbing possibility made Jack want to dig deeper but he resisted the urge and switched to a search for Esma's address. The usual people-finder sites showed it blocked, a protection that would keep away stalkers and telemarketers. But not a stubborn ex-cop like Jack who knew of other ways to obtain such information. According to property title records, Esma Kaya lived in Anaheim Hills on a street called Glastonbury Oval.

For quick reference Jack jotted down directions, along with Esma's phone number, on the back of a Chinese take-out menu. He checked his watch. Traffic was sure to be bad, always a factor in the Southland, but if he left now he could probably make it down there in about an hour.

With Claire out cold, Jack changed into dry clothes, then went down the hall and knocked on Mrs. Woo's door. As he explained the situation to his kindly neighbor and left her with Claire, Mrs. Woo gave him a wink of approval.

There was a parking ticket under the windshield wiper when Jack returned to his car. He chucked it in the back seat to keep his father's book company and pulled away. Before getting on the freeway, Jack stopped at a convenience store to grab a snack and coffee for the drive down to O.C. As he paid, he noticed an open lunch bag on the counter behind the clerk, its contents peeking out: a half-eaten pastrami sandwich and a pint of vodka.

Stoli, Jack's one-time poison of choice.

Jack felt his stomach tighten. The liquor bottle was no different than all those he had seen and passed without temptation in the last year since getting sober. But something had changed. This time Jack had a sudden, overwhelming craving to drink. It hit him so fast and hard that he spilled the coffee and left it behind with his change in order to get out of there as quickly as possible.

Jack drove onto the Hollywood Freeway at North Main and ramped over to the Harbor Freeway heading south. He turned on the radio. He turned it off. He tried thinking about old girlfriends, world capitals, anything to distract himself, but the harder he tried, the more his mind returned to what had happened back there.

Jack knew that feeling.

He knew what it meant.

He didn't need a shrink to tell him the events of the last couple days were beginning to take a toll.

15

SALAZAR

n the back booth of a smoky pool hall, a white plastic bag dropped on the table in front of Salazar with a soft thud—the bag Reaper had tormented Pearl with.

"There," Reaper said. "That's all the *baboso* had on him. No stuffed animals or rosaries like the kids of the dealers and coyotes we usually target. How'd you find this joker anyway?"

"I told you," Salazar said. "Personal connections."

Salazar emptied the contents of the bag in the jaundiced light.

"Did he put up a fight?" Salazar asked.

"Naw, too scared."

"And you didn't talk to him?"

"Not a word," Reaper answered. "Like you said."

Salazar doubted it was true but decided to let it pass. While Reaper had useful talents, he was too green to understand the importance of such details. He would learn, thought Salazar. He had better, or he would be dealt with accordingly.

Pool balls clattered in the background as Salazar pushed aside coins and keys and picked up a brown leather wallet. He opened it to find a Massachusetts driver's license inside.

"Joseph William Pearl," Salazar read. "Five-foot eleven, hazel eyes, age sixty-one. Lives in Boston."

Reaper chugged his beer.

"I had an uncle from there," he said. "Or maybe was Boise. Well, y'know, not my real uncle. I had a lotta them growing up."

Not listening, Salazar searched the wallet and found a Harvard University faculty I.D. There was also an appointment reminder card from a doctor's office, an oncologist.

"It appears this man has health issues," Salazar said. "And that he is a college professor."

"No shit? Maybe he can teach me Moby Fucking Dick."

"He teaches philosophy."

"Whatever."

"Philosophy. Do you even know what that is?"

"Who gives a fuck? What's he worth is all that matters. Speaking of which, it's been over a day since we grabbed him. When do we call his *familia*?"

Salazar remained composed.

"Soon," he said.

"Let's hope they want him back real bad, enough to cough up some serious coin."

"It's not only the families that pay," Salazar said. "Sometimes there are others who care more, others with the means and motivation to bear the burden."

"Like a rich homie, you mean?"

"Or a lovesick girlfriend."

"Whoever it is, why not contact them now?"

"Better to wait and let them worry. Drives up the price."

While that was often true, it did not apply in this case. But there was no reason to share that with Reaper. Salazar knew that the prospect of a bigger pay-day would placate the kid.

"I guess you know what you're doing," Reaper said.

"Always," Salazar said. "Now why don't you make yourself useful and get me another beer."

From the money in Pearl's wallet, Salazar extracted a ten dollar bill and pushed it across the table. Reaper glared in outrage and rubbed his neck tattoo. As Salazar knew, the tat was a portrait of Reaper's ex, Carmen, and their baby, Raoul. It wasn't hard to guess what Reaper was thinking: once he scored his cut of the kidnapping money, Carmen might take him back and they could be a family again, but until then he would have to suck up to Salazar.

Reaper swiped up the cash and trudged away to the bar. Glad to be rid of him, Salazar returned to searching the wallet. In one of its compartments he found an expensive-looking business card with a name engraved in metallic gray:

ESMA KAYA

Salazar held up the card and stared at the name, as if it held some private meaning for him. In another slot he discovered an orange Post-It with words scrawled on it—written in anger, it appeared, because the pen strokes were so heavy that they had torn through the paper:

WHAT WOULD KANT SAY?

Salazar pondered its meaning. Then, tucked behind a credit card, he came upon an old, faded photograph. It was a candid shot of a younger Pearl, perhaps in his thirties, caught in a happy moment with a young boy and a woman with compassionate blue eyes.

Intrigued, Salazar placed the photo next to the one in Pearl's driver's license and noted how much older Pearl looked, but not from aging. It was the look of weary acceptance that came from experiencing a great personal loss—a look Salazar knew well, the same one he saw in the mirror every day.

Of all his kidnappings, Salazar thought, how fitting that this would be his last victim: a thoughtful man, a man for whom family was important, a man worn down by the travails of life.

A kindred spirit.

With the respect it deserved, Salazar returned the photo to the wallet and folded it shut.

16

JACK

For Jack, love Dad.

Jack remembered the inscription halfway to Orange County. For the rest of the drive he puzzled over it. What could have possessed his father to write something so personal? This, from the same absentee parent who had always forgotten Jack's birthday growing up. Who, as far as Jack could remember, had never once used the L word. Could it be that after their phone call, his old man had been seized by a pang of paternal regret? Was this an olive branch? If so, had his dad, an expert in the meaning and power of language, struggled to get the words just right, in the end deciding that less was more? Or was Jack reading too much into it?

A million questions.

Every one raised ten more.

God help me, Jack thought, I'm starting to think in circles like a philosopher.

Yet all the questions pointed to a deeper mystery, one that seemed to be at the heart of the matter: was the timing of Joseph Pearl's call to Jack simply a coincidence? Or had he wanted to talk to his son about more than their past, something that might explain why he was missing?

Jack drove on. Along the way he passed the usual oddities seen only on L.A. freeways. A surfboard flattened like road kill. A phalanx of Hells Angels in dress leathers riding together in a funeral procession. And, most spectacularly, a double-decker tour bus engulfed in flames on the shoulder as its stranded passengers snapped selfies with morbid glee. While the blaze posed no danger to traffic, cars slowed down to rubberneck which backed up the freeway for miles. By the time Jack reached Anaheim Hills he had been on the road for nearly three hours and was ready to strangle someone. He was also concerned about those plans Esma's assistant had mentioned, which meant there was a good chance Esma might not even be home when he got to her place.

The moment Jack turned onto Glastonbury Oval he realized that finding Esma wasn't going to be a problem, but that he now faced another one. At the end of the cul de sac was a gated estate matching the address Jack had jotted down on the take-out menu, where a bevy of female valets in red satin tuxedo jackets were taking Jaguars and Bentleys from well-dressed guests arriving for a party. So that explained why Esma was so busy, Jack realized. He glanced down at the shirt and jeans he was wearing. Not exactly elegant attire. A tie would come in handy right now, except Jack didn't own a tie. The last time he had worn one was at his mother's funeral.

No sweat, Jack thought. Party or not, he would breeze in there and find Esma and she would explain his dad's whereabouts and how the whole thing was a big misunderstanding. Then Jack could go back to his nice, happy life and never have to think about his old man again.

And in that world where rhinos fly...

Jack pulled up and turned over his car to one of the valets, then followed the flow of guests past manicured gardens and a tennis court to a palatial mansion.

A pair of greeters, a man and a woman, were working the entrance, welcoming invitees while checking their names off a list. Both wore Secret Service-type earpieces which told Jack this was going to be more complicated than he had counted on. One thing was sure: that stunt he had pulled at the W to get up to his father's room wasn't going to work here.

Jack sized up the greeters, observing that the woman was being more careful in her checks, so he stepped up to her male counterpart, a linebacker type with fire-hydrant biceps and a chin-strap goatee.

"Hi," Jack said. "I'm here to see Esma."

Goatee gave him a quick up and down.

"Your name, please?"

"I'm not on the list."

"Sir, this is a private party."

"I know, but—"

"Sir, please. I'll have to ask you to leave."

As Goatee signaled two security men, an idea came to Jack.

"On second thought," Jack said, "Maybe I am on the list."

Goatee's eyes narrowed.

"Your name?"

"Pearl."

The security men waited for Goatee to check his list. When he did, he frowned with surprise.

"First name?"

Jack was surprised too but remained poker-faced.

"Joseph," he said.

Guests were backing up behind Jack. Goatee checked the name again and shrugged, deciding it wasn't worth causing a scene.

"Sorry for the inconvenience, sir. Enjoy your evening."

As Goatee stepped aside, Jack walked into the mansion. Back in his days on the force, he had a few occasions to visit places like this, homes in the ultra-exclusive zip codes of L.A. where, despite the best security money could buy, crimes of one kind or another were committed. But this was hands down the most opulent residence Jack had ever stepped foot in. The two-story living room was wedding white and large enough to fit ten of Jack's lofts inside, with twin marble staircases at one end and a Steinway grand piano at the other. On the walls were paintings that could rival those of any museum. Jack recognized a Paul Klee and a couple Hockneys, even a Picasso nude—not those hand-painted repros sold in the Glendale Galleria but the real deal.

All through the house guests were chatting and mingling, the soiree spilling out onto the back lawn where a Mariachi band was playing *Guantanamera* near an infinity pool. Jack wasn't there to have fun but in an effort to blend in he grabbed a red wine off the tray of a passing server. Not until he brought it to his lips did he realize what he had done. He pulled the wine away but it was too late. The rich taste and aroma had fired off the liquor-deprived synapses in Jack's brain and brought on a wave of craving like the one he had experienced in the convenience store, only stronger.

Jack looked around for help and noticed a collection of framed family photos on the nearby grand piano, arranged with care to look as if they had been placed there informally. He ditched his wine glass behind the photos, displacing a few, and headed off in search of Esma.

It didn't take long to find her. She was impossible to miss in a splashy cocktail dress and statement necklace of rough-hewn amethysts, a clash of styles that on anyone less beautiful or confident would have come off looking tacky. With the effortless skill of a seasoned hostess Esma was trading embraces and air kisses with her guests. Jack intercepted her as she was leaving one group to check on another.

"Excuse me," Jack said. "Esma?"

Esma breezed around to face him.

"Bonjour, hello, welcome," she said. "Forgive me, have we met?"

"Actually, no, we haven't. But I believe you know my father, Joseph Pearl."

A look of utter delight came over Esma.

"Joseph? He's here? How wonderful! And how nice that he brought you with him!"

"Well, the truth is—"

"So you must be Jack. At last, I have the pleasure of meeting the splendid son I have heard so much about."

Jack was taken off guard, both by her knowing his name and that his old man had mentioned him. More than mentioned, it sounded like. 'Splendid'? Or maybe she was just being polite.

"It's been forever since Joseph and I have seen each other," Esma said. "When he called to say he was in town, I made him promise to come."

Jack was still processing the 'son I've heard so much about' part, wondering what specifics his dad had told Esma about him.

"He didn't bring me," Jack said. "I'm trying to find him."

"So you came separately then?"

"What I meant was he's gone missing. I was hoping you might have some idea where he is."

Esma smiled, smoothing the amethysts at her throat.

"Delayed by his conference, no doubt. You know how your father puts everything second to his work. Don't worry, I am sure he will be arriving soon."

It wasn't her fault for misunderstanding, Jack thought. He had been less than clear. Rather than try again, he decided to take the path of least resistance.

"You're right, I'm sure he's on his way," Jack said. "I hope you don't mind my showing up first, looking like this."

"Don't be absurd," Esma laughed. "Life is too short! I understand you work in law enforcement. How interesting. I want to hear all about it, but first tell me, how is your father?"

"Elusive."

"Yes, of course."

"Hard to pin down."

"I know what you mean."

She didn't, Jack mused. But it didn't matter. It was time to probe.

"You mentioned he called you?"

"Yes," Esma said. "The day before yesterday."

"Just wanting to catch up?"

"And to ask my advice as someone who collects art. He was wondering where he might go to find the ideal complement to his next masterpiece."

Jack frowned.

"Sorry, you lost me."

"As I am sure you know," Esma said, "It is a source of lively debate within the philosophy world: what work of art will Joseph Pearl choose to grace the cover of his latest book? And what does it mean? The pieces your father is drawn to tend to be primitive and soulful, achingly human. When it comes to appreciating things of beauty, he has a special gift."

Coming from a woman so attractive, Jack wondered if the statement had some personal significance.

"Aren't book covers chosen by publishers, not authors?"

"There's a bit more freedom in the academic world," Esma said. "Especially when the author is someone as important as Joseph Pearl."

"I see," Jack said, "So for his upcoming book, he was looking for some drawing or painting to put on the cover?"

Esma nodded.

"A pre-Columbian artifact. He was quite specific. I happened to know someone who specializes in that area, whose pieces could be counted on to be authentic and not too expensive."

Jack flashed on what Esma's assistant had told him on the phone. So that must have been the 'suggestion' that Esma hoped 'went smoothly'.

"Did you go with him to pick something out?"

Esma shook her head.

"Joseph said he had a morning lecture to give, then lunch plans, but that he hoped to look up Henry in between."

"Henry? I'm assuming that's the art dealer you recommended?"

"More a custodian of art, I would call him. He handles consignments at his pawn shop."

"Pardon?"

Esma's eyes sparkled with wisdom.

"You would be surprised where great art pops up," she said. "Often in places you least expect."

"And the name of this pawn shop?"

"'Henry's'. Easy to remember. It's on a little side street off Melrose, near the Fairfax District."

Across the room, guests were waving to Esma to join them.

"Go," Jack said. "We can talk more later."

Esma took his hand in both of hers.

"Please make yourself at home, Jack. And promise you will come get me the moment your father arrives. We will find a nice quiet corner where we can all catch up. Ciao."

As she flitted away, Jack stood there alone for a moment, an island of forced restraint in a sea of revelry. The craving from before had subsided but in its place had come fatigue. And more heartwarming thoughts about his father.

Jack hated him.

He hated feeling that he had to look for him.

Most of all, he hated that he was starting to worry about him.

On his way out Jack saw a waiter remove his wine glass from the Steinway grand, repositioning the picture frames so everything was returned to its fragile appearance of order.

Among the photos was one of Esma smiling with her arm around someone, which Jack failed to notice. If he had, it would have changed everything.

17

JACK

As Jack drove away from the Elysian splendor of Anaheim Hills, he flashed on something he had forgotten about or, closer to the truth, had chosen to ignore: those needy voicemails from Lim. He still owed Lim a call. Jack's thoughts drifted back to a year ago when he had finally gotten himself clean and sober, back when he still took the Twelve Steps to heart. The last Step, about carrying the message to others, was the reason he had agreed to sponsor Lim, a teen alcoholic Jack knew nothing about except that Lim had suffered a messed-up childhood and was about to have more abuse heaped on him by the juvenile justice system. In other words, a slightly more damaged version of himself. Only later did Jack realize what he had gotten himself into. With Lim, it was always the same pattern. First would come some personal calamity, followed by frantic texts and calls, then silence. Days later he would reemerge from the wreckage and Jack would help him get back on his feet until it happened all over again. Crisis, crash, repeat. Lately, the cycle had been getting shorter, and with it Jack's tolerance. But guilt always seemed to reel Jack back in. It made him pull out his cell phone and speed-dial Lim's number.

Lim answered on the second ring.

"G-go to hell," he said.

Great, Jack thought, at least the kid hadn't deleted him from his contact list.

"Lim, I'm sorry."

"Yes...yes, you are."

"I'm checking to make sure you're okay."

"Oh, so now you give a shit?"

"Did something happen?"

"Two guesses where I was when I called before? Try County."

Jack frowned.

"Jail?"

"Bingo! No more juvie since I turned eighteen last week. But hey, n-no problem cuz my sponsor bailed me out. Oh wait. No, you didn't, did you? So I had to call my crazy crackhead cousin who kicked me out of his crib."

"Wait," Jack said. "Back up."

"Yeah, that's right. I'm homeless again. But it's all good cuz I didn't drink. Not one drop, can you believe it? So you're off the hook. No r-relapsing Flips on your conscience."

Flip, Jack knew, was a colloquial term signifying Filipino descent, an acronym for Fucking Little Island

People. It was a word Lim detested, the reason he was throwing it out there. One of Lim's special talents, knowing how to get under Jack's skin.

"Why don't we try this over," Jack said.

"So you can get my hopes up again? Here's a better idea. Tell me to fuck off. At least that would be honest."

Jack hesitated.

"C'mon, man," Lim said. "Straight out, 'stead of that phony-ass crap you call help. Let's hear you get real for once, assuming you even k-know what that is."

"Is that what you want? Honesty?"

"Doesn't everyone? Go ahead, say it. S-say it if you've got the balls!"

"Okay," Jack said. "Fuck off."

The line went dead. Jack clicked off his phone and felt a cold wave of shame, acutely aware that he had treated Lim with the same indifference he resented in his old man. At least Joseph Pearl could blame his lack of empathy on a dedication to his work. Jack had no such excuse. That made him a jerk as well as a fraud. Nevertheless, he was relieved. Besides, Lim deserved someone more dependable to be there for him. Someone less damaged. Jack told himself it was all for the best.

While the cell was still in his hand he thought about checking in with Mrs. Woo but realized it was unnecessary. Claire was safe and in good hands. Instead, Jack went online to get a phone number for Henry's Pawn Shop. There was no reason to believe that calling the place would shed any light on his father's disappearance but it was worth a try. When Jack punched in the number, he was greeted by a folksy recorded voice:

"Hi. It's me, the eponymous Henry. I'm either with a client or grabbing something in the back, so please try again later. Or better yet, just come on by. We're open 'til six."

Jack clicked off and checked the time on his cell. It was four-thirty. Traffic was moving at a good clip, in contrast to his trip down to Orange County. There was no reason he couldn't make it to the shop in plenty of time before it closed.

Instead of taking the I-10 to Fairfax Avenue which could be slow during rush hour, Jack caught the Hollywood Freeway to Melrose and headed west. In L.A., Jack knew, there were always several ways to get where you wanted to go. Making the right choice could save you a lot of headaches, as in poker and relationships and pretty much everything else in life. So you could get to your other headaches faster.

Jack cruised through the trendy section of Melrose Avenue, past shops with names like Vinyl Fetish and Retail Slut. The typical denizens were out in droves, neo-punks and bikers and Midwestern tourist families and bands of young Japanese girls dressed in Goth Lolita outfits. As Jack continued down Melrose the foot traffic thinned and the stores appeared more and more run-down. Others had been boarded-up and plastered with graffiti and peeling rock concert posters, victims of changing taste and the fickle economy.

A couple blocks before Fairfax Jack found the side street he was looking for and turned right. A row of sad-looking businesses came into view, all long-abandoned except one, a corner shop abutting the service alley that ran parallel to the main drag. Above the door was a hand-painted sign with the outline of some previous store moniker behind it. The sign read:

HENRY'S PAWN SHOP

Jack parked across the street and ambled over. Because of the late afternoon glare from the sun, he didn't realize the shop was dark until he reached the door. Jack tried it. The door was locked. He cupped his hand against the window and peered inside. Along with the usual eclectic clutter typical of hock shops Jack could make out several shelves in the back lined with primitive artifacts. Whether they were pre-Columbian or not Jack had no way of knowing. What was clear, however, was that no one was around. It seemed that Henry or whoever ran the shop for him had closed up early and gone home.

Jack searched the door and window for an after-hours number but there wasn't one. Frustrated, he gave the door a sharp kick. It caused a bell inside to jingle.

Patience, Jack knew, had never been his strong suit. The same went for accepting defeat, especially after what happened three years ago. It made Jack think about Franco and the hell he put his ex-partner through, not only straining their friendship but placing Franco in danger—all in Jack's obsessive attempt

95

to bring down the ghost who disappeared with all that money. That nameless, faceless killer who somehow knew that Jack was closing in on him, and set that trap for him to take the fall.

Someone, Jack believed, who could only be a cop.

Jack shook it off and returned to his car. As he sat there gripping the wheel but going nowhere, statistics from his detective days filled his head.

30: the number of hours his dad had gone unaccounted for.

2300: the number of Americans reported missing each day.

6: the percentage of those over the age of eighteen.

Of that small number of missing adults, all belonged to one of four subgroups: young men, people with psychiatric problems, people with drug or alcohol addictions and seniors suffering from dementia. None of those fit Joseph Pearl which suggested to Jack that his old man fell into a more serious category of missing persons known in law enforcement as E or I, Endangered or Involuntary.

That raised another statistic.

48: the number of hours after which the odds of finding an E or I alive dropped off the chart.

The implications were clear. Either Jack picked up the pace and pulled out all the stops or he risked running out of time.

Assuming he hadn't already.

18

JACK

Jack headed back to Chinatown. On the way he put in another call to Gary. Now that Jack was clear on the seriousness of the situation, there were some basic checks that needed to be made: passport, credit cards, bank accounts. If any belonging to Joseph Pearl had been used in the last couple days, it might provide a clue. Over the phone Gary explained to Jack that accessing that kind of security-protected data was outside his purview. But he had a friend in Nigeria, a bank employee who ran phishing schemes, who could get the job done fast. He told Jack to expect an e-mail from the Nigerian by tomorrow morning at the latest.

Next, Jack called the W, the morgue and all those area hospitals he had rung the night before. Good detective work, Jack knew, required dogged checking and rechecking to make sure no stone, not even a pebble, had been left unturned.

For better or worse, nothing had changed.

Jack turned onto his block and parked. As he killed the engine, he caught himself reaching toward the glove compartment for his service revolver, the one he had been stripped of along with his shield. It gave Jack a bad feeling. The last time he had pulled the gun from the glove box was during his last week as a cop, when Jack suspected he was being followed and that his cover had been blown. For those next few days the weapon never left his hand, even as he slept in his car in different locations each night while telling Becky more and more elaborate lies about why he couldn't come home, in order to protect her—all the while drowning his fears the best way he knew how, in ever larger quantities of alcohol.

Until the night fate rewrote his life in indelible ink.

But that was three years ago. Why, Jack wondered, would he be reaching for a weapon now? Could it be that his unconscious was warning him of a new danger, one somehow connected to his father's disappearance?

The unsettling thought continued to eat at Jack until he walked into his loft to find it empty. Claire was gone. So was Trouser. For a second Jack froze with alarm, all sorts of dark explanations filling his head, until the obvious one registered. He went down the hall and knocked on Mrs. Woo's door. A moment later the Chinese woman answered it with an affectionate scowl.

"Out playing games of chance again?"

"No," Jack said. "I told you, it was personal matter."

"One day you learn," Mrs. Woo said. "Right now, dinner ready. Zhangcha duck, your favorite."

Over her shoulder Jack could see Trouser batting around a chewed-up tennis ball with Muffin and Fu. Then Claire emerged from the kitchen with a bowl of rice in her hands. She was no longer in the wet clothes Jack had left her in, now wearing a pair of matronly slacks and an ugly sweater with butterflies on it. Her hair was still damp from a shower and her tear-stained makeup had been scrubbed off.

"Oh, hi," Claire said. "You're back."

"Sorry I took so long."

"Did you find Joe? Where was he? Please say you didn't mention me..."

"Of course not."

"Thank God."

"Even if I had wanted to," Jack said. "He's still missing."

Claire's look changed to one of concern. Mrs. Woo saw it.

"Sound like important things you two need talk about," she said. "Best postpone our dinner another time."

Claire put down her bowl and gave the woman a warm hug.

"Thank you for everything. Oh, your clothes—"

Mrs. Woo shooed her away.

"Remember, dear. Time. Best medicine."

As she saw them to the door, Mrs. Woo threw Jack a matchmaker wink. He pretended not to notice and led Claire back down the hall to his loft with Trouser trailing behind.

"Such a kind woman," Claire said. "I'm sure she had a million questions but she didn't ask me any. Well, one maybe."

"What was that?"

"She asked if I knew what a good man you are."

They reached Jack's door. He held it open for Claire but she remained outside as Trouser bounded in.

"Sweet friend you've got there," Claire said.

Jack nodded with a smile.

"He's a goofball. Only one who'll put up with me."

"His name's Trouser?"

"When we first met, he wouldn't let go of my pant leg. He's seen me through a lot. C'mon, I'll make you some coffee."

Claire hesitated.

"I think it's better if I don't come in."

"A few minutes, that's all," Jack said. "We need to talk."

Claire wrung her hands.

"Look," she said. "I realize this is awkward and inconvenient, and please forgive me if it sounds cold, but I need to stop thinking about Joe."

Jack wasn't sure how to respond.

"It's all I've been doing for days," Claire said. "And the reason I tried to...so stupid, pathetic...I mean, I haven't even thanked you for saving me. As if I ever could."

Claire attempted to brighten her expression but it collapsed under the weight of too many emotions.

"What I'm trying to say is...Joseph, your father... wherever he is I'm sure he's okay. But I don't know anything about it. If I did, I would tell you. What I need to do right now is take care of myself for once and go."

"Go where?"

"Back to Yale," Claire said. "I'm fine, I'm better now. I think you can see that. In the morning I'll catch the first flight home, then take some time off to get my bearings again."

Jack didn't answer. Claire reached out and touched his arm.

"Again, I'm so grateful," she said. "And sorry for all the trouble I've caused you. If I can use your phone, I'll call a cab to take me back to my hotel. Then I promise you'll never have to see me again."

19

JACK

Jack insisted on driving Claire to her hotel. She was the closest thing he had to a lead and all he had to work with at the moment. That was how he justified it to himself. If there was another motive, Jack didn't want to think about it.

"There's something I keep bumping on," Jack said as he maneuvered his car through traffic. "Two people have a fight and break up. One vanishes, the other tries to take her life. It feels like more than a coincidence."

Claire's back went up.

"What are you implying?"

"Did something happen that might explain why he's missing?"

"Do we have to talk about this again?"

"Is there some reason you don't want to?"

"I told you why."

"What are you leaving out? What are you not telling me that's important?"

Resentment filled Claire's eyes. Then it drained away into sorrow and she gave a sarcastic shrug.

"Okay, you got me," she said. "I confess. I made him drink a cup of hemlock like Socrates, for dumping me. Then I felt so horrible and guilty about it I wanted to kill myself."

She turned away but Jack could see her lips trembling. The shadows of passing lights caressed the contours of her face.

"Sorry," Jack said. "I never meant to suggest..."

"Sure you did. Not that I blame you. What do you know about me? Nothing. Except that I'm some crazy woman who felt wronged by a man for all the clichéd reasons. Not just any man, your father. Why should you believe me? I wouldn't."

"So to be clear," Jack said. "You're saying?"

"I'm saying there's nothing I can tell you. I don't have the slightest idea where he is. I realize that's not what you want to hear and it's not very helpful but it happens to be the truth."

Claire raised her chin to meet his gaze. All the police interrogations that Jack had conducted, both court-worthy and not, had taught him how to read people with exceptional accuracy. At the poker tables it was his greatest strength and the single most important factor in the game: being able to discern the difference between a look that was protecting hidden information and one that was not. Already having a baseline on Claire, Jack studied her eye movements, skin tone and micro-expressions, all the things that gave people away. While he did, Jack thought about how damaged he was to be mentally polygraphing Claire as if she were a common criminal or card shark. Damaged or not, Jack was relieved to see nothing but honest sincerity in Claire. In fact, it had been a long time since he had looked deep into the eyes of someone so open and defenseless, so willing to bare her soul. It stirred up feelings of attraction in Jack before he reminded himself who Claire was and forced his attention back to the road.

Their destination came into view. Jack separated from traffic and pulled up to the curb. About to reach for her door, Claire blanched as she saw the big white W in front of the hotel.

"Wait," Claire said. "This isn't where I'm staying."

"I need you to help me with something," Jack said. "It won't take long."

Claire shrank back in her seat and hugged herself.

"Why are you doing this? I don't understand. If you're so worried about Joe, why haven't you contacted the police?"

"I know what the police would do and it isn't much."

Claire shook her head.

"Enough," she said. "Please..."

"Look," Jack said. "I get where you're coming from. He's not my favorite person either. But he may be in trouble. And in a way, you owe him."

"Meaning what?"

"Meaning if my dad hadn't gone missing, I wouldn't have followed you to find him. And you wouldn't be here right now having this conversation."

Claire flinched as if he had slapped her hard across the face.

In icy silence, they rode the elevator to the eighth floor. Using the key card he had pocketed the last time he was there, Jack unlocked the door to Room 811 and entered with Claire. She kept her head down as if entering a sacred space where she knew she didn't belong. Yet at the same time her eyes darted around with longing, clearly trying to soak up the energy of the man who had stayed there.

Jack was equally conflicted. Sure, desperate circumstances called for desperate measures. But it was also a pretty good bet that if his father knew about this, he wouldn't approve.

Everything was the same as before, Jack observed, except the white shirt on the bed was now folded over a chair. It meant housekeeping had returned sometime after he had left that morning.

Only twelve hours ago.

To Jack, it felt like a month.

The red light on the room phone was blinking again, undoubtedly more messages from colleagues wondering why Joseph Pearl was skipping conference events. The more, the better, Jack thought. Any tightness in a voice or veiled reference might yield a direction to pursue. While Claire hung back by the door,

Jack went over and hit the voicemail retrieval key along with the speaker button so both of them could hear the messages.

"What do you want me to do?" Claire asked.

"Tell me if you know any of these people."

Jack waited for Claire to come over. As the voice prompt announced there were three new voicemails, Claire squirmed.

"One of those messages is from me," she said. "I don't want you to hear it."

"I already did."

Claire blushed.

"I've left messages like that," Jack said. "Worse, much worse. I felt like that about someone once."

"What happened?"

"I got over it."

Claire gave him a glance to say she knew he was lying as Jack punched up the first message:

"Hey, Joe. Julian Wade here. Just calling about that matter we discussed. No need to ring back. Oh, and break a leg on Saturday. Looking forward to the clash of the titans."

Jack turned to Claire.

"Wade," he said. "Isn't he your friend? The one you talked into presenting your paper this morning?"

Claire furrowed her brow.

"How did you know that?"

"I followed you, remember?"

"He's not a friend. I met him for the first time yesterday after a lecture."

"What do you know about him?"

"Not much. Teaches at Duke, I think he said. Kind of a jerk but charming and knows how to work it."

"A player?"

Claire shrugged.

"What male professor isn't? It's the dirty little secret of these conferences, the real reason most of them come, to prey on sycophantic grad students looking for jobs or references. Like wolf spiders eating their young."

Sycophantic. Good word, Jack thought. There was something incredibly sexy about a woman with a well-endowed vocabulary.

"What did he mean by 'clash of the titans'?"

"One of the big draws of the conference," Claire said. "A debate between Joe and another big philosopher from Berkeley, Arthur Constantius. Classic archrivals. Sort of like Wittgenstein and Popper but with W.M.D.'s instead of a poker."

Jack had no clue what she was talking about. He moved on to the next message. It was a voice Jack remembered from before, that man who had identified himself as Milton. This time the voice sounded upset:

"How many times do I have to call, Joseph? I know you're avoiding me. What happened to forgive and forget? Don't make me beg."

Jack shot a look at Claire again.

"Oh, that's Milton McGurk," she said. "Father Milty, as his students affectionately call him. He used to be a Catholic priest. Sweet, nerdy. All but worships Joe."

"'Forgive and forget'?"

"I have no idea what he was referring to."

Jack played the last message. It was different from the others: eerie silence, followed by a trill of electronic tones, a phone number being punched in by someone who didn't realize the line was live. Then it ended with an abrupt hang-up.

Claire watched him play it again, twice.

"Bad habit," Jack said. "I seem to have trouble letting things go."

Claire said, "I'm the queen of that."

Between the electronic tones and the hang-up Jack could make out what sounded like a short, tight inhale. Almost a gasp. It prompted Jack to pull out his cell and replay the message once more to record it. He also jotted down the time code, seven forty-six A.M.—shortly after he left the room, Jack realized, when he went to find Claire at the university.

"Only a few more," Jack said.

Claire shifted uncomfortably, knowing one had to be hers.

Jack keyed into the messages he had heard before. The first was from McGurk which Jack skipped over, having covered him. Next was the agitated voice of the man with the Indian accent.

"I'm pretty sure that's Deepak Singh," Claire said. "He teaches at Princeton. Nickname, the philosoraptor. A legend in his own mind."

"Unlike other philosophers, you mean?"

"He has this thing for writing notes on Post-Its. Orange, they have to be orange. Rumor has it, he once went postal on a teaching assistant who moved some of the notes on his desk. The T.A. had to get a restraining order against him."

And I thought my old man was bad, Jack mused. Philosophers. Who knew? They probably had their own chapter in the Diagnostic and Statistical Manual of Mental Disorders. A very long chapter, if not several.

Jack clicked to the next message. It was that deep imperious voice complimenting Joseph Pearl on the lecture he had given.

"That's him," Claire said. "That's Constantius."

"The archrival?"

"Like Joe, he's one of the few in the field who lives up to his rep. In fact, he recently came out with a new book that some are comparing in importance to Heidegger's *Being And Time*."

"Fascinating."

Not really, Jack mused. He knew about Heidegger from a metaphysics class he had taken at Cornell before dropping out. He knew Heidegger was a philosopher. That was all he remembered. That was more than enough.

"This Constantius," Jack said. "What else can you tell me about him?"

"Lone wolf type," Claire said. "Cool, sexy-dangerous. You could see him being a Russian spy or a black market arms dealer. Surgical and ruthless in his thinking, yet unpredictable. He would kiss you, then slit your throat."

"Sounds like a big Joseph Pearl fan."

"You mean the knife-in-the-back flattery? That's nothing. Wait until the debate."

"Assuming they're both there to have it," Jack said. "Wade said it was on Saturday, right? That's day after tomorrow."

Jack hung up the phone. Claire looked at him.

"You missed one."

"Did I?"

Jack shrugged as if not knowing what she meant. For the first time since entering the room, Claire smiled.

"Thank you," she said.

On a nearby table Jack spotted the pale green conference program, the one that had led him to Claire. As he picked it up and scanned the list of events, Claire eyed the door.

"So, if there's nothing else..."

"According to this," Jack said, "Neither Constantius or Singh are on the schedule tonight. But looks like McGurk is doing some panel. Guess we have to start somewhere."

Claire looked ambushed.

"*We?*"

"You're from the philosophy world. He'll trust you. I need you to question him without being obvious."

Claire backed away, violently shaking her head.

"What you need is to call the police," she said. "Or not. Just leave me out of it!"

Like a spooked horse, Claire fled the room. The suddenness of it held Jack there for a moment, then he chased her.

"Claire, wait!"

"Stay away. Please. No more."

"You're right," Jack said. "It's my problem, not yours. Another bad habit of mine, pretending I still wear a badge."

Claire stopped and turned on her heels to face him.

"Yeah," Jack said. "Believe it or not, I used to be a cop."

Claire looked bewildered.

"Then why are you doing this alone? All the more reason to contact the authorities. If you're so worried about your father, why haven't you filed a missing person report?"

"I told you, I have my reasons."

There was bitterness behind Jack's words but they came out sounding distant and detached. From the way Claire looked at him, Jack could see he reminded her of someone else who talked that way.

20

SALAZAR

Salazar put on a conservative suit and tie, like a chameleon changing its colors, and drove to the Beverly Hills branch of his bank. He walked in a few minutes before closing time as planned. On his way to the elevators he passed the lifelike wax security guard that had stood in the lobby for as long as Salazar had been going there, its paraffin hand resting on the butt of a holstered gun. How telling, thought Salazar. The wax figure hinted at the truth behind most financial institutions: security was mostly about appearances and easy to get around.

Salazar rode the elevator to the second floor and strode into Entertainment Services. The place had the look and feel of a first class airport lounge and catered to people in the film and music industries. Not that anyone checked. All you had to do was say you were a studio executive or record producer with boatloads of cash to deposit and, presto, you were assigned a personal banker to attend to your every need.

Salazar had an excellent rapport with his banker. Her name was Alice. She was young and pretty but not his type which was one of the reasons Salazar had chosen her. An unabashed opportunist like himself, Alice had an entrepreneurial attitude about banking secrecy, thanks to the generous monetary incentives Salazar had provided to her over the years. That didn't mean he trusted her. Before taking her into his confidence Salazar made Alice understand what would happen if she ever compromised him in any way, arrangements he had put into place even if he wasn't around to initiate them himself. Merely mentioning a few intimate details about Alice's twin sister in Seattle had seemed to get the point across.

As an assistant escorted Salazar into her office, Alice rose from her desk. She wore a form-fitting mauve dress and the diamond Cartier brooch Salazar had given her the first time they met.

"Wonderful to see you again, Mr. Salazar."

"You too, Alice."

The two shook hands.

"Can we get you anything? Coffee, tea?"

"I'm fine," Salazar said. "Thank you."

Alice turned to her assistant.

"No calls, please."

Once the door was closed, Alice unlocked a drawer in her desk and pulled out a charcoal gray folder which she slid across to Salazar.

"Per your instructions," Alice said. "I ran a final inventory of the offshore transfers. All untraceable, of course."

"How much?" Salazar asked.

"In each account?"

"Total."

"Eighteen million, give or take. Not including the three-point-six we re-routed through Caracas to cover the closing costs on your island property."

Salazar's eyes glistened.

"You wouldn't believe the view," he said.

Alice returned a coy smile.

"Twenty acres overlooking the Caribbean. What I wouldn't give to come visit. Under different circumstances, of course."

Having left the folder unopened, Salazar slid it back to Alice along with something he had extracted from his pocket.

"A small token of my appreciation," Salazar said. "You've earned it."

Alice blinked with surprise. It was a platinum Bergdorf Goodman gift card. She had never mentioned to Salazar that Bergdorf's was her favorite store in New York City, nor that she was planning a trip there with her boyfriend next weekend. But she understood the subtext. It was Salazar's way of reminding her that there would always be eyes on her. Always.

"Thank you," Alice said. "When are you flying out?"

"Saturday. Only two more days to wrap up one final piece of business. My work should be completed by then."

"As soon as I receive the second payment from your client for services rendered, I'll let you know."

They shared a parting handshake.

"I'm going to miss you, Alice."

"Be careful, sir."

"Always."

"Oh," Alice said. "And don't forget this."

From behind her desk Alice pulled out a sleek aluminum briefcase and handed it to Salazar.

"Have a safe trip, Mr. Salazar. Enjoy your new life."

On his way out of the bank Salazar thought about Alice, how dependable she was in contrast to Reaper. It had been a rare lapse in judgment for Salazar to have taken on an impetuous street thug to help him do a job—in particular this job, his last. Or maybe he was being too hard on himself. Soon none of it would matter. The kid would be a distant memory, as forgettable as the wax security guard standing in the bank lobby.

Salazar climbed into his car and placed the briefcase on the passenger seat. He clicked on the sound system to Manifest, his favorite song about getting what you want and what you deserve. Yes indeed, Salazar thought. Another seventy-two hours and he would be gone. He could already feel the warm, wet island breeze.

21

JOSEPH PEARL

With the setting of the sun, Pearl watched the light fade through the cracks in the boarded-up windows and with it, his spirits. Once again he would be compelled to brave a night of hushed darkness in the abandoned factory, relieved only by the passing trains and, he hoped, a few fitful moments of sleep.

With his ordeal had come unexpected insights. One of them pertained to his work. He had discovered that evaluating philosophical concepts under normal conditions was very different from evaluating those same concepts while forced to smell the stench of urine and feces, especially when it came from oneself. Equally dispiriting, he had observed that the popular claim that pain cannot be felt in two places at once was untrue. With hours of nothing else to do but test it, Pearl had found that in fact he could experience up to four pains simultaneously. These included the ache from lying there too long, the burn in his wrists rubbed raw from the handcuffs, the stomach pangs from not having eaten in two days and, strongest of all, the throbbing in his right eye which now was swollen shut from being kicked. Yet it could be worse, Pearl reminded himself. At least the captor had let him live.

Ever since their encounter, Pearl had struggled to reconcile the words and actions of the young man with the neck tattoo with his own recollection of what had happened before he had awoken to this nightmare. Pearl remembered walking into the pawn shop where he had introduced himself to Henry, the old gentleman whom Esma had been kind enough to refer him to. Upon hearing Esma's name, Henry had brought out his finest pre-Columbian pieces for inspection. One in particular had caught Pearl's eye, even though it appeared to be damaged. It was a figurine from Ecuador, over a thousand years old, of a female priestess with a steely, ethereal gaze and one of her bare breasts missing. With pride, Henry had explained that such pieces had a ceremonial function for healing and bringing fertility, and were broken in rituals after their power was believed to be used up. Of course Pearl, himself an expert on primitive art, knew this and more but he was charmed by Henry's affection for the piece. At the same time Pearl had found himself imagining the figurine on the cover of the important new book he was finishing. He felt certain that the rich symbolism of the broken, naked relic would exemplify the provocative theme of his book: how persons were human artifacts, physically embodied yet culturally emergent.

It was at that moment that the bell over the door had jingled behind Pearl. He seemed to recall Henry looking up. Had Henry frowned? Pearl wasn't sure. He had been too lost in thought to be paying attention. That was the last thing Pearl remembered yet he could deduce what happened next, thanks to the gash on the back of his head. The person who entered the shop, ostensibly his captor, had hit Pearl from behind with a blunt object. Then, instead of robbing him and leaving him there, the captor had gone to the considerable trouble of transporting him to this remote location where Pearl regained consciousness to find himself handcuffed to the pipes.

Everything about it implied premeditation. It suggested, preposterous as it seemed, that Pearl had been abducted for ransom. If so, it meant that calls were being made behind the scenes in an effort to extort money in exchange for his release. How much was an old philosopher worth? If not for the painful reality of his circumstances, Pearl would have found the idea amusing. But it raised a troubling question, the same one Pearl put to his students at Harvard on his final exam:

Why?

There appeared to be two possible answers. The first presupposed that Pearl was meant to be the target. *Prima facie*, that seemed illogical. For it to be true, the captor would have had to know that Pearl planned to be at the pawn shop. Yet there were only two people who had that information. One was Esma. The other was a colleague from the conference who had offered to drive Pearl there. While both had reason to bear a grudge against Pearl, neither seemed capable of devising such an odious scheme.

That suggested a more prosaic explanation: Pearl had simply been at the wrong place at the wrong time. The captor must have gone to the shop to abduct someone else but had seized Pearl instead. Only later, after the captor examined Pearl's wallet and other items he had taken by force—presumably to supply proof of life to whomever he intended to extort money from—had the captor realized his error. That would also explain why the tattooed young man had never returned to the deserted building.

What you need is to pray, the captor had said. *Pray to God or Whoever is up there.*

Like most philosophers, Pearl was a confirmed atheist. Turning to prayer was literally the last thing he would do.

So we can get rid of you.

Might the captor have an accomplice? Whether he did or not, Pearl seemed to be facing the same fate, one that had kindled the imagination of great thinkers through the ages. On that subject, Pearl was reminded of one of his favorite maxims, from Epicurus's letter to Menoeceus:

When death is, we are not.
And when we are, death is not.

To Pearl, it meant there was nothing beyond death and therefore nothing to fear. When death came, we were no longer around to worry about it and as long as we were living, there was no death to suffer.

But what of dying? Was Pearl prepared for that? He hoped he would not be rattled by it. He would have to be patient and await the inevitable. Whether he had the ability to do that with dignity he did not know. He had enjoyed a full life. He had been reasonably healthy and had been working at the same pace, perhaps even better, than when he was younger. The idea that he had been able to enjoy sixty years more or less on his own terms was just a piece of luck. And when the time came for it to be over? The wisdom of Epicurus offered peace of mind, equanimity. There was no ground for superstitions or unreasonable fears. One had only to live one's life with that assurance.

As for regrets, Pearl had none. He didn't have the feeling of having failed to live his life effectively or productively, and he had no illusions about how much better he might have handled the lives of others who came his way. Or did he? Certainly he had not anticipated being pulled away from his life so abruptly. Upon reflection, Pearl had to admit there were two people he wished he had dealt with in a different way.

One of them was Claire. Their romantic interludes, at philosophy meetings in different cities, had been a pleasurable diversion. While Pearl was more a creature of the mind than of the heart, he had developed an affection for Claire—her razor-sharp intellect, her zest for life, her vulnerability. Pearl's error was allowing Claire to believe, in the absence of any statement to the contrary, that their affair was more than it was and might even evolve into something more serious. By the time Pearl had tried to extricate himself it was too late. Claire had come to care about him more than he deserved.

Pearl's second mistake was Jack. If there had been any doubt about how much pain his son still carried around, it had been put to rest in their brief phone conversation. Jack's pain was palpable. As for the invitation to lunch, well, who could blame his son for not being interested in meeting? Nevertheless, Pearl had intended to go to the restaurant on the chance that Jack might have had a change of heart. Now he hoped his son had not. If indeed Jack had shown up, Pearl shuddered to contemplate the added lack of resolution his absence would bring to their already tenuous relationship. It mattered little that Pearl's intention had been the opposite. At the lunch, the philosopher had planned to discuss the tragic events of ten years ago, first and foremost to listen to his son and give him a chance to express his feelings, but also to make his own difficult admission: that with time Pearl had come to understand that his emotional detachment had contributed to what had happened to Ann, Jack's mother, a truth made all the more painful because Pearl had genuinely loved her. And that he now wanted—no, *needed*—to ask for Jack's forgiveness.

A shifting shadow jolted Pearl back to reality. He braced himself, thinking his captor had returned, only to realize the shadow was his own. As the philosopher relaxed again, he could feel his quartet of pains returning, exacerbated by the suffocating darkness. To distract himself, Pearl went through the vast library in his mind and selected Hume's *Treatise of Human Nature*.

22

JACK

As Jack exited the W with Claire, the doorman gave him a private nod. So did the valet before dashing off to get his car. It was that certain acknowledgment reserved for a man leaving a hotel with an attractive woman. In his mind, Jack heard himself explain who Claire was and why he was with her. It made him wonder who he felt the need to set the record straight for, others or himself.

"I'll walk," Claire said.

"You sure?"

"My hotel's only a few blocks over."

Claire gave Jack a parting look.

"I hope you find him," she said. "I know you will."

Her eyes lingered as if there was more she wanted to say, then she gave a weary shrug and walked off into the night. Jack watched her go. When the valet came with his car, he drove away in the opposite direction toward UCLA.

He got lucky and found a metered parking space across from the venue where McGurk's panel was being held. By the time Jack slipped into the lecture hall, he had managed to put Claire out of his mind.

The place was packed. Jack jostled past a row of people in the back to grab one of the few empty seats. All eyes were on four scholarly-looking men at a table up front, one of them speaking with rhetorical fervor:

"—The notion is already embedded in the views of Hegel and Kant, and calls for commitments that, on a reasonable interpretation, would be incompatible with pragmatism."

Jack groaned to himself, a little too loudly judging by the death glare he got from an androgynous preppy in the next seat. As the other panelists weighed in on the subject Jack sized up each of the men. None matched Claire's description of McGurk so he turned to his new preppy friend.

"Excuse me," Jack said. "Which one up there is McGurk?"

The preppy gave Jack another warm and fuzzy look.

"None," the guy said. "Uncle Milty was a no-show."

"Pardon?"

"He didn't show up."

Jack knew what a no-show was.

"Did anyone say why?"

The preppy shook his head, more at Jack than at the question, and turned back to the panel discussion.

Great, Jack thought, one more dead end to add to his growing collection.

He was about to leave when he noticed a collage of color on the other side of the room: bright orange Post-It notes being scribbled on by a boyish-looking Indian man in a black suit. Jack recalled Claire telling him about the Princeton professor with the Post-It habit—Singh, that was his name. With nothing better to do, Jack kept an eye on the man, not sure what he was looking for, while the panel droned on. After about twenty minutes, Singh pulled out a cell phone and read a message on its screen. Whatever it said appeared to fluster him. He gathered up his Post-Its and slipped out a side door.

Jack checked himself. For all he knew Singh had received a text from his wife reminding him to get ice cream on the way home. Rather than chase another long shot, Jack thought, maybe he should do what his old man would do if he was there right now: sit back and enjoy some intellectual stimulation.

"—But if that is so, then prudence and morality are not coextensive and an agent may act rationally though not in accord with given prudential interests."

Scratch that idea, Jack decided. In his haste to leave he stepped on the preppy's foot.

Jack burst out the back of the hall and into the lobby. It was overflowing with conference goers, several events having ended at the same time. Through the congestion Jack caught a glimpse of Singh moving at a fast clip out of the building. Jack started after him when he heard a female voice from somewhere.

"Jack!"

He turned to see someone cleaving through the crowd. It was Claire. Her cheeks were flushed as if she'd been running.

"You're still here, thank God," Claire said. "I was afraid I might have missed you."

Jack shot a look over his shoulder. Singh was gone.

"What are you doing here?" Jack said.

"I remembered something that might be important. I thought you'd want to know."

"Great timing."

Claire caught the edge in Jack's tone.

"Sorry," she said. "Were you going somewhere? Did you already talk to McGurk?"

Once again Jack checked himself. It wasn't Claire's fault he had nothing to show for his efforts. Much as he wanted to unload on someone, Claire was the last person who deserved it.

"Never mind," Jack said. "You said there was something you remembered?"

This time he lost the attitude. Claire looked relieved.

"It happened a couple weeks ago," she said. "At another philosophy conference in Chicago. I overheard Joe having a private talk with Constantius. No, talk is the wrong word. They were having an argument."

"What about?"

"Something involving the book Constantius published recently, the one that's won so much praise. I only caught the tail end but I heard Joe say something like 'Don't blame the messenger, you dug your own grave.'"

Jack frowned with interest.

"What did he mean?"

Claire shook her head and shrugged.

"All I know is, I've never seen Joe so confrontational with a colleague, or someone react the way Constantius did."

"React how?"

"Like a dangerous animal backed into a corner."

"Did you bring it up with my father?"

Claire nodded.

"He was concerned that I knew," she said. "And not very happy about it. He refused to discuss the matter. For my own sake, he said. He made me promise not to mention it to anyone."

"Did you?"

"Not a word. Well, until now."

Claire swallowed with emotion.

"Look," she said, "I'm not saying there's any connection, and maybe I'm looking for something to blame, but it was right after that that Joe started to become distant toward me."

"So this argument you witnessed. You believe it might have something to do with my dad's disappearance?"

"If it didn't, then what would explain that message from Constantius on Joe's voicemail?"

Jack saw where she was going.

"You mean, why would he leave it?"

Claire nodded.

"With their debate coming up, Constantius had to be worried that Joe might go public with whatever they sparred over. So why pour oil on the fire by baiting him with false flattery? Over the phone, no less? In a voicemail? It makes no sense. Constantius is way too smart to do something like that."

"Yet he did," Jack said.

"So it would seem."

"Any doubt the voice on the message was his?"

"None."

"So what motive could he have?"

"Maybe to point the finger away from himself," Claire said. "Knowing the message would be heard once Joe was reported missing."

It was the kind of double bluff Jack saw in poker all the time. But if Constantius was as brilliant as Claire was suggesting, even his ruse might be hiding something more ominous.

"Anything else you want to share?" Jack said.

Claire tucked a stray strand of hair behind her ear.

"Only that I'm sorry I was so wrapped up in my own pain that I didn't mention any of this before, when you asked what else I knew. I guess it didn't sink in until now that Joe might really be in trouble."

"That's honest."

"How's this for honesty? I hate your father. Part of me wishes he were dead."

Jack let a smile escape.

"I used to feel that way when I was a kid," he said. "Except in my fantasies I'd be the one killing him."

His candor surprised Claire and seemed to reassure her.

"So," Jack said. "I guess I better have a chat with this Constantius character. Only one problem, how to find him."

"If we can figure out what hotel he's staying at, you could give him a call."

Jack shook his head.

"Too easy for him to blow me off."

"Or maybe he's at that party tonight," Claire said.

"Party?"

"Some Berkeley alumnae thing. I think I saw a flyer about it in my registration packet. Which is back at my hotel."

Jack didn't have to think about it. Thinking meant choices and there were none on the table at the moment.

"Okay," he said. "Let's go."

23

JACK

J ack held open the passenger door for Claire as they returned to his parked car. Driving off again, Jack pulled out the envelope he had taken from his father's hotel room.

"What's that?" Claire said.

"Something important," Jack said. "Or maybe not."

He handed it over while hanging a right. Claire stiffened slightly as she recognized Joseph Pearl's chicken scratches.

"Sorry, I can't decipher it," she said. "Any more than I could the person who wrote it."

"What do you make of this?"

Jack pointed out the notation 'NO 2 OC' circled in red. Claire squinted at it and shrugged.

"Maybe some brainstorm Joe had in the middle of the night. He'd often get up to jot down ideas, then would end up working into the next day. He doesn't sleep much."

Jack remembered that from childhood. How he would wake up and fall asleep to the sound of the typewriter in the attic. Jack imagined Claire naked in bed somewhere while his old man searched for a pen and paper to heed the clarion call of his philosophy. Unsettled by the image, Jack steered his attention back to the envelope.

"Or maybe it's a reminder," Jack said. "To say 'NO' to someone. About a matter of importance, given how he circled it. Some person with the initials 'O.C.'"

Claire looked amused.

"You're being too literal. Thinking in two dimensions. Joe thinks in three, six, ten."

"Okay, what then? If you had to make a guess?"

"Well," Claire said. "Instead of initials, 'O.C.' might be the beginning of a word. Like, say, occasionalism."

"Ah yes," Jack said. "But of course."

"It's a philosophical theory which states that all events are taken to be caused directly by God."

"I'm pretty sure my father doesn't believe in God."

"You're right, he doesn't. In fact, he once said that if he ever did, even in the privacy of his own thoughts, it would be the end of his philosophy."

"Okay," Jack said. "So, something else then."

Claire traced the red circle with her finger.

"Instead of 'NO' in the negative sense," she said, "It might refer to the second part of something. Number Two of O.C. Which could be an abbreviation for anything. Old Covenant, Ockham's Razor, Oxycontin."

"Oxycontin?"

131

"Shows you where my mind goes."

"Thanks for that," Jack said. "From now on whenever I think of my dear old dad, I'll picture him reading the Bible while popping O."

Claire suppressed a laugh and handed back the envelope. Jack eyed the notation again. Something told him it was relevant, maybe crucial. But how?

It wasn't long before they pulled up to the Palomar, a boutique hotel on the Wilshire Corridor where Claire told Jack she was staying. As Claire broke open her door, she gave Jack a vulnerable look.

"I'll wait here," Jack said.

"What? Oh sure, of course. No, I was just thinking about my car. I remembered it's still out there with my purse in it."

Jack recalled finding the red Mustang abandoned off P.C.H., the handbag lying next to the empty pill bottle. He had forgotten about it.

"No big deal," Claire said. "There's nothing in it I care about. Well, except for a locket my dad gave me. Anyway, let me go get the flyer. Be right back."

She slipped out and disappeared into the hotel.

Jack waited. His eyes drifted to the hotel flags stirring in the breeze. Their ocean colors reminded him of Laguna Beach, that funky little motor inn where he and Becky had once stayed, right after they first met in court on opposite sides of a case. What followed were two days of nothing but sex and room service. By the end of the weekend they'd had their first fight. Then came the warmth and tenderness that always followed. The contradiction was a defining feature of their relationship and, much as Jack was loathe to admit it, one he missed.

His thoughts returned to Claire's Mustang and the yellow Hertz tag he had observed on the keys left dangling in the ignition. It prompted him to pull out his cell phone and punch up a local number for the rental company.

When Jack hung up a few minutes later, the passenger door opened and Claire jumped back in. She had changed out of Mrs. Woo's frumpy clothes and into her own, a pale blue cashmere sweater and dressy jeans that showed off her figure. She was also wearing glasses again, a spare pair, as well as a touch of makeup. And she had let her hair down. The full effect brought out an understated beauty that would have made most men stare. Jack tried not to.

"Much better," Claire said. "I can see you now."

"Good, great."

The way Jack averted his gaze made Claire smooth her sweater self-consciously.

"Is everything okay?"

"Yeah, fine."

"I mean, I can change into something else if..."

"No, you look great."

"Really?"

"*Really.*"

It came out sounding a little more captivated than Jack intended. He changed the subject, holding up his cell phone.

"By the way, I took care of your car," he said. "The rental agency promised to deliver your purse here to the hotel."

Claire smirked.

"Yeah, right."

"Tomorrow morning, they said. Noon at the latest."

Claire realized he was serious.

"Wait, but how? I mean, how could you possibly know which company I rented from?"

"Ex-cop, remember?"

"Wow, I don't know what to say. Thank you."

For a moment Claire forgot about everything else, amazed and touched by what Jack had done. Then she remembered the flyer in her hand and straightened her glasses to read it.

"Okay, so the party," she said. "Says here it's being held at the Getty Museum."

"Convenient," Jack said. "Only ten minutes away."

The wind shifted, disturbing the hotel flags, as they drove off again.

24

SALAZAR

A fire truck screamed past Our Lady Queen of Angels, its siren reverberating through the candlelit sanctuary. The old church was empty except for Salazar. With his head bowed in prayer, he made the sign of the cross and sat back in his pew.

As he waited, he rested his hand on the aluminum briefcase Alice had given him at the bank and admired the gilded panels behind the altar depicting hallowed saints and scenes from the Bible. Salazar knew each one by heart. He had grown up in this church and had come here every Sunday until the gang wars forced him to flee to Guadalajara. With a sad smile, Salazar remembered how, as children, he and his brother Ignacio would make funny faces during the long services to get each other to laugh until their grandmother would give them both a rap on the ears. Dear Ignacio, who was so pure. So full of life. Everything going for him.

Until, one week before his tenth birthday, he was cut down by a bullet meant for Salazar.

The peaceful serenity of the church was disturbed by the echo of someone approaching. Salazar looked up as Reaper slouched out of the shadows and slid into the pew.

"Of all the crazy-ass places to meet."

"You're late," Salazar said.

"I went to check on our investment."

Salazar's expression darkened.

"I said no more contact."

"Chillax," Reaper said. "The *cabron* didn't see me. And no, I didn't give him nothing, not even water. He's still chained there in a pile of his own piss and shit. Hanging on, don't ask me how. But he won't last much longer. I hope you know what you're doing."

"You can be sure of it."

"So," Reaper said, "What's this big important thing you said couldn't wait?"

Before Salazar could answer, Reaper noticed the briefcase.

"Don't tell me his peeps came through? About fuckin' time!"

Salazar pushed the case toward Reaper who placed it in his lap and hit the lock buttons. The lid sprang open to reveal stacks of money inside.

"Oh yeah," Reaper said. "Sweet!"

Reaper's eyes shimmered as he raked his fingers over the cash. But then his excitement faded as he realized the stacks were made up of twenties, not hundreds.

"Wait, how much is here?"

"Ten grand," Salazar said.

"That's all we got for him?"

"Your share. For services rendered."

"What's that supposed to mean?"

"It means this is where we part ways."

Reaper stared, blindsided.

"No, man," he said. "That's fucked. My cut was twenty percent. I'm the one who grabbed him, remember? The one who took all the risks."

"For which you are being well paid."

"More like cheated outa what's mine. Fuck that. I'm not some *panocha jota* you can kick to the curb."

Salazar's gaze didn't waver.

"Ten grand," he said. "Take it or leave it."

Reaper rubbed his neck tattoo and slammed the case shut.

"*Me cajo en la hostia!*"

The kid spat on the pew and stormed off with the briefcase.

Salazar remained deathly still, the words ringing in his ears. Literally, "I shit in the communion wafers." It was more than a personal insult to Salazar, it was a desecration of the church. *His* church. Had the remark been made anywhere else, Salazar would not have hesitated to act. Before Reaper could get the words out, Salazar would have pulled out his gun and blown them back into the kid's mouth.

Salazar eyed the gob of phlegm on the pew, glistening in the candlelight. As the saints appeared to watch from the gilded panels, Salazar made the sign of the cross three times and used the sleeve of his jacket to wipe away the mess.

25

JACK

t was one of the unwritten rules of the road in Los Angeles that shitty cars got the right of way. It made sense. What owner of a luxury vehicle, of which there were a disproportionately large number in the city, would want to risk kissing bumpers with some uninsured clunker? It allowed drivers like Jack a certain reckless abandon when getting around, especially on the Westside. Claire watched Jack weave in and out on their way to the Getty, then looked at her hands in her lap.

"You know all my secrets," she said. "But I know nothing about you except that you're Joe's son."

"What else would you like to know?"

"What kind of cop were you?"

"Undercover," Jack said. "Drug cases mostly."

"Until something happened?"

"Something I didn't see coming."

"Involving others in your department, I'm guessing. The reason you don't trust the police anymore. Which is why you didn't report your father's disappearance."

Jack gave Claire an amused glance.

"No need to be shy," he said.

"Am I right?"

"Being a missing person isn't a crime. And unless there's evidence of one, the police are way too busy to check out every disappearance."

"You didn't answer my question."

"Do I trust the LAPD? No. And vice-versa. My last case involved several murders, some missing money and a dirty cop from another precinct. It would take too long to explain. Suffice it to say, the money was never found and the cop is still out there somewhere."

Jack made a right turn onto Sepulveda. A ribbon of light from a passing car haloed Claire's face.

"What about relationships?" she said.

"You mean am I in one? No."

"Because?"

"Life is complicated enough."

"I take it the last one ended badly."

"What makes you say that?"

"The message I left for Joe. You said you had left worse ones. Or was that only to make me feel better?"

"No," Jack said. "That was real."

"Mind if I ask her name?"

"Rebecca. Becky, I called her, unless we were fighting."

"How often was that?"

"More often than not. Any more questions?"

"Just one."

Claire reached behind him, into the back seat, and picked up Joseph Pearl's book lying there.

"What's your take on this?" she said.

"Pardon?"

"I mean, obviously it's an amazing overview of the whole trajectory of western philosophy, but do you think it lives up to the title?"

After Claire's probing questions, her deadpan humor was a welcome relief to Jack. Until he saw her expression.

"Wait," he said. "You're serious."

"Why wouldn't I be?"

Jack shook his head.

"I'm the wrong person to ask."

"C'mon, you must have an opinion."

"Not really."

"As his son."

"It's not my thing."

"Which part?"

"All of it."

Claire's eyes became saucers.

"Have you even read it? You haven't, have you? Then why are you carrying it around?"

"Good question."

"But you've read other things he's written? At least you're familiar with his ideas?"

"Not the ones you're talking about."

Claire shook her head in astonishment.

141

"Wow, I'm sorry," she said.

"Why's that?"

"Because he's your father, that's why. Who happens to be one of the most important living philosophers in the English-speaking world, doing things in the field no one else is doing."

"If it's any consolation," Jack said, "I don't think he would care. But I'm sure he would be pleasantly surprised to hear you defending him."

Claire flashed a defensive look, not sure of his tone or what to do with the book in her hand. She tossed it over her shoulder. It landed on the back seat with a thud.

26

JACK

Jack wasn't the museum type. The last time he had been to one was on a blind date arranged by Franco in an attempt to help him get over Becky. Jack remembered how his date, an old sorority sister of Franco's wife Kate, tried to give him an art history lesson while all Jack could think about was getting toasted. Luckily the feeling passed. Still, it left an unpleasant association in his head.

Jack and Claire pulled up to the Getty and parked in the underground visitors' garage, then took the elevator to the entry plaza where a dozen academic types were queued up for the funicular tram to the museum. When it came, they rode up the hill. Jack admired the twilight views of the city and wondered what his dad was looking at right now. Assuming, Jack thought darkly, that his old man was still around to see anything.

Claire tugged on Jack's sleeve as they pulled into the arrival area where everyone got out. Rock music blared from the direction of the white marble museum. They followed it through a rotunda to an open-air terrace amid the art pavilions where a sizeable crowd was drinking and dancing to an 80's cover band.

Jack shook his head and chuckled.

"Weird," he said.

Claire looked at him.

"The music? Or watching philosophers dance?"

"Neither," Jack said. "A memory that popped into my head. Something my father once said to me at a bowling alley."

Claire smirked.

"Wait...Joe...*bowling*?"

Jack nodded.

"He used to take me as a kid whenever my mother had one of her breakdowns. To spare me seeing her like that, I guess. Anyway, I remember this one time I bowled a strike and my dad's face lit up. For a second I thought he might even do something completely out of character like hug me, but instead he gripped my shoulder with this pretend-serious face and said 'Jack, you're a good egg...but who likes eggs?'"

Claire grinned.

"Sweet."

"Yeah," Jack said. "I think that was the closest he ever came to saying 'I love you.'"

"Nice memory."

"Apropos of nothing. So what made me think of it just now? What does it have to do with being here?"

"Well," Claire said. "A philosopher might say it holds some profound significance. And then, of course, another philosopher would disagree."

"And they'd spend the next ten hours arguing about it."

"See?" Claire said. "You're catching on."

They shared a smile and turned their attention back to the party.

"Okay, we deserve some luck," Claire said. "Let's hope Constantius is here."

"Might help if I knew what he looks like."

Claire was already on her iPhone searching Google Images. When she showed Jack a photo of the Berkeley philosopher, he was surprised at how unattractive the man was.

"You described him as sexy-dangerous," Jack said. "All I can see is the dangerous part."

"Trust me," Claire said. "He's hot."

"Are you speaking from personal experience?"

"You mean have I slept with him? No, but I could have. He made a pass at me once. I told Joe about it. Want to know what he said?"

"Not really."

"Nothing. Not a word. I could have been standing there with my hair on fire, telling him I'd fucked every philosopher in his department, and he wouldn't have batted an eyelash."

Benign indifference. Jack knew it well. It was the way his father treated everything except his work. Jack wanted to tell Claire how many times he had felt the same way growing up, but he decided to keep it to himself.

"That was the moment I realized how much I despised him," Claire continued. "And yet how's this for sick? I also loved him. More than I have ever loved anyone. I still do."

She swallowed and turned away but Jack caught the look in her eye, like that of someone holding onto a ledge and feeling their grip slipping.

They both searched the crowd again for Constantius but there was no sign of him.

"Oh well," Jack said. "It was worth a try."

"It's early yet. He might still show. C'mon, I need a drink."

Claire took Jack by the arm and led him away. Through the sea of people, Jack thought he saw someone watching them, an indistinct figure lurking in the shadows across the terrace. But when some guests passed between them and Jack looked again, there was no one there.

Claire turned to Jack as they arrived at the bar.

"I'm having a martini," she said. "You?"

"Coffee, thanks."

"That's no fun. It's a party."

"And I'm the designated driver," Jack said. "Next time."

"Okay, I'm going to hold you to that."

Claire gave Jack a light-hearted bump. She appeared to be in good spirits again. That look of distress Jack had noticed before was gone.

They paid for their drinks and found a table with a good vantage point. As Jack caught a whiff of Claire's perfume and tried not to let it distract him, Claire took a generous sip of her martini.

"As long as we're stuck here, maybe we could talk."

"Sure," Jack said. "What about?"

"Something you should know, but obviously don't."

"And what would that be?"

"Your father's philosophy."

Jack laughed.

"Good one," he said.

"Just the basics," Claire said. "In layman's terms."

There was a gleam in her eye, mischievous but serious.

"Please tell me you're joking," Jack said.

"You'll be fascinated, I promise."

"I promise you, I won't."

"How do you know? Five minutes, then I'll stop if you want. Besides, it might help you find him."

"Uh-huh."

"Wouldn't it be useful to understand the way Joe thinks? Maybe someone was threatened by it. Constantius, or someone else perhaps. I mean, you'd know better. You're the detective."

"Was."

Jack felt his face scowling.

"Why do you care so much?" he said.

"What difference does it make?"

"Clearly, it does."

Claire traced the rim of her glass.

"Knowing your father...it's important. I didn't think it was either until I lost mine when I was twelve."

So that explained her relationship with Joseph Pearl, why she had fallen for a sixty-year-old narcissist. Textbook daddy complex, Jack figured. No wonder Claire had gone into philosophy. It was either that or psychology, become another screwed-up therapist.

Jack checked the crowd. Still no Constantius.

"Alright," he said. "You win."

"You won't be sorry."

"If I had a dollar every time someone told me that..."

"It's actually pretty cool," Claire said. "Basically it breaks down into three parts. The first two are radical notions of ideas that have been around since the beginning of philosophy. Plato, Aristotle. You've heard of those guys, right? The third part is pure Joseph Pearl. It's an idea that builds on the other two to create a unique way of looking at the world that has tremendous implications, not only on a theoretical level but in terms of how we live day to day."

"That's a pretty hefty claim."

"Interested?"

"Part Three. What's the gist?"

"Uh-uh. Have to keep you in suspense. Besides, you won't get it unless you understand Parts One and Two first."

Jack gulped his coffee and raked the crowd again.

"Five minutes," he said. "Clock's ticking."

Claire leaned closer.

"Okay, here goes. The first theme is the most inclusive. It's simply this: the only constant in life is change."

"Change?"

"As opposed to changelessness. Which by the way is what Constantius preaches. Joe would argue that 'flux', as he would call it, is more resourceful and reflective of the truth of human experience than the idea of changelessness or invariance."

Jack could already feel himself getting sleepy.

"Go on," he said.

"In western philosophy, there's been a history of thinking that has passed through a number of phases. The beginning was to emphasize invariance, fixed laws of nature. And then to account for the reality of change in terms of invariance. And then to say, well, we no longer know how to establish invariance—in science, morality, laws, *anything*—which then means that all order has a conjectural character to it. It holds for an interval, we don't know how long, and we keep improvising new ways of construing the world depending on our practical interests and needs. Are you with me so far?"

"Yeah," Jack said. "I think so."

"So there's a kind of deep provisionality to science and to thought. That is the most radical position we've been able to think of. If Joe were here, he would tell you that almost no one until recently was prepared to

149

go with that idea, even though it is the most inclusive thesis. It is one which most people, including great thinkers, have tended to resist."

Whatever shortcomings Claire had, intelligence was not one of them. Her eyes sparkled with passion for the subject.

"Why would people resist that concept?" Jack asked.

"Because it's frightening."

"What's frightening about it?"

"People think they have to be anchored in something. They tend to be worried about getting their bearings correctly. But living without invariant rules is actually freer. There are more possibilities of thought and also there is less likelihood of deceiving yourself into believing you have found the way, the true way, which then also makes for a kind of inflexibility."

Inflexible. That's me, Jack thought. He had always tended to see things as black or white, right or wrong, good or evil. It was the reason he became a cop and it had always worked for him. That is, until everything got turned upside down.

Jack eyed the crowd again. The band was playing Duran Duran.

"So let me see if I have this straight," he said. "According to Joseph Pearl, there are no changeless truths in life."

"That's right."

"Not just in the physical universe."

"As science bears out."

"But also in every aspect of our lives we can think of."

"And even the ones we can't."

"Or to put it another way, there's no single, correct way to experience the world."

Claire nodded.

"And therefore," she said, "We should recognize that all presumption of fixity in human life is itself a prejudice, and a conservative one at that."

"A prejudice we struggle with. Because we're afraid."

"Not only that, we internalize that fear contrary to our own interests. We criticize ourselves for being who and what we are."

That struck a chord with Jack, even if his head was beginning to hurt.

"Look," Claire said, "Obviously it's more complicated than that. I'm giving you the Cliff Notes here. But if you can accept the idea that change is more reflective of the truth of human experience, then you're ready to go on to Part Two."

"No thanks. I think I'll quit while I'm ahead."

"Sorry?"

"Five minutes," Jack said. "Time's up."

27

JOSEPH PEARL

Pearl dreamt of a fire burning in a cave. Around it sat three men, a trio of intellectual giants who only in a philosopher's mind could be in the same place and time, and in such an exposed state. Literally. The men were naked.

Aristotle was the first to speak.

"We all know why we are here."

"To help," Hegel said. "By lending our collective wisdom."

"In an effort to uncover the hidden truth behind the crisis at hand," Nietzsche said.

"In time," Aristotle said. "Before it is too late."

On the sepulchral walls of the cave their shadows loomed large.

"As is often the case, the answer is already known, though not in a conscious way."

"It is always hardest to see that which is staring one in the face."

"Therefore, take heed."

Together the naked philosophers raised their hands to the fire, its reflection flickering in their eyes.

"Revenge is at the heart of the matter."

"Exacted by someone with a secret to protect."

"And a purpose far more ingenious than meets the eye."

"But be doubly warned. For in the mix are other, unpredictable forces which threaten any who would come to your aid, including those you care most deeply about."

"Which leaves you but one hope."

"An act of faith."

"You must turn away from the shadows that imprison you, from everything you hold to be real, and free yourself by stepping into the sunlight to behold the truth."

Pearl bolted awake in the dark. A mournful train horn wailed past, splinters of light flashing through the edges of the boarded-up window. For a moment Pearl thought he was still dreaming. Then the pain returned, reality.

How strange, thought Pearl. He never dreamt, at least never remembered his dreams. But this one was so vivid. Could it be trying to tell him something?

It felt significant that the men who had appeared in the vision happened to be Pearl's favorite philosophers: Hegel, the first to reinterpret the field in terms of cultural history; Nietzsche, the most salient critic of conventional academic thought; and of course Aristotle, without a doubt the greatest of the ancient philosophers, who still counted in comparison and competition with those of the modern world. Who better than these three to deliver a message of importance in, of all places, a cave, a transparent reference to Plato's allegory and also to Pearl's circumstances. Just as the prisoners in Plato's scenario had only their shadows to keep them company, so too did Pearl.

But why had the philosophers in the dream appeared unclothed? Pearl thought back to the cocktail party where the allegory of the cave had come up. He recalled the question Singh had posed about the shadow watchers being naked. Perhaps Pearl's sleeping brain had added that detail to the dream for a bit of sardonic color. Or it could be more than that.

Revenge is at the heart of the matter.

Of all the people Pearl knew, who had a motive for revenge? Three colleagues came to mind, each for a different reason:

Singh, because of his suspicions about his wife and Pearl.

McGurk, because of what he had stolen from Pearl.

Constantius, because of the secret Pearl knew about him.

Forces which threaten any who would come to your aid, including those you care most deeply about.

Pearl did an inventory. He had many colleagues but few friends, none of whom elicited feelings he would characterize as deep caring. The two people who did, he was forced to admit, were the same two he had managed to push out of his life.

Claire was one. Again, Pearl felt sorry for the hurt he had caused her which would be compounded if Claire noticed he wasn't at the conference. Almost certainly, she would misinterpret his disappearance as an effort by Pearl to avoid her.

Pearl also cared deeply about Jack. Once more, he hoped his son had not shown up to the lunch. It was what Pearl deserved. Yet a small voice inside him, the voice of self-preservation, held out hope that Jack had cared enough to meet—his son, who worked for the police, in what capacity Pearl was ashamed to admit he had never bothered to inquire about—and that Jack would be angry enough at being let down one more time by his father that he would investigate his absence. If so, Pearl might still have a chance of being saved, by virtue of his poor parenting as irony would have it. But in trying to find him, would Jack be exposing himself to danger as the dream had implied?

The dream. So much of it had been troubling to Pearl, in particular the idea that, locked in his subconscious, he might know more than he realized without understanding how to avail himself of it. However, one part of the dream had caused Pearl a deeper concern, the prophetic last words of the philosophers:

Which leaves you but one hope. An act of faith.

In both religion and philosophy, faith was the traditional source of justification for belief in a higher power, a belief antithetical to everything Pearl had built his life and work on. Faith was one of those loaded words he would never use except to point out its problematic nature. And yet there it was in the dream, a dream he had authored. It not only invoked faith but called him to turn away from the shadows and step into the light, to take action which, even with its Platonic allusion, sounded uncomfortably like having a religious conversion.

It called into question the content of the dream itself and whether Pearl could trust his own mind. Was this what the beginnings of madness felt like? If so, how much longer could he hold out?

28

JACK

t had been over an hour since Jack and Claire had crashed the Berkeley party. The band had played everything from Jon Bon Jovi's *Livin' On A Prayer* to a cheesy cover of *Super Freak*, but there was still no sign of Constantius.

Having returned to the bar for a second martini, Claire was bringing the drink back to the table when she grabbed Jack's arm and pointed to someone.

"There," she said. "There he is."

Through the crowd Jack spotted Constantius with his entourage, shaking hands and slapping backs as he made his way into the party. He looked unclean. The word *feral* came to mind. In a police lineup he would have been picked out for his lawless demeanor, yet his eyes were soft and sensual like those of a silent film star. Together with the confidence he exuded like a pheromone, he came across as weirdly handsome. A glance at the females around him, all striking, made it clear he knew how to work it for more than professional gain.

Claire turned to Jack.

"Okay," she said. "So how do we do this?"

Jack wasn't sure. Every minute that passed was a minute his father was also passing somewhere, in circumstances that were sure to be unpleasant and likely to get worse. If Constantius had information pertaining to Joseph Pearl's whereabouts, Jack needed him to cough it up. And fast. But would he?

It was something Jack should have thought out in advance. Now that he could see Constantius in action, Jack realized the answer was *no*. Whether the Berkeley professor knew anything or not, he would deny that he did and no amount of threatening or cajoling would make any difference. Clearly the man was too cagy and vainglorious to help his archrival Joseph Pearl, let alone incriminate himself.

That left only one card to play.

"Jack?"

Claire was still waiting for an answer.

"You mentioned Constantius hit on you once," Jack said. "Any chance he would recognize you?"

Claire shook her head.

"It was ages ago, and he was drunk at the time."

"How good are you at bluffing?" Jack said.

"Why? What do you have in mind?"

"If I was involved in someone's disappearance, what would I do if I ran into some girl at a party who told me she had just seen that person?"

Claire raised an eyebrow.

"Very clever," she said. "But why not tell him yourself? He doesn't know who you are."

"I've got a feeling you'd sell it better. Besides, you're more his type."

"You mean female?"

"And pretty."

Claire looked flattered but a little embarrassed.

"I'm not that pretty, but okay."

She considered the martini in her hand, took a swig for courage, then placed the glass on the table and headed away.

Jack watched her weave through the crowd to Constantius who was lavishing his attention on a voluptuous beauty with flaming red hair. For several minutes Claire hovered nearby, waiting for a chance to talk to him alone. When none came, Claire ordered a wine and accidently-on-purpose bumped into the redhead, spilling the drink on her. The minute the girl huffed away to clean herself up, Claire engaged Constantius in conversation.

As Jack kept watching, his eyes strayed to Claire's martini sitting on the table. It was half full yet somehow that made it even more tempting, as if the damage of drinking it would only be half as bad. Jack imagined guzzling it down, even licking the glass, before he forced his attention back to Claire.

She was still chatting up Constantius. Then Jack saw the philosopher react to something Claire said, a thin film of tension spreading across his ugly-handsome face. He appeared to press Claire for details but what-ever answer she gave seemed to disturb him even more. When the redhead returned, Claire managed to extri-cate herself as nimbly as she had gotten to Constantius, and hurried back to Jack with a hopeful look.

"He definitely knows something," she said.

"You told him you'd seen Pearl?"

Claire nodded.

"An hour ago at the W," she said. "I also worked in Joe's room number, and that he seemed upset about something. Which, in case Constantius was interested which he was, explained why Joe planned to be alone in his room all night."

"Nice job," Jack said. "Looks like he took the bait."

As Jack nodded in Constantius's direction, Claire followed his gaze to see the philosopher cup his mouth to the ear of the redhead who glanced around with a furtive look. Then the two of them hurried away through the crowd, toward the museum exit.

"Yeah, looks like something's up," Claire said. "But why is he taking the girl with him?"

"Maybe she's part of whatever this is about," Jack said. "We'll find out soon enough."

Jack led Claire away. Together they tailed Constan-tius and the redhead back to the tram. When it pulled up and let out arriving guests, Constantius and the red-head slipped into the front car with others leaving the party. Claire grabbed Jack's hand to hurry him into the back car before the doors hissed shut.

The tram slithered down the hill to the entry plaza where everyone got out. Once again Jack and Claire shadowed the pair. They veered down a side path. Then, unexpectedly, Constantius stopped short and looked over his shoulder. Before Jack could react, Claire yanked him into the bushes where suddenly they found themselves jammed up against each other, faces inches apart. Jack could feel Claire's left hand crushed against his chest as well as her breath on his neck.

"Awkward," he muttered.

Claire tilted her head demurely.

"Don't try anything," she whispered.

Through the branches they watched Constantius grab the redhead and kiss her like a lion feeding on a baby gazelle. When the girl kissed back hard, Constantius slid his hand under her dress and between her legs. Claire drew in a gasp. Her body tightened and shifted against Jack's. The redhead pulled away from Constantius, laughing lustily, and wiped her lips with the back of her hand as if checking for blood. Then the two composed themselves again and continued down the path.

With teenage clumsiness Jack and Claire disentangled and staggered out of the bushes. Jack could still feel Claire's hand on his chest and smell her scent on him but he shook it off as they continued to follow.

Twenty yards ahead, the path rounded a building and opened out onto the busy main entrance of the Getty Center. Constantius stopped there with the redhead. They shared a few words and another rough kiss.

Then they split up, the girl angling away toward a line of taxis while Constantius hurried off in the direction of the parking structure.

Claire perked up, frowned.

"Oh, great," she said. "Now what?"

Jack nodded toward Constantius.

"When in doubt, follow the money."

"But what about the girl? Like you said, she might know something. No worries, I'll take her. Quick, give me your cell number so we can stay in touch."

Claire whipped out her iPhone for him to enter it.

Jack shook his head.

"No," he said.

"Hurry," Claire said. "Before you lose Constantius."

Jack balked. Claire had done a good job of hiding her pain, for someone who only twelve hours ago had been willing to give up her life to make it go away. But Jack could see it was still there right under the surface, thick and tender, the hurt of being rejected by a man she was now helping Jack try to find. Why? In hopes that Joseph Pearl would be so grateful for her efforts that he would want her back? If so, Jack wondered, was he doing Claire a favor by keeping her involved, or merely prolonging her agony? Or worse, was he putting her back in the water but this time with no one to pull her out?

"Jack?"

Claire was still holding out her iPhone. Against his better judgment, Jack punched in his digits.

"Be careful," he said.

"You too."

"No, I mean it."

Claire squeezed his arm.

"Don't worry, I won't make you have to save me again."

As she hurried away toward the redhead now getting into a cab, Jack took off after Constantius.

He reached the parking structure to find the philosopher waiting with others for an elevator. Instead of falling in behind them, Jack rushed down a stairwell back to his car and roared out of the garage. Then he pulled over to wait. It wasn't long before Constantius drove out in a midnight blue Tesla.

Jack let a few other vehicles pass before pulling out to follow the Tesla. Déjà vu, he thought. Just like his undercover days. He glanced at the medallion hanging from his dash, the one of St. Michael, the patron saint of police officers.

The Tesla cruised south, driving fast. As Jack changed lanes to keep up, he checked his rear view mirror and noticed a black sedan with a broken headlight nosing out several cars behind before it drifted back behind traffic. Jack continued to follow the Tesla. At Santa Monica Boulevard it took a right, heading west now. Jack made the same turn and checked his mirror again to see the sedan with the broken headlight doing the same.

A coincidence, Jack thought. Or was it?

When the Tesla reached Barrington Avenue, it hung a left. So did Jack. So did the sedan. Then the

"

Tesla turned right again onto a smaller street, as if nearing its destination. Before copying the turn Jack slowed down to get a better look at the sedan but it sped up and roared past, its license plate obscured by a trailer hitch, the driver hidden behind tinted windows. Unsettled, Jack returned his focus to the Tesla and tailed it another four blocks until it pulled into the parking lot of a place called The Boardroom.

The sign out front identified it as a "Gentleman's Club" which meant a strip joint with a fancy name to justify its fancy prices. The same kind of place that Franco had tried to get Jack to consider for a job. But why, Jack wondered, was Constantius here? And what did it have to do with his father vanishing?

Jack parked, paid the exorbitant cover charge and made his way into the main room where strippers were dancing and hustling customers. At first, the dim lighting and carnival atmosphere made it hard to find Constantius. Then Jack spotted him across the room, settling into a seat near the stage.

For the better part of an hour Jack watched Constantius order drinks, tip girls, even get a lap dance. He kept waiting for something meaningful to happen. Finally the truth sank in. Constantius's reason for being there had nothing to do with Joseph Pearl or philosophy or anything else but the obvious: that primal urge that reduced all men, including distinguished intellectuals, to their lowest common denominator.

Jack walked out in disgust and thought of Claire. The least he could do was call her so she didn't waste her time on the redhead. But as he pulled out his phone, Jack realized he didn't have Claire's number. Foolishly, he hadn't bothered to get it from her when she had asked for his.

Jack marched back to his car, furious at himself, and peeled away into the night. He drove and drove, not sure where to go or what to do next. As he turned the car back toward home, his gaze fell on a bright neon sign up ahead, flashing like a lighthouse beacon in a storefront window:

LIQUOR

Jack tore his eyes away. Not fast enough. He could feel his heart racing, a chill of need entering his bloodstream. Digging deep, he summoned every last ounce of self-control and managed to drive past the sign. But then something stronger made him pull a wild U-turn and swing into the alley behind the store.

In a trance, Jack entered. He pulled a fifth of Stoli off a shelf and brought it to the counter. When the clerk took his money and brown-bagged the bottle, Jack grabbed it and left.

He tried to make it back to the Wagoneer but he couldn't wait. In its shadows he broke the seal and fumbled the bottle to his lips when he caught his reflection in the car's taped-together side mirror. Instantly Jack was seized by a wave of revulsion and self-loathing that jarred him back to his senses. He flung the bottle away. It shattered against a dumpster.

A splash of vodka had spilled into Jack's mouth. Its sting made him shudder in ecstasy and horror as he staggered back behind the wheel.

Tears came.

Jack looked at his trembling hands and covered his face in shame. Broken. He needed a refuge, a safe haven, somewhere to go to pull himself together again. But where? There was only one place he could think of and it wasn't A.A.

29

JACK

J ack pulled up to The Commerce.

Still shaky, he walked his usual route past the Asian games to the poker floor where the familiar buzz of activity and jangle of chips had an immediate restorative effect. It was a busy time of night when the jackpots were doubled, paid out not to the best hand but to the best bad beat, a losing hand of aces full of tens or better. People could always tell when someone hit by the lusty victory cry, followed by players from other tables rushing over to witness the miracle as if its powers might rub off and make them next.

Jack didn't care about that. All he wanted was to get out of his head and kill time with a circle of strangers, most of whom were there for similar reasons.

He gave his initials to a guy manning the wait board. When a seat opened up, the floor man waved him over to a table. From the wad of cash he had won last time, Jack peeled off a couple hundreds for a rack of chips and ordered two large black coffees.

He played. The cards were cold. He resisted the urge to read anything into it. It seemed to help. The hands started to turn around. He wasn't winning a lot but at least he wasn't losing.

Between hands Jack thought about Claire—her scent, her touch, the way she had looked at him when they were pressed together in the bushes. It had been a long time since someone had that effect on Jack, made him feel something. Anything. Broken through the armor. Of all people, a woman who had slept with his father.

Why hadn't he heard back from her, Jack wondered.

The dealer passed around a fresh round of cards. Jack checked his to discover a pair of queens. He reminded himself what happened the last time he had drawn that hand. Somehow it was no longer his favorite. The pot was raised. When the action came to Jack, he folded.

He drained both his coffees and looked for a waitress to order another. None came so Jack got up to go to the casino cafe, figuring it would be faster. He was halfway across the card room when his cell phone rang. Claire, Jack thought. Finally. He answered it.

"Where are you?" Jack said.

"Getting on with my life. Unlike you, apparently."

It was a female voice but not Claire's.

"Who is this?" Jack said.

"Not funny, Jack. I thought we agreed, no contact."

The sweetness with an edge, the cutting direct-ness. There was no mistaking it. Jack stopped short.

"Becky?"

"Even for you this is a new low. And don't pretend you don't know what I'm talking about."

Jack felt his throat constrict with old emotions, ones he didn't know he still had. Somehow he got his voice to work.

"What's wrong?" Jack asked. "What happened?"

"I'll tell you what happened. I'm here working late, trying to finish an emergency brief, when who should I get a call from but one of your drinking buddies."

"Excuse me?"

"Some person named Lim. He said you told him I would help him out with some legal mess he got him-self into."

Jack was dumbfounded.

"Lim? Wait, Lim called you?"

"As if I don't have enough on my plate."

"He's not a drinking buddy."

"No, of course not."

"I don't drink anymore. And I didn't tell him to call you. I would never do that."

"Then how did he get my name and number?"

"How the hell should I know?"

"Okay, Jack, whatever. I don't want to fight any-more. All that was over a long time ago."

She hadn't changed, Jack thought. She was the same passionate hothead, intense and stubborn, all those things Jack hated and loved and missed. The weight of it made Jack close his eyes. He dragged his fingers through his hair.

"Becky," he said. "Listen to me."

"No, you listen. As a once-only courtesy to you, I'll handle his arraignment tomorrow afternoon, then get him assigned to a public defender if necessary. But that's all, on condition you promise me this won't ever happen again. From now on you will respect my boundaries."

"Can I say something?"

"No."

"Jesus."

"Promise me."

"I promise."

"Thank you."

"Now listen."

"Goodbye, Jack."

"Wait—"

Jack heard a click.

"Becky?"

There was no answer.

"Rebecca?"

She had hung up.

Jack punched the SEND button to call her back. The screen read RESTRICTED. He madly scrolled through his contact list before realizing he had deleted Becky from it in a moment of drunken despair soon after their break-up.

In a spasm of rage, Jack threw down his cell phone and stomped on it as if to kill something that had bitten him. The thing broke apart like a cheap toy. Passing gamblers threw Jack curious glances but not with particular surprise. Outbursts of extreme frustration were nothing unusual here.

Jack stared at the shattered phone. He looked around at the thrumming casino. He wondered what Joseph Pearl would think if he could see his son now.

Where was he when Jack needed saving?

Where was his father three years ago?

PART TWO

30

JACK

Jack opened one eye. Staring back at him was a regal stallion with its head held high. As it startled Jack awake he realized it was the ancient clay horse on the cover of his father's book which was pressed against his face. Jack batted it away and raised his head to find himself in the back seat of his Wagoneer, parked in the far corner of a Toys R Us lot a few blocks from the Commerce Casino.

It all came back to him. After his wonderfully uplifting chat with Becky, he had returned to playing poker and lost everything he won before and more, whereupon instead of having the good sense to go home he pulled over to crash in hopes of waking to find that everything that had happened in the last couple days was a bad dream.

No such luck.

Jack climbed over the seat and back behind the wheel. As he rubbed the sleep from his eyes, a random thought hit him.

He had been hating his father for the wrong reason.

It was the kind of insight that came with defeat or exhaustion or both, one that had been knocking around in the back of Jack's head since getting that surprise call from his father. Ten years ago, he had blamed his dad for not saving his mother from herself, even as Jack knew deep down there was nothing anyone could have done. Yet Jack had continued to shun his old man for all these years and now he understood why. It was because Joseph Pearl was not, nor would he ever be, the father Jack always wished he was.

Had the philosopher shown up for their lunch date, Jack might have had the guts to admit that to him. Maybe his dad would have opened up too and shared his own feelings on the subject. But the opportunity had been lost for reasons unknown, and more and more it looked as if it would never come again.

Jack was famished. He drove to a Denny's a few blocks away and ordered a Grand Slam breakfast, paying with plastic since he had gambled away all his cash. Then he found a Verizon store and bought a replacement phone for the one he had trashed. The first thing Jack did was call Mrs. Woo.

"Not worry," Mrs. Woo said. "Trouser fine."

"You're a saint," Jack said.

"And you foolish young man. Bit by gambling bug. Sure you not Chinese?"

Knowing better than to defend himself, Jack thanked her profusely. As soon as he hung up, he checked for a voicemail from Claire but there was nothing. It was possible she had tried to reach him without leaving a message but if so, Jack knew, any record of the call would have been lost with the rest of the data stored on his old cell phone—including, he realized, that strange hang-up on his dad's hotel messages that he had recorded. Like the dumb mistake of not getting Claire's number, Jack had failed to take the extra few seconds to send the cryptic aborted message to himself as an e-mail attachment for safekeeping. Now, whatever clues it might have yielded were gone.

Thinking about e-mail reminded Jack of the one he was expecting from Gary's contact in Nigeria. When he checked his inbox, he found it waiting there with PERSONAL AND CONFIDENTIAL in the subject line. Jack held his breath. He clicked it open and a message popped up on the screen:

```
Good day Sir,

Regarding the subject of your enquiry,
please be advised that no financial
accounts or personal identity informa-
tion have been accessed in the last for-
ty-eight hours.

Faithfully yours,
Dr. Kassim Biobaku
Managing Director, Afribank Nigeria PLC
```

177

Jack exhaled. He wanted to believe there might be some mistake but he knew better. To be recommended by Gary, the Nigerian was sure to be one of the best cyber trackers on any continent, his finger firmly on the pulse of the electronic ether circling the planet. Even the tiniest shred of data pertaining to Joseph Pearl would have been picked up on his radar.

One more dead end.

Jack felt tired and discouraged. Constantius had been a bust. McGurk and Singh were still persons of interest but, without more to go on, low percentage plays at best. That left only one box unchecked: the pawn shop. Going back seemed like an exercise in futility, but Jack hated loose ends.

He drove off again and clicked on the radio, catching a ballad by Coldplay. *I know I'm dead on the surface, But I'm screaming underneath.* Jack changed the station. A few blocks down he found an entrance to the I-5 and headed north, flowing along in six lanes of traffic through downtown. Then he made a smooth transition onto the Hollywood Freeway and got off at the Melrose exit. At the bottom of the ramp a young sunburned woman held up a sign that read WHY LIE? I NEED COLD BEER. As Jack roared past, the woman made an obscene gesture.

Jack continued west on Melrose toward the pawn shop. He was a few blocks away when he heard a siren behind him. As he pulled over with other cars, a red Fire Department rescue ambulance howled past. Jack watched it race down the street, then veer into a tight passageway between buildings and disappear. Further down, a parking enforcement vehicle blocked off the next side street. An officer was waving cars along as if there was a traffic light out, except there was no light at that corner and the officer's wave appeared tense.

An alarm went off in Jack's head. To a blast of horns he swerved around cars and shot into the passageway the ambulance had taken. He followed its dust trail to a service alley running behind the stores on Melrose. As he cut a sharp left Jack was met by a sea of flashing red lights. The alley was swarming with detectives and CSI's as well as patrol cops guarding the perimeter. Having unloaded a gurney from the ambulance, two paramedics bobbed under yellow police tape and entered the back door of a business which seemed to be the focus of activity. Above its door was a sign:

HENRY'S PAWN SHOP
PLEASE USE FRONT ENTRANCE

The alarm in Jack's head was screaming now. As he ran out of the car, a rookie cop intercepted him.

"Stay back, sir."

"What happened?"

"Don't worry, everything's under control."

Jack tried pushing past but the rookie grabbed his arm.

"Hey, mister, you can't go over there."

"It's okay," Jack said. "I'm a cop."

In the heat of the moment it was all Jack could think to say. It made the rookie release him. But simultaneously Jack was body-blocked by someone else with a blunt, gravelly voice.

"You're a *what*?"

Jack turned and came face to face with a human Rottweiler named Trigwell, a suit from Hollywood Division who Jack had had the distinct displeasure of sharing a few cases with in the past. But Trigwell was not just any suit. He was the one Jack had always suspected of being involved in the matter that had ended his career—the dirty cop who had set that trap and made off with the missing drug money—although Jack had never been able to prove it, even with Franco's help.

"I must be going deaf," Trigwell said, "Because I could have sworn I heard you say you were still a police officer."

Jack wasn't listening. All that registered was what kind of detective Trigwell was. Homicide.

"Is there a body in there?" Jack said.

"That's no concern of yours."

"I need to see it."

"What you need is to get back in your car right now and leave."

Jack tried to shove past but Trigwell checked him.

"The hell is wrong with you, Pearl? Soiling your badge wasn't disgrace enough for you?"

"You don't understand."

"Understand *this*," Trigwell said. "One more step and I will arrest your sorry ass!"

Jack glanced around. Other cops had stopped what they were doing to see what the commotion was about. Jack didn't know any of them but even if he had, none would have backed him up.

Trigwell jutted his chin at the rookie.

"Officer, please escort this man back to his vehicle."

"That won't be necessary," Jack said.

He returned to the Wagoneer and backtracked out of the alley. Under any other circumstances, running into Trigwell would have caused Jack to obsess about the past again. But there was something more pressing right now, the identity of the homicide victim in the pawn shop. It was all Jack could do to keep from fearing the worst.

He swung back onto Melrose and drove several blocks east, far enough away to be sure he was out of sight even if Trigwell came out to check the street. Then Jack pulled over and waited.

And waited.

For what felt like an eternity.

Finally, as expected, the ambulance sped out of the alley, its siren wailing. But instead of heading in the direction Jack was pointed, toward the L.A. Coroner facility downtown, the ambulance sped off in the opposite way without turning off its siren.

Jack felt a rush of shock and hope. He knew it could only mean one thing. Whoever was inside the ambulance was still alive.

31

SALAZAR

I n a taqueria downtown, a World Cup soccer match played on an old television behind the counter. The excitement was electric as Mexico scored against Argentina.

"Gol!"

Salazar exchanged nods with others watching the game. When the TV switched to a commercial, Salazar went back to eating his *huevos con chorizo* and thought about his unusual hostage, the philosopher Joseph William Pearl.

From his own experience during a hunger strike in prison, Salazar remembered that seventy-two hours was the turning point when deprived of food or water. After that, the painful gnawing receded and the body went into a kind of protective trance. Without being exposed to the sun or other harsh elements a human being could remain in that state for a fairly long time, even a week or more as had been shown with survivors trapped in the rubble of earthquakes—assuming, of course, that the person in question was otherwise healthy. In the case of the hostage it was probable, given his age, that whatever ailments he suffered from would be worsened by his captivity. But that was not Salazar's problem. The client had been clear: no comforts of any kind, not even a bucket to piss in, until further directions were provided.

The client.

As a rule Salazar preferred to choose his own targets. That made it easier to control all the elements and reduced the chance of something going wrong. But sometimes situations arose where people wanted others punished or worse, for which they were willing to pay handsomely. When providing his services in such cases, Salazar exercised even more caution than usual. Every client was vetted. Communication was kept to an absolute minimum and conducted through secure channels. Above all, Salazar made sure his own true identity remained a secret so that, even if all else failed, he could vanish without a trace.

As he finished his meal, a cell phone chirped inside his pocket. Salazar extracted it, a cheap prepaid throwaway, and read a text message on the screen:

2$ X ?

It was from Alice, the only person who had that number. The shorthand indicated that the second and final wire transfer from the client had not yet been received. Alice was asking for instructions.

Salazar consulted his watch. It was ten A.M., two hours after the payment was due according to the pre-arranged timetable.

Someone less experienced might have lost his cool over such a gaffe and deviated from the plan. But Salazar knew that was the way people got caught. Besides, the client had been reliable so far. It was just business. Complications sometimes arose. Salazar was sure there was a logical explanation which the client must have detailed in a safeguarded message. Still, he would need to make sure before answering Alice.

Disappointed that it meant missing the soccer game, Salazar tossed some money on the counter including a generous tip and walked out.

A church clock rang on the quarter hour as Salazar entered the art deco grandeur of the Central Library a few blocks away. Instead of heading for the busy media center on the lower level, he took the stairs to the reference section where he found a free public computer in the corner that was not being used.

Before logging on Salazar took several moments to sanitize the machine, creating a temporary firewall that would prevent any of his keystrokes or pathways from being traced. Then he typed in the address to an anonymous e-mail account he had set up through a hyper-secure web service that provided such accounts for a nominal charge.

As expected, the inbox was empty but there was one message in the draft folder. Salazar eased back in his seat. Why bother sending e-mails when drafts were more efficient and protected? It was the perfect way to communicate in secret, a system favored by white collar criminals and terrorists alike. To send a message Salazar would write what he wanted to say to someone and save it as a draft. The recipient would then log onto the same account and read the draft, then change it with a confirmation message. That way the exchange was never sent into cyberspace, preventing interception and making it untraceable.

With a click of the mouse, Salazar pulled up the draft. As soon as he read it, his eyes turned to stone. All that was written there was the message he had left for the client two days ago, acknowledging receipt of the first of the two payments due. The fact that it had not been deleted and replaced with an explanation, why the follow-up payment had not been wired to Alice on time, indicated a lapse on the part of the client, a deviation from the plan. It could be nothing more than a careless oversight or it could mean something serious.

Salazar decided to give the client the benefit of the doubt. He deleted what he had posted before and composed a terse new draft message:

YOU'RE LATE
PAY BY 3PM OR SERVICES TERMINATED

Salazar clicked off. Careful to a fault, he made sure the firewall had erased all evidence of his visit before leaving the computer. As he headed back to the first floor he pulled out the pre-paid cell and fired off a text:

DEAD 3

Alice would know that meant the deadline had been extended to three P.M. For Salazar it also had another meaning: what would happen to the hostage if the client failed to make good.

He reached the bottom of the stairs and was about to exit the library when he noticed a security guard watching a small portable TV on his desk. Salazar remembered the soccer game and wondered what the score was. He stepped over to ask the guard and heard a female news reporter on the TV:

"—Still no word on the victim's condition or his connection to the pawn shop where he was found."

Salazar stopped in his tracks.

"According to police," the reporter continued, "The man was rushed to an area hospital with, quote, very serious injuries. Reporting live from West Hollywood, this is Kelly King, Eyewitness News."

The guard noticed Salazar staring.

"Can I help you, sir?"

Salazar regained his composure.

"No, thank you," he said. "Everything's fine."

With a polite nod, Salazar turned and left the building.

32

JACK

T hanks to all the congestion on Melrose caused by the crime scene, it took Jack longer than expected to turn his car around to tail the ambulance. By the time he had, the emergency vehicle was gone. Jack stuck his head out the window in hopes of hearing its siren but even that had been swallowed up by the cacophony of the city.

The nearest hospital was Cedars-Sinai. However, Jack doubted the ambulance was headed there. Given the police presence around the pawn shop it was a good bet that the injuries of the person being transported were serious, even life threatening, which meant the destination would be a hospital with an E.R. set up to handle severe trauma. There were two major ones in Los Angeles, Jack knew: USC Medical Center in Boyle Heights and UCLA Med on the Westside. Besides being closer, UCLA was in the direction the ambulance had headed.

It took Jack twenty-two minutes to get there. He pulled into the emergency parking area adjacent to the ambulance entrance. In its arrival bay, as Jack hoped, was the LAFD rescue vehicle with its back doors flung open. Standing nearby was a uniformed police officer Jack recognized from the crime scene. The officer was talking to a triage nurse who was scribbling notes on her clipboard. The fact that a cop had ridden along in the ambulance confirmed the gravity of the situation. Except in circumstances where a suspect was injured, the lone reason for a police escort was in case a victim might make a dying declaration en route regarding who caused the injuries or any other crimes that might have been committed. Unlike similar statements made elsewhere, dying declarations in ambulances were not considered hearsay and therefore were admissible in court.

Jack didn't want to risk a replay of what had happened with Trigwell so he steered clear of the cop and darted into the E.R.'s walk-in entrance. The place was a zoo. Patients who had been able to get there on their own were waiting in various states of discomfort alongside friends and family of others who had already been taken in for treatment. Some looked sick with worry, knowing that what had brought them there would alter their lives forever. In one corner, a young Asian mother was crying while clutching a doll that had been scorched by a fire.

Jack looked around. The only security guard on duty was flirting with an admissions clerk, both of them turned away from a set of double doors that read RESTRICTED AREA, AUTHORIZED PERSONNEL ONLY. Jack marched straight past the guard, doing his best to look authorized, and pressed the button on the wall which made the doors swing open.

He hurried through. Sleep-deprived doctors and nurses were moving about, too busy to notice him. With no idea where to go, Jack continued down the hall toward a suite of curtained treatment beds. He made it past a nurse's station when a stern-looking RN spotted him and sprang to her feet.

"Excuse me, excuse me! Are you a patient?"

She knew he wasn't.

"The police just brought someone in," Jack said. "I think it may be my father."

"You can't be in here."

"Please," Jack said. "I need to know if he's okay."

Something, maybe the crack in his voice, made the RN soften.

"Your father's name?"

"Joseph Pearl."

"Wait here. Stay. Do not move."

The RN disappeared around a corner. Jack paced. Sooner than he expected, the RN returned.

"A John Doe came in a few minutes ago," she said. "About sixty, gray hair, average height and build."

Jack stiffened.

"Sounds like him," he said. "What's his condition?"

"Critical. He's lost a lot of blood."

"What happened?"

"He was stabbed, multiple times."

Jack felt his stomach drop.

"Can I see him?"

"He's been taken to surgery."

"When will he be out?"

"Hopefully soon," the RN said. "Meantime, what can you tell us about him?"

"Tell you?"

"Blood type? Allergies to medications? Does he have any preexisting conditions?"

"I...don't really know."

The RN's eyes narrowed.

"You did say he was your father?"

"It's been awhile since we saw each other."

The RN wasn't buying it.

"You'll have to leave now," she said. "As soon as they know anything, you'll be called."

She put her hand on her hip to let him know the conversation was over. Jack returned to the purgatory of the waiting room and took an empty seat.

He waited. As the minutes dripped by, Jack's thoughts drifted to his mother. He remembered her soulful blue eyes and Zorba The Greek smile, even when life was crumbling around her. She too had been rushed to a hospital with mortal injuries but had died before Jack had the chance to say goodbye. Would history repeat itself?

A familiar voice interrupted Jack's thoughts.

"Twice in one week. What are the odds?"

Jack looked up to see Franco coming over, still sporting his beard and biker jacket. With him was a young black guy in dreadlocks.

"What happened," Franco said. "Truck hit you? Jesus Christ, man, you look like shit."

Jack didn't need to ask Franco how he happened to be there.

"Trigwell," he said.

Franco conceded a shrug.

"He called me about your run-in. Figured you'd follow the meat wagon here. Gave me a heads-up to keep you out of trouble."

"To keep me on a tight leash, you mean."

The black guy smirked. Franco gestured to him.

"This here's my partner, Kevin Russell. Kev, meet Jack Pearl."

Kevin shook Jack's hand.

"Franco has told me a lot about you."

"I'll bet," Jack said. "So I guess you know all about the bad blood between Trigwell and me?"

Franco shot him a weary look.

"Not again, Jack."

"Ever since that little present Trigwell left me three years ago," Jack said. "The gift that keeps on giving."

"Back to the situation here," Franco said. "What's the story, Jack? Who's this vic you're so interested in?"

"What did Trigwell tell you?"

"He's not positive yet."

"Neither am I. But I'm pretty sure it's someone I know."

"How well?"

"Not very."

"Be thankful for that."

"Just my father."

Franco's eyes widened. He turned to Kevin.

"Give us a sec."

As Kevin made himself scarce, Franco settled into the seat next to Jack.

"No offense, buddy, but I've never heard you talk about your old man. Not once in all the years. I just assumed..."

"He was dead?"

"Yeah."

"He was, pretty much. As far as I was concerned."

"He lives here in L.A.?"

"In Boston," Jack said. "He flew in for a conference a couple days ago. He's a philosopher."

"You mean the cerebral type."

"No, I mean that's his job. He teaches, writes books on the subject."

Franco looked impressed.

"So then, you *do* come from smarts. Even if they skipped a generation. But how does a philosopher come to be knifed in some pawn shop in Hollywood?"

"All I know is he disappeared the day before yesterday. I've been trying to find him ever since."

Before Jack could elaborate he heard his last name being called. He turned to see a doctor in scrubs standing by the double doors. Franco sprang to his feet but hung back as Jack met the doctor halfway.

"Joseph Pearl," Jack said. "I'm his son. How is he?"
The doctor shook his head.

"I'm sorry," he said. "We tried everything we could."

A hot chill shot through Jack's veins. Death was nothing new to him. He had seen more than his share in the line of duty, but it was one of those things a person never got used to, especially when it hit close to home.

"We'll need you to identify him," the doctor said. "Please come with me."

As Jack followed the doctor back through the double doors he glanced over his shoulder at Franco who returned a solemn nod of support.

Jack walked down a maze of corridors with the doctor. Along the way he remembered working one summer during high school as a hospital janitor. The cancer ward. Every time a patient would expire on his shift, the Jamaican floor nurse on duty, who was superstitious about being alone with the dead, would grab Jack and make him accompany her to the morgue with the corpse.

The doctor escorted Jack through the O.R. wing and into a cold, stark post-op room. On a steel gurney lay a body draped in a white sheet, stained with blood and iodine. Jack forced himself to walk over and pulled back the sheet. Staring back at him was the John Doe. His face was purple-gray and contorted by fear. One eye was open a crack and lolled to one side, as if looking at the scar on his right temple. Across his exsanguinated neck and chest were hideous, open stab wounds. Other defensive slashes crisscrossed his hands and arms from fighting for his life.

A surge of horror hit Jack, along with relief.

It wasn't him.

The John Doe was not Joseph Pearl.

33

SALAZAR

When Salazar put something behind him he rarely looked back, but what he had learned from the TV at the library demanded his full attention. He called Reaper. There was no answer. He went to his apartment. No one was there. He drove to hangouts he knew Reaper frequented, to no avail. It occurred to Salazar that the kid might have used the pay-off money to skip town in order to get away from him, knowing how dangerous he was, but he dismissed the idea. Reaper wasn't that smart. More likely, he was burning the cash up his nose or in some other mindless pursuit of pleasure.

With cold-blooded efficiency, Salazar kept searching. In due course he tracked down Reaper at a whore bar in Watts, getting a blow job in a bathroom stall. Before the kid knew what hit him, he was dragged out, pants around his knees, into the alley where Salazar flung him into a pile of garbage.

"What the hell, man! You *loco*?"

"I warned you," Salazar said. "No mistakes."

Reaper struggled to his feet and pulled up his pants, only to have Salazar jam the Kimber .45 under his right ear.

"Something wrong with your hearing?" Salazar said. "Did I not tell you explicitly not to go into the shop? To wait for the target to leave before grabbing him?"

"Whoa, easy—"

"Fast. Clean. No one else involved."

"I got him, didn't I?"

"After sticking the owner, which may have been caught on a security camera. And you with it. A small detail you forgot to mention."

"The guy was taking a long time in there. I thought—"

"You *thought*?"

Without the slightest hesitation Salazar fired his gun, blowing half of Reaper's ear clean off. Reaper screamed, blood splattering his face. As his legs buckled Salazar held him up while keeping the gun on him.

"Give me one good reason not to kill you."

"Please...another chance..."

"Who else knows where the hostage is?"

"No one, I swear..."

"I can't take any chances. He needs to be moved to the backup location. The one we talked about, remember?"

Reaper pushed out a nod, moaning and clutching the shredded remnant of his ear. Salazar pulled out a new pre-paid cell phone in a Ziploc baggie and tucked it into Reaper's shirt pocket.

"Don't let him out of your sight, until I call. To tell you whether to kill him or cut him loose. Either way, make sure it's clean this time. And that I never see you again."

Reaper shook his head, beyond pain.

"Never," he said. "Never..."

"Or what?"

"I'm dead."

"Not just you."

Salazar pressed his gun against Reaper's blood-soaked neck tattoo, using the barrel to caress the faces of the pretty Latina and her child.

Reaper gulped.

"No..."

"Your sweet Carmen."

"Oh God..."

"And baby Raoulito."

"No, please..."

"Not quick. Slow. So they suffer."

Wetness stained Reaper's pants as he soiled himself. Salazar felt satisfied that the point had been scorched into the kid's psyche. He withdrew his weapon.

"Don't forget," Salazar said. "Now go."

The second he was released, Reaper ran away with both hands clutching his ear as if his brains might fall out.

197

34

JACK

Jack returned to the waiting room and filled in Franco, starting with the lunch with his father that never happened. He told Franco everything, including the part about saving Claire. It was the first real talk the two of them had had since the events that caused their partnership to end. When Jack finished, Franco drew in a breath.

"So what do you think?" Jack said.

"I think you have reason to be concerned."

"That's why I need your help."

Franco nodded.

"I'll tell Trigwell. He's a raging asshole but a good cop, despite what you think. Now that this is officially a homicide, he'll put a team on locating your dad, if for no other reason but that he may be a material witness."

Jack shook his head.

"By help, I meant you," he said. "Alone."

Franco tightened up.

"Come again?"

"By the time this gets case-filed, it'll be too late."

"Tell me you're not saying what I think you are."

"In hopes of saving a man's life."

"Breaking the rules, Jack. Same thing that hung your ass out to dry three years ago."

"Not just any man, Franco. My father."

Jack's eyes were smarting. He looked away.

"Jack? You okay?"

"Guess my anchors aren't working anymore," Jack said.

"Sorry, your what?"

"Those invariant rules I've been living by."

Before Franco could ask what he was talking about, Kevin came over juggling coffees. He offered one to Jack.

"Franco mentioned you take it black."

"Along with all the dirt he told you about me?"

"Damn straight," Franco said, "Including that you're a world class pain in the ass. C'mon, Kev, there's a hock shop in Hollywood we need to check out."

Jack looked at Franco.

"Thank you."

"Yeah, yeah," Franco said. "I must be outa my mind."

Jack bumped fists with Franco who led Kevin away. The sounds of the waiting room faded back in. Jack glanced around. The Asian mother in the corner was no longer there, the burned doll left behind on the seat. Jack focused again. Odds were, the John Doe from the pawn shop was Henry, the 'custodian of art' Esma had told him about. With a pang of guilt, Jack realized that Henry was probably there at the shop when Jack had stopped by the day before to find it closed. Most likely, Henry was behind the counter or in the back storage room, unable to move or cry out because of his knife wounds, when Jack had kicked the door and caused the bell to jingle. How differently things might have turned out, Jack thought, if he had only broken into the shop instead of walking away.

Pretty soon a police team would arrive at the hospital to identify the body through prints and dentals. Jack thought of a faster way, someone who might give him a new angle to pursue while Franco was working the crime scene.

Esma.

Jack walked back to his car where he found the take-out menu with Esma's number on it. He called the number, expecting to get the assistant again. To his surprise, Esma answered.

"Hello?"

Something was different. The cheer in her voice was gone.

"Esma, it's Jack Pearl. Joe's son, remember?"

"Oh, Jack...yes, of course."

"Am I calling at a bad time?"

"No, forgive me, I was...a difficult family matter I was attending to. How are you, Jack? And where did you disappear to yesterday? I'm sorry to say your dear father never showed up. I was so looking forward to seeing him, after all these years."

Was she being sincere or evasive? Jack couldn't quite tell.

"Esma, I need your help," Jack said. "Please don't ask me to explain. I need you to describe Henry, the owner of the pawn shop you referred my dad to. What he looks like, any distinguishing features."

There was a momentary silence on the other end. When Esma spoke again she sounded anxious but obliging.

"A description of Henry? Let me think. Middle-aged, hazel eyes, Mediterranean features. I seem to recall a scar from a childhood accident. On his right temple, I believe."

Jack remembered the scar on the stab victim. Confirmation.

"Do you know if he had any enemies?"

"I beg your pardon?"

"Someone he owed money to or had wronged in some way? Anyone who might have wanted to hurt him for any reason?"

"Oh dear. I'm afraid I didn't know him that well."

"Anything he confided to you? Anything out of the ordinary? Anything at all?"

"No. Please, Jack, you're scaring me."

"One last question. Did you tell anyone that my dad would be going to the pawn shop?"

"No," Esma said. "Why do you ask?"

"Even in passing?"

"My God, what's happened?"

"Turn on the news. My father was involved some-how. If you think of anything, please call me at this number."

Jack hung up. As he pulled out his keys to leave, he was struck by an uncomfortable thought. What if he had gotten it all wrong? Instead of being the victim of foul play, suppose Joseph Pearl had been the cause of it, the one who had stabbed Henry—over an argument, in self-defense, for some other reason only the two of them knew about—and then had fled in fear or shock or to cover his tracks. What if that was the real reason his father had dropped out of sight? It seemed crazy, impossible. But was it?

If Jack had learned anything as a cop, it was that people could surprise you. People were capable of any-thing, particularly when emotions were involved. In the heat of the moment, anyone could commit a crime, even murder. Anyone. Even someone you thought you knew, let alone someone you had never had the chance to.

An electronic sound interrupted Jack's train of thought, the default ringtone of his replacement cell phone. Was it Esma calling back, Jack wondered. He checked the screen to see a number he didn't recog-nize. He answered it.

"Pearl here."

"There you are," a woman's voice said. "I was start-ing to think you had forgotten me."

The voice was one Jack recognized, similar to Esma's in its cadence though less self-assured.

"Claire?"

"I sent you several texts. Why didn't you answer?"

So that explained why he hadn't heard from her. Like the rest of the data on his old phone, Claire's messages had been ground into the carpet at the Commerce.

"I must have deleted them by accident," Jack said, wincing at how lame it sounded. "What did they say?"

"First tell me about Constantius."

"He's not involved."

"You sound certain."

"Sorry you wasted your time chasing his girlfriend."

"You might change your mind when you hear what she had to say," Claire answered. "Yeah, I talked to her. The reason I texted you. She told me something about Joe. Something disturbing, involving Singh."

Jack felt his attention sharpen.

"Disturbing in what way?"

"I'd rather tell you in person. Can we meet?"

Jack took a second to think. It might be awhile before he heard back from Franco. In the meantime he needed to check out every lead.

"Okay," Jack said. "Where are you?"

"At Moore Hall, back at the conference. Singh is scheduled to do graduate reviews here all morning. I just saw him go in."

"I'm on my way."

"I'll be waiting out front."

There was a click as Claire hung up.

203

Jack rubbed the slope of his nose pensively. Part of him wanted to see Claire but another part was resisting. It all started at the Getty when Jack had smelled her perfume and wondered if she had put it on for him. No, Jack admitted to himself, it started way before that, in the whirlwind of forced intimacy that had surrounded their first meeting, when Jack had rescued her from the ocean and carried her in his arms.

As a kid Jack had once done a school project on rare medical conditions. He wondered if there was one for a son attracted to a woman his father had rejected. If so, it was deserving of shame. And probably incurable.

Jack shoved the car key back in the ignition and roared away.

35

JOSEPH PEARL

P hilosophy and violence. In the clutches of both, Pearl pondered the connection. On the surface, there appeared to be none. Philosophy was a product of mental discipline, a search for an understanding of values and reality by chiefly speculative means. In contrast, violence was innately physical and required no discipline whatsoever. Mind and body: as different as night and day. Yet Pearl's profession was rife with examples of the power of the one provoking the fury of the other.

Perhaps the most famous was an incident involving Karl Popper and Ludwig Wittgenstein. Popper, an esteemed philosopher at the London School of Economics, was invited to present a paper at a meeting of the Cambridge Moral Science Club which was chaired by his legendary colleague, Wittgenstein. According to eyewitness accounts the two began arguing about whether there existed substantial problems in philosophy or merely linguistic puzzles. As the exchange heated up Wittgenstein grabbed a red-hot poker from the fireplace and jabbed it at Popper, challenging him to state an example of a moral rule. Popper replied, "Not to threaten visiting lecturers with pokers", whereupon Wittgenstein threw down the iron and stormed out, stoking the fires of philosophical debate for years to come.

A less amusing episode involved Moritz Schlick, a logical positivist who was shot dead by a former student on the steps of the University of Vienna. As part of his defense the student claimed that Schlick's philosophical arguments had undermined his moral restraints.

And then there was Louis Althusser, a French post-structuralist who murdered his wife while working out the influence of empiricism on Marxist theory. Althusser told his psychiatrist he was massaging his wife's neck when he discovered he had strangled her.

Philosophers were a strange breed.

As he lay there in agony, still handcuffed to the pipes, Pearl wondered if his ordeal would someday be added to the lore of his profession. Perhaps he would best be remembered for the groundbreaking new work he was on the verge of completing, his legacy. It was Pearl's modest hope that the radical notions contained in his unfinished book, the one whose cover art he had sought to find at the pawn shop, would stir a fresh debate in philosophy. It might even revitalize the field at a time when many people wondered about the relevance of philosophy in the fast-changing world. If so, Pearl could take comfort in that, even if he would not be around to see it.

From somewhere below a sound reverberated through the gloom of the factory: those familiar steel-tipped boots clanging up the metal stairs. All thoughts of philosophy abandoned, Pearl struggled to raise his head.

When Reaper came into view, Pearl almost didn't recognize him. The young man was ashen and appeared to be drugged with a bloody bandage covering his right ear.

"The fuck are you looking at?" Reaper said.

Pearl's gaze shifted to a baseball bat in Reaper's hand.

"*You*," Reaper said. "That's who I got to thank for this. Only right I return the favor."

He swung the bat down on Pearl, smashing him into the pipes. Through the ferocious pain, Pearl watched as Reaper stepped over to finish him off. Instead, Reaper pulled a key from his pocket.

"It'll hurt ten times more if you try anything," Reaper said. "And I am really hoping you *do*."

He unlocked Pearl's left handcuff. Like dead weights, Pearl's hands fell away from the pipes.

"Get up," Reaper said. "*Now*, or you won't ever again."

Pearl wasn't sure he remembered how to stand. Somehow he managed to pull himself to his knees. Reaper wrinkled his nose.

"Phew, man. *Hueles a mierda.*"

He reattached the cuff to Pearl's raw and bloody left wrist so his hands were bound in front of him again.

"Okay," he said. "Let's move."

Pearl choked out a hoarse whisper.

"Where...?"

"You'll see."

Reaper dragged him away. With every step, Pearl felt fear rising in his throat. When they reached the top of the stairs Pearl jerked back.

"Keep going," Reaper said.

"Can't..."

"I won't ask you again."

Reaper turned his head to spit, taking his eyes off Pearl for a fraction of a second. From somewhere deep and instinctual, Pearl's fight-or-flight response kicked in. He mustered every last scintilla of strength and rammed Reaper with his shoulder, knocking him off balance. Reaper swiped at Pearl but missed, already pitching backward. As he screamed and toppled down the stairs, Pearl heard sharp edges gashing skin and breaking bones until Reaper slammed to the cement below.

A hush fell over the factory. Pearl stared from the landing, his heart beating out of his chest. He kept expecting Reaper to get up and come after him but there was nothing but silence. For a full minute Pearl waited to make sure, then he edged down the metal stairs.

He reached the ground floor where Reaper lay sprawled, the baseball bat a few feet away. I just killed a man, Pearl thought. Anyone else would have felt justified, but in his weakened state Pearl was stopped by the idea and the moral questions it raised, questions he had addressed in books and articles over the years yet never had to confront firsthand. With difficulty, the philosopher pushed the thoughts away, promising himself he would give them the consideration they deserved at some later time when he was more able. Right now he had a more pressing need, to stay alive.

He limped away, the cuffs still cutting into his wrists, when he heard something behind him, a sound like air leaking from a tire. He turned to see Reaper stirring. Pearl hemorrhaged with horror. In his panic to escape he tripped into one of the cobwebbed factory machines and gashed his thigh.

From somewhere behind, a wounded roar pierced the dark.

"Where are you...you're dead, motherfucker!"

Because of the echo, Pearl couldn't tell if Reaper was still by the stairs or was coming after him. Pearl fled. As he searched the rows of machines for a way out, he noticed blood dripping from the gash on his leg. He grabbed his thigh with his cuffed hands to cover his trail and hobbled on. Then he spotted a rat behind a machine sniffing the edge of an open drain hole in the floor, a space barely large enough for a man to crawl into. In one last all-or-nothing stab at survival, Pearl dragged himself behind the machine and into the hole.

Suddenly he was sliding down a drainage chute and into pitch darkness. He fell fast, out of control. Then he catapulted out and splash-landed in the black void of a sewer tunnel.

The impact knocked Pearl unconscious.

36

JACK

Claire was there to greet Jack as he walked up to Moore Hall. Once again she looked distractingly pretty, this time in an orange tank top, white skirt and sandals. Jack glanced down at the clothes he had on, realizing he hadn't changed or showered in two days.

"You're fast," Claire said.

"Not always."

"We have to stop meeting like this."

She smiled and brushed her hand against his arm, letting it linger. Her temperature ran warm to Jack. Feeling it raised his.

"Oh, before I forget," Claire said, "Thank you again for that call you made to the car rental place. They delivered my purse this morning as promised. And this."

She touched a silver locket at her throat.

"The one your dad gave you?" Jack asked.

Claire nodded.

"Shortly before he died. Wearing it helped me get through that difficult period. Seems like a good time to start wearing it again."

"Okay, I'm all ears," Jack said. "What's this disturbing news involving my father and Singh?"

"Actually," Claire said, "It involves Joe and Singh's wife."

Claire saw Jack's expression change and smoothed her skirt.

"Yeah, it was a shock to me too," Claire said. "Not so much that Joe would cheat on me but that he would stoop so low as to sleep with the spouse of a colleague."

Jack frowned.

"The redhead told you that?"

Claire nodded again.

"According to a mutual friend who Singh's wife confided in, it's been going on for some time."

"I have to say that sounds..."

"Pretty scandalous. Yeah."

"I was going to say out of character for my dad. I mean, granted I haven't been around him for a while but from the way he treated my mom growing up, he always seemed incredibly respectful of the institution of marriage."

Claire gave Jack a doleful look.

"I guess that's another thing we have in common, besides that we both love him. For different reasons we both keep wanting to believe he's the person we wish he was rather than the man he really is."

Her words stung Jack. It was the kind of painful truth that Becky would bring to his attention back when they were together, either in the sweat-drenched quiet after making love or during one of their fights.

"So Singh found out?" Jack said.

"Evidently he was devastated."

"What did he do?"

"According to what his wife told her friend, he was going to enlist someone's help to teach Joe a lesson. I asked the redhead what that meant but that was all she knew."

Claire could see Jack was still skeptical.

"Don't take my word for it," she said. "Ask Singh yourself."

"Where is he?"

"Meeting Room C. It's on the second floor."

Claire pointed toward the building but didn't move.

"Aren't you coming?" Jack said.

"You've had to put up with enough of my drama. I'm sure you'll do better without me."

In her eyes Jack saw all the things she couldn't bring herself to say: "I'm still fragile, I'm hurt, I'm torn between wanting to help and wanting to run." And underneath that, something deeper: "I can't be attracted to you, it's wrong, but I am and it scares me." Or maybe he was seeing what he wanted to see, Jack thought, what he was feeling himself. Claire sensed what he was picking up and lowered her eyes.

"Go," she said. "I'll wait for you here."

Jack turned and headed into Moore Hall.

The lobby was empty except for a few stragglers from the conference coming and going. Jack made his way to the second floor and found Meeting Room C. Stuck to the door was an orange Post-It:

GRAD REVIEWS, DO NOT DISTURB

Jack peeked through the small window in the door to see Singh inside. Wearing all black again, the Indian professor was seated with a student whose dissertation Singh was tearing to shreds by the looks of it. The philosoraptor in all his glory. Off to one side, two other students were waiting their turn with the joyful anticipation of vestal virgins about to be sacrificed. The scene reminded Jack of his time at Cornell, how much he struggled before accepting that he would never be an academic like his old man, and that he was okay with that, free to pursue his own path which led to his becoming a detective and not a bad one at that. Until the unforeseeable happened.

Jack brushed his clothes to make them appear a little less rumpled, then barged through the door. The students glanced up in surprise. So did Singh, with a lemon-sucking expression.

"Excuse me," he said. "This room is reserved."

Jack whipped out his wallet and flashed his driver's license as if it were a badge, too fast for Singh to get a good look.

"Detective Russo, LAPD," Jack said. "Sorry, my suit's at the cleaners. Are you Professor Singh?"

Singh's unibrow furrowed.

"Yes I am," he said. "Why?"

Jack motioned to the students.

"You're free to go," he said. "Please leave."

As the students bolted out of the room, Singh shot up from his chair.

"What's the meaning of this?"

"Have a seat, professor."

"What happened? What's wrong?"

"That's what I'm here to find out."

Jack grabbed a chair and signaled Singh to do the same. To sell his act, Jack was prepared to launch into a speech about Singh's rights and other official-sounding doublespeak but he could see it wasn't necessary. Singh was already convinced. If only it were that easy in poker.

"I'll get right to the point," Jack said. "This concerns Joseph Pearl and his recent disappearance."

"What did you say?"

"We have reason to believe you may be involved. In fact, we have a witness who says you threatened to harm Pearl."

Singh drew back.

"What? No, there must be some mistake. Joseph is a colleague, a friend. I had no idea he was even missing."

"A friend?"

"In the professional sense."

"But in the personal sense, you hate his guts."

"That's absurd."

"For screwing your wife."

Singh's jaw dropped.

"Who told you that?"

As Jack remained silent, Singh hung his boyish head in shame. It took a moment for him to find his words.

"Alright," he said. "Yes, I learned my wife had been unfaithful. When I confronted her, she claimed that Pearl had pressured her into having an affair."

Jack could hear doubt in the professor's voice.

"But for some reason you didn't believe her?"

"Sir, I love my wife very much. But it's not the first time she has strayed."

"So you were unsure who she was messing around with. But you confronted Pearl just in case?"

"In a careful way," Singh said. "All the years of boot-licking I've had to endure to climb the ranks of the profession...I wasn't about to throw it all away by confronting a philosopher of Pearl's stature."

"So what did you do?"

"I slipped a note in Joseph's conference materials where I knew he would find it. A message vague enough to be ignored by someone who was innocent, yet specific enough that a person guilty of philandering, someone with Joseph's encyclopedic knowledge, would understand the reference and be warned off by it."

"And the message was?"

"'What would Kant say?'"

Jack frowned.

"Pardon?"

"Kant, sir, was known for his philosophy of pun-
ishment. He believed in retribution proportionate to
the moral gravity of the offense."

"In other words," Jack said, "If you keep fucking
my wife I'll cut off your balls."

"That is a crude way of putting it."

"Which you acted on, by arranging for Pearl to
disappear."

"No!" Singh said. "I told you, I don't know anything about that!"

He didn't, Jack could tell. Or else he was a mas-
terful bluffer, the kind who would eat Jack alive in a
poker game.

Jack got in Singh's face.

"Look," he said, "Either you stop bullshitting and
tell me where he is or I'll have you arrested on suspicion of kidnapping and possibly murder."

For a moment Singh looked intimidated, as if he
might give up the ghost. But then a wall went up and
his eyes narrowed.

"What did you say your name was, Detective?"

"Russo. Now let's hear it."

"May I please see your badge again?"

Jack had pushed too hard, he realized. The kind of
blunder that could blow a case, were he still a cop. His
performance was over. It was time to go.

"You can see my badge when I come back with a
warrant," Jack said. "Enjoy your freedom while it lasts."

He walked out, leaving Singh looking dazed and
confused.

Jack took the stairs back to the lobby. What had caused him to be so careless? If he was trying *not* to find his father, he was doing a kick-ass job. Distracting thoughts, Jack realized, had made him lose his focus. Thoughts of someone besides Claire who Jack hadn't stopped thinking about since hearing her voice the previous night.

Jack reached the exit doors to see Claire standing outside where he had left her. She was talking to Julian Wade, the cocky-looking guy she had asked to read her paper before she attempted to take her life. Jack hung back to watch them chat, then Wade nodded goodbye and headed off across the quad. Once he was gone, Jack walked out of the building and rejoined Claire who seemed pleased that he was back.

"So how did it go?" she asked. "Did you talk to Singh?"

Jack nodded, trying to hide his disappointment.

"Another strange and tortured member of your profession who has nothing to do with Joseph Pearl missing."

Claire pursed her lips.

"But what about Singh's wife?"

"Turned out to be bogus," Jack said. "Whatever indiscretions you have reason to blame my father for, that wasn't one of them."

While he hoped it was true, Jack was no more certain of that than Singh had been. But it had the desired effect on Claire. She appeared relieved.

"By the way," Jack said, "Wasn't that Wade you were just talking to?"

Claire seemed only mildly surprised that Jack had noticed. She nodded.

"He was on his way to a lecture," she said. "He invited me to come but I told him I couldn't go."

"Why not?"

"Because I have more important things to do like being with you. To help, I mean. That is, if you'll let me."

Jack could see she was eager to please. But he didn't want to have to explain about Henry, the pawn shop, Franco.

"If you want to help," Jack said, "Go meet Wade. Try to find out what matter he discussed with my father, the one Wade alluded to in his voicemail. It might be relevant."

Claire didn't look thrilled with the idea.

"What about you?"

"There's something I need to do," Jack said.

"Another lead?"

Jack shrugged.

"I'll call you later."

"Or maybe we could meet up for a drink," Claire said. "Y'know, to compare notes."

"A drink?"

"There's a cool little bar at my hotel."

In spite of Jack ordering a coffee at the Berkeley party, Claire seemed to have no clue that he was an alcoholic. Another thing Jack didn't want to have to get into.

"I don't know," Jack said. "This might take a while."

"I don't mind waiting. Come find me when you're finished."

Claire brushed his cheek with a kiss and hurried off.

Jack felt an endorphin rush, another surge of attraction. Just what he needed to add to his already confused state. He was glad to feel his pulse returning to normal as he headed away.

37

JOSEPH PEARL

Pearl awoke to new darkness, new agony. His first sensations were nausea, dizziness, uncontrollable shivering. Then the stench of raw sewage and reality rushed in.

He heaved to vomit but nothing came out. As his mind cleared Pearl realized he was drenched from head to toe, sprawled face down in a small stream of sewer water. It was too dark to see but he could feel its lazy current trickling across his face and leaking into his mouth.

He tried to raise his head but he was too weak. Straining, he managed to work his cuffed hands out from under his broken body and used them to shift his weight and roll onto his side. The memory of the escape that had caused him to be there came flooding back. He perked up his ears but there was nothing to hear except for the echo of his own labored breathing.

It appeared to Pearl that he had eluded certain death at the hand of his captor. But now he faced the prospect of dying slowly and painfully in the wretched darkness of the sewer tunnel, cut off from the outside world, where even the chance of someone finding his remains would be remote.

God help me, he thought.

Pearl blinked, taken aback. Where had that thought come from? Had it popped into his head as an expression of frustration? Or was there more to it than that?

Pearl's views on God had been formed from an early age. He had nothing to say about God. He found it mysterious that people were so certain of God's existence. He couldn't see what they were driving at when they talked about God's character as if they were talking about the melting point of gold. The act of praying, too, was meaningless to Pearl. Prayer might be a voicing of one's sincerest hopes. Pearl could understand that. Everyone spoke in that theatrical way and longed for things they didn't have. But prayer could also mean addressing some Being who might, out of miraculous concerns, make something possible. To Pearl, that was nonsense.

He had been in some tough spots in his life, including coming to terms with Ann's death and learning recently of a stage II carcinoma at the base of his spine. At neither of those times did Pearl pray nor could he imagine any situation so disturbing that he would be moved to call upon a higher power he did not believe in. Until now. Now he found himself in uncharted territory. In light of the questions raised by his dream and his growing self-doubt, Pearl realized that he had to prepare himself for a daunting possibility: as his inevitable demise drew near, even his most deeply-held convictions, those upon which he had built his life and his work, might crumble into dust.

He struggled to pull himself up. A stabbing pain radiated from his right leg. Pearl screamed, filling the pitch black tunnel with distorted echoes. His shackled hands trembled as he groped his leg and felt a bone sticking out, apparently broken by the fall.

It's over, Pearl thought, I can't go on. But something would not let him surrender: the voice of one of the naked philosophers from his dream, Nietzsche, whispering in the back of his mind:

He who has a 'why' to live can bear any 'how'.

Pearl closed his eyes to concentrate. He dipped a bloodied finger into the sewer stream. He could feel the direction the water was flowing, the direction he had to go. Somehow he marshaled what meager shreds of strength he had left and began dragging himself away in the dark.

38

JACK

J ack returned home for a much-needed shave and shower. Then he took Trouser for a walk. It was the same walk they took every day but Trouser was just as excited every day. As they stopped at a dog park and Trouser played with his canine friends, Jack thought about Becky. Before hanging up on him, Becky had mentioned that she would be handling Lim's arraignment. In the afternoon, she had said. That didn't leave Jack much time to find out where it was being held if he wanted to see her.

He called Becky's law firm. When he was put through to her secretary, Jack identified himself as Lim's probation officer and said he wanted to confirm the time and place of Lim's court appearance. Happy to oblige, the secretary checked Becky's calendar and told Jack it was scheduled for two o'clock in Courtroom 313, Department 134, of the Clara Shortridge Foltz Criminal Justice Center downtown.

Of all places, Jack thought. It was the same court-house where O.J. Simpson, Phil Spector and other high profile defendants had been tried, and where Jack had first met Becky. At the time, she was defending the CEO of a pharmaceutical company who Jack and Franco had busted using one of Gary's wiretaps. Before they even got to testify, Becky made a motion to suppress evidence. The judge granted it, her client walked free and Jack followed Becky down the street to the Water Grill where they sat at the bar for the next three hours arguing the merits of the case. Too many vodka martinis later, they were laughing and kissing and on their way to Laguna.

Another lifetime ago, Jack thought.

After Trouser led the way home with the leash in his mouth, Jack kissed him on the head and rubbed his favorite spot under his chin. Then he headed off alone again.

He made it to the courthouse in forty minutes.

As usual a line of people, mostly jurors returning from lunch, were waiting to go through the metal detectors. Jack checked a wall clock. No need to rush. With the court docket sure to be full, it was doubtful that Lim's case would have been called yet.

After clearing security Jack stepped on a crowded elevator and checked his breath. He tried to recall the last time he had seen Becky but couldn't. Either he was too drunk at the time or the memory was too painful and he had blocked it out. In the elevator's mirrored button panel Jack caught his distorted reflection and tried to imagine what Becky's reaction would be when she saw him. It elicited a wave of doubt. What was he doing, Jack thought. And why now? In the midst of something more urgent: trying to find his father who might be dying if not dead. Before he could change his mind the elevator doors opened on the fifteenth floor.

The moment Jack entered Courtroom 313, he saw her. She was at the county clerk's desk providing documents—tailored suit, hair in a loose bun, beautiful as ever—while the judge heard a motion for a bail reduction in a burglary case. Jack found a seat in the gallery and watched Becky traverse the well to join Lim who was waiting with other lowlife defendants and their lawyers. He was wearing the same jacket and tie Jack had bought him the first time Jack accompanied him to juvenile court. Lim was doing what he always did when he got nervous. He was rubbing his philtrum, the groove between the nose and upper lip. Unlike most people's, Lim's philtrum was flat and smooth, a telltale symptom of fetal alcohol syndrome.

The judge disposed of several more cases. Then he called Lim who approached the bench with Becky.

"I see a petition here, counselor, for the case to be reassigned to the public defender's office."

"That won't be necessary, Your Honor," Becky said. "After reviewing the police report and conferring with my client, I will be continuing as his attorney."

Jack frowned. Becky was a corporate litigator who billed out at five hundred dollars an hour. Why was she volunteering to take on a two-bit criminal defense matter?

"Very well," the judge said. "How do you plead?"

Lim straightened his jacket.

"N-not guilty, Your Honor."

"Preliminary hearing will be set for ten A.M. on the twentieth of this month. Bailiff, call the next case."

Becky gave Lim an encouraging look. On their way out of the courtroom they walked right past Jack but neither of them noticed him. Jack followed them out into the hall.

"Two people I never expected to see together," he said.

Lim turned first and did a doubletake.

"Jack? The h-hell...?"

Hearing his name made Becky spin around and freeze.

"What are you doing here?" she asked.

"Are you really taking him on as a client? I thought you said you already had too much on your plate."

Becky stared daggers.

"That's not an answer."

"I need to talk to you," Jack said.

"I thought I made myself clear."

Lim said, "R-rejection, Jack. Ain't it a bitch?"

Jack ignored Lim, his gaze still locked on Becky.

"Two years together," he said. "I think I deserve two minutes."

For a long moment Becky glowered back at him. Then she straightened up and gave Lim an apologetic look.

"This won't take long."

As Lim stayed behind, Becky followed Jack away for privacy. She stopped him halfway down the corridor.

"Okay," she said. "I'm listening."

"My father is missing."

"That's it? The thing you came here to tell me?"

"It's brought up a lot of stuff for me," Jack said. "Made me think about choices I've made. Mistakes, regrets."

"Because of your absentee dad?"

"No, you don't understand."

"The one who was always too busy being brilliant?"

"By missing I didn't mean—"

"I'm sorry, Jack. I thought I could do this but I can't."

Becky started away. Jack grabbed her arm.

"What happened to us?" he said. "You don't have what we had and then suddenly it's gone."

Becky looked Jack straight in the eye.

"No, you're right," she said. "Feelings like that don't just go away. It takes time to get over them."

"Maybe I haven't."

"But I have."

"I refuse to believe that."

"Jack, I'm engaged."

Her words jolted him. He fired a glance at her hand to see a ring there. Impossible to miss, yet somehow he had.

"That's right," Becky said. "I'm getting married."

"Who is he?"

"I'm happy. That's all that matters."

Jack tried to hide his hurt but Becky saw it and eased up.

"Did I love you?" she said. "Yes. More than you could ever know. Maybe that's why I'm here helping your friend, to show you that. But I'm a different person now. I've changed. The person you're looking for is gone."

Becky searched his eyes for a response. When Jack remained silent, she touched the back of her Modigliani neck.

"It was good seeing you, Jack. I'm glad we talked. I hope things work out for you, and with your dad. Believe me, I know how it feels, to realize you've lost someone even if that person was never there. Who knows, maybe someday you'll find him."

She walked away and returned to Lim who threw Jack an ambivalent glance as they left together. For several moments Jack stood there thinking about what Becky had said. Instead of feeling sorry for himself, Jack was strangely relieved. There was still a longing there but he cared too much about Becky not to be happy for her. Now that she had moved on with her life, maybe he could do the same.

Jack exited the courthouse and headed back to where he had parked his car. On the way he noticed a yellow Corvette with a custom-framed vanity plate:

LUV 4EVR

Perfect, Jack thought. The universe was telling him that everything was going to be okay. Kumbaya. Then, out of nowhere, an idea clicked in Jack's head. He shot another look at the Vette's license plate, then he reached into his pocket and pulled out the envelope, the one with his father's writing on it, and stared at the notation circled in red:

NO 2 OC

What if...

Jack whipped out his cell and called Franco. When his ex-partner answered, Jack could hear cop chatter in the background.

"Great minds," Franco said. "Was about to call you."

"Anything yet?"

"A name to go with the stiff. Turns out he's—"

"The owner of the pawn shop," Jack said. "Henry."

"Yeah, how'd ya know?"

"What else?"

"Well, seems an old leather satchel was found in a dumpster a couple blocks away. No identifying items inside, other than some lecture notes and a program for a philosophy conference."

Jack swallowed.

"Jesus," he said.

"There was also a trace of blood found," Franco said. "But only on the handle which suggests it was Henry's, transferred there by his killer when whoever it was fled and threw away the bag."

Jack hoped to hell Franco was right, that the blood wasn't his father's.

"How about the pawn shop?" Jack said. "Did it have a security camera?"

"For appearances only," Franco said. "Hadn't been used in years. But we found another one outside a comedy club across the street that might've caught something. Trigwell's over there now."

"Trigwell."

"Put it to rest, Jack."

"No, I meant...better to keep this on the down low."

"Of course," Franco said. "Oh, and one more item. I seem to be having memory problems. Yeah, strangest thing. Seems I grilled some professor named Sing or Song who called in a complaint about it, yet I can't remember talking to him for the life of me. Any suggestions?"

Jack suppressed a smile.

"I'm sure it won't happen again," he said.

"That a promise?"

"In exchange for one more favor."

"Here we go again."

"I need you to run a license plate," Jack said, reading from the envelope. "November-Oscar-Two-Oscar-Charlie. Check tags both here and in Massachusetts. And to cover all the bases—"

231

"FBI data bank. On it."

"Thanks, Franco."

"Don't worry, buddy. We'll find your old man."

Jack hung up feeling encouraged. For the first time since his father had vanished, he had something tangible to pursue. A playable hand.

39

SALAZAR

Behind the wheel of his parked car, Salazar let Manifest clear his mind. While the Caribbean rhythm played, he pulled down his sun visor. Attached to the back was a postcard of Playa El Agua, a beach of uncommon beauty on Isla Margarita off the coast of Venezuela. His beach, Salazar thought. Once he received confirmation from Alice that the client had paid, he would be on the first plane to Caracas.

With his characteristic patience, Salazar watched the clock on his dashboard change minute by minute. When the clock read two fifty-nine, he checked it against his atomic wristwatch, its satellite-calibrated signal accurate to the millisecond. At precisely three o'clock an alarm pulsed from the watch.

Salazar clicked it off. He looked at the throwaway cell phone on the passenger seat next to his Kimber .45. Its screen remained blank. There would be no confirmation text from Alice. The client had stiffed him.

It had happened once before in Phoenix, the reason he had relocated to L.A. Although the circumstances were different, Salazar had taken swift action to eliminate both the hostage and the client. In a business where the stakes were so high, zero tolerance reduced the risks as well as enhanced his reputation, allowing him to command higher prices.

None of that was of consequence to Salazar anymore. If he had it to do over again, he would never have taken this job, even for the obscene amount of money the client had offered. Now all he cared about was closing the books on his life here so he could begin his new one.

Salazar reached into his jacket and pulled out a second cell phone. He punched in a number that matched the untraceable cell he had given to Reaper. It rang and kept ringing. Salazar's eyes hardened. After the twentieth ring, he hung up and flung the phone on the seat with the throwaway and the gun.

He had warned Reaper.

He knew what he had to do.

Salazar opened his glove compartment and pulled out a photo. It was a grainy surveillance shot of a young woman playing with her toddler in a playground, taken without their knowledge: the pretty Latina and child from Reaper's tattoo. Salazar turned over the photo. Written on the back was a name and address:

CARMEN ORTIZ
599 SHIRLEY PLACE
BELL GARDENS

Salazar drove away. He ramped onto the 5 freeway and headed east, then transitioned onto the 710 south to Bell Gardens. At the Florence Street exit, he got off and cruised past Garfield, then hung a left on Shirley Place, a working class residential street lined with jacarandas. He checked addresses against the one on the photo and pulled up to a two-story stucco house with toys littering the front yard.

The driveway was empty but several windows were open. The faint drone of a vacuum cleaner could be heard from inside.

Salazar took a moment to look up and down the street. No one was around. He picked up his Kimber from the seat, the ultimate concealed carry weapon which he had chosen for its incredible accuracy and precision. More stopping power. Bigger hole in the thoracic cavity. With the gun still empty, Salazar dry-fired it three times—pull, rack pull, rack pull—another superstition he had picked up from his days with the Mexican Federal Police. Then he slid in a ten-round magazine and stuffed the gun under his shirt.

He checked the street again.

It was quiet, peaceful.

A study in calm, Salazar got out of the car like a family man coming home from a long day at the office and walked toward the house.

40

JACK

Jack returned to the loft to wait for Franco's call. Trouser was there to greet him with his usual slobbery face licks. He pawed the leash on the hook by the door.

"Not now," Jack said.

Trouser woofed.

"Sorry, kiddo," Jack said. "I can't."

Trouser drooled with a tongue-hanging smile.

"No fair," Jack said. "Don't give me that face."

Trouser squinted and flopped down on the floor. For a while he watched Jack pace back and forth, then he yawned and retired to the couch for a nap.

Jack's cell phone remained silent. As Jack squeezed the bridge of his crooked nose in frustration, his eyes fell on the manila envelope lying in the same spot it had been for the past three years. Something made Jack step over and pick it up. He brushed away the film of dust covering the envelope and felt the weight of its contents. It almost stopped him. Then he tore open the seal and pulled out an inch-thick report with an official cover sheet attached:

```
INTERNAL AFFAIRS
Case File #2475/531
Official Investigation into Use Of
   Deadly Force
Officer Involved: #4376LAPD, Det. Jack
   Pearl
```

Gingerly, Jack flipped through pages until he came to an interview transcript. One section jumped out at him:

```
PEARL: It started two months ago when we
stumbled on a smuggling ring, me and my
partner Franco.

IA: That would be Detective Francis
Russo.

PEARL: A big coke operation. Huge. All
we knew was the person behind it was
some ghost known as El Otro.
```

Jack flipped through more pages, remembering:

```
IA: How long were you and Russo undercover?

PEARL: Too long.

IA: Which began taking a personal toll.
```

PEARL: Being around nothing but drugs, violence, people who would kill you in a heartbeat if they ever suspected.

IA: You started drinking. Is that correct?

PEARL: It covered my cop smell.

IA: Despite repeated warnings from your partner. Which is why you told him the Feds were taking over the case, so you could keep working it alone.

PEARL: El Otro was always one step ahead, as if someone was feeding him information. Someone on the force, most likely. Franco had family, a beautiful wife and kids. I couldn't risk putting them in danger.

Before Jack could read any more, his phone rang. He checked the screen to see Franco's number and answered it.

"About time," Jack said. "What took you so long?"

"Had a mani-pedi appointment," Franco said. "Then I went to Nordstrom's. They were having their semi-annual white sale."

"Very funny, smartass."

"So you wanna hear about the tea towels I bought or are you gonna ask me about those plate numbers?"

Jack sat up.

"Please tell me you got a hit," he said.

"Not in Massachusetts. But I scored a match here in Cali. Make that two. One tag spelling with O's, the other with zeros."

"Registered to?"

"The first, a Fred Cox," Franco said. "Age 70, lives up in Oakland, 2010 Camry. The other vehicle is a '95 Impreza belonging to a Carmen Ortiz, age 23, address in Bell Gardens."

"Either one have a criminal record?"

"Not unless you count parking tickets and a couple moving violations. Correction: Cox once got cited for threatening a neighbor whose dog kept pooping on his lawn."

"Shit."

"Literally. Not what you were looking for, I take it?"

"If only I knew what I was looking for."

"Want me to dig deeper?"

"It'll probably go nowhere," Jack said. "But yeah. Whatever personal info you can get, especially on the Ortiz woman since she lives in the L.A. area."

"I'll put Kev on it," Franco said. "He's good at that stuff."

Jack clicked off.

Another disappointment.

Now what?

Besides Franco doing background checks on the two car owners, Jack could count on his ex-partner to follow up with the crime lab regarding his father's leather satchel. Also, a bit trickier, with Trigwell concerning the comedy store security camera. But it might take days before anything came up and even then it might not help.

Trigwell. Why did he keep going there, Jack wondered. Was it the same itch under his skin that made him believe Trigwell was the cop who had helped El Otro elude capture? Or had Jack, in the process of trying to find his father, somehow dislodged a clue from the past without knowing it, one that had been hiding in plain sight, the key to the case three years ago that might exonerate Jack and help him win back his life?

Jack shook it off. His thoughts returned to Claire. Maybe she had learned something from Wade. Worth a call, Jack decided. Once more, he picked up his cell and scrolled to the number Claire last phoned him from.

It was then that Jack remembered her invitation.

41

JACK

Jack pulled up to the Palomar. As he climbed out of his car, he noticed a muscular guy breezing out in Raybans and a baseball hat pulled low over his eyes. The man slipped into a Dodge pickup and drove off. Jack only saw him for a second but he looked a lot like Goatee, the security man at Esma's party. Obviously mistaken, Jack shrugged it off and headed into the hotel.

Across the lobby Jack spotted Claire sitting at the bar. She was circling the rim of a martini while talking on her iPhone, too engrossed in conversation to notice Jack walking up.

"—What about the eight o'clock? Not even in first class? I see. Well, thank you for checking. No, I better stick with the flight I'm on."

Claire clicked off and stared at the iPhone as if something fragile had died in her hand.

"Going somewhere?" Jack asked.

Claire swiveled in surprise.

"Oh hi," she said. "I...wasn't expecting you. What I mean is, I didn't think you'd come."

She put on a smile and brushed at her eyes as if to wipe away dust but Jack could see they were red from crying.

"So," Claire said. "How did it go? Your lead?"

"Not the way I hoped."

"Oh, I'm sorry."

"Me too," Jack said. "I thought it might be what I was looking for, but it turned out to be a mistake."

Something in Jack's words appeared to hit a nerve with Claire. She looked away.

"Claire, what is it?"

"You wouldn't understand."

"Try me."

Claire searched Jack's eyes to see his concern was genuine.

"I'm not safe here anymore," she said. "With my feelings, I mean. I need to go back to Yale."

"When is your flight?"

"Tonight. I'm catching a red-eye to New York."

Claire drained her martini.

"You must think I'm a freak," she said.

Jack shook his head.

"What's that saying? 'All are lunatics, but he who can analyze his delusions is called a philosopher.'"

Claire returned a sad smile.

"Sounds like something Joe would say," she said.

242

A bartender came over. Claire pointed to her empty glass.

"Another martini," she said. "And one for my friend here."

Jack held up his hand.

"No thanks," he said.

Claire winked at the bartender.

"Don't listen to him."

"Really," Jack said. "I can't."

It was too late. The bartender had already headed away to mix their drinks. Claire gave Jack a nudge.

"I said I would hold you to it, remember? And the next round is on you, for making me go meet Wade."

The next round? Jack was still trying to figure out how he was going to avoid the one she had ordered.

"Why?" Jack said. "What happened with Wade?"

"He took my showing up to mean I was looking for more than intellectual stimulation. But it turned out to be worth it. Wait until you hear what I found out."

"About the matter he discussed with my father?"

Claire nodded.

"It had to do with a review Joe had been asked to write by The Philosophical Quarterly, a highly respected journal which Wade helps edit. A review of Constantius's latest book."

"You mean his magnum opus? The one Constantius and my dad had words over in Chicago?"

Claire nodded.

"When I pressed Wade for details, he pushed back a bit, saying that Joe had spoken to him in confidence.

243

But I heard enough to realize it wasn't just any review. It was a nuclear bomb about to go off."

Jack frowned.

"How do you mean?"

"According to Wade, Joe had proof that the central thesis of Constantius's work had been heavily borrowed from a dissertation written by one of his students."

Jack frowned at Claire.

"Plagiarism?"

"It'll all come out when the review is published next month," Claire said. "But Wade said that Joe was also going to raise the issue at the debate tomorrow."

The wheels turned in Jack's mind.

"'You dug your own grave'. So that's what my father meant."

"And why you might want to take another look at Constantius," Claire said. "Hell hath no fury like a famous philosopher about to be ruined."

She was right, Jack thought. He made a mental note.

"Anything else?"

"Actually, yeah," Claire said. "Joe's absence at the conference came up. Wade said he'd heard that Joe had gone to some private place to rest up for the debate."

"Who told him that?"

"McGurk," Claire said.

"My father's colleague at Harvard?"

"The one you first wanted to check out. One more reason to. Kind of makes you wonder if there's anyone in the profession who doesn't have some hidden agenda."

At that moment, the bartender returned with their martinis. Jack looked at his with dread. Claire raised hers.

"What should we toast to?" she asked.

"I better not," Jack said.

"To the wonderful, brilliant, impossible man we both love," Claire said. "Even at our own expense. Here's hoping he's safe and sound, and that he turns up soon."

Claire waited for Jack to raise his glass. Maybe it was the toast or the timing or that he was tired of worrying about his old man but Jack felt himself surrender. One year of hard-fought sobriety out the window, just like that. With the guilty excitement only another addict could appreciate, he took his martini, clinked it against Claire's, then brought it to his lips and felt a soft, hot wave of euphoria spread to every pleasure receptor in his body. Claire seemed to savor hers with equal abandon. She closed her eyes and shuddered.

"The best feeling," she said. "Like sex without the guilt."

Jack took another sip. First panic came over him, then shame, then the sweet suppression of all his uncomfortable feelings that had been too much to bear.

"Speaking of brilliant," Claire said. "I still haven't told you the second theme of your father's philosophy."

"Let's not spoil the moment," Jack said.

"I know you're dying to hear it."

"Yeah, right."

"C'mon. Live dangerously."

She leaned close. Jack took another generous sip of his martini. There was no turning back.

"Okay," he said. "What the hell."

"Really?"

"Before I change my mind."

"Great! So let's see, where did we leave off?"

"Part One," Jack said. "Life is about change."

"Which allows us to grow."

"And Part Two?"

"The second idea overlaps the first," Claire said. "It's basically this: reality is unset Jell-O."

"Cute," Jack said.

"No, I'm serious," Claire said. "Most people go through their lives thinking that everything they observe has an independent character that they need to reckon with. Traits that are set in stone. But Joe would say that nothing could be further from the truth. He would argue that it's the act of being conscious of something that defines it and brings it into existence."

Jack licked a drop of vodka off his finger.

"Can you give me an example?"

"Well," Claire said, "Take quantum physics. When we dive down into the nature of matter, everything we know about the natural world dissolves. There are no objects anymore, there are only relationships. Not only that, it's impossible to describe or measure those relationships without the observer affecting them. So in a very real sense it's the marriage of the two, the ultimate inseparability between the observer and the observed, that creates the entire universe."

"In other words," Jack said, "Everything is relative."

"And intertwined."

"By seeing you, I see part of myself."

"It's more than that," Claire said. "It's that there is no *me* and no *you* without our coming into contact. And whatever we perceive is as real as anything can ever be in this world, as real as this martini glass, but is no more or less reliable than anyone else's perception."

Jack could relate. For most of his adult life he had felt justified in resenting his old man, based on his own personal observations which he considered to be profoundly reliable. But were they really? If one couldn't even be sure of the 'right' or 'wrong' of physical laws, how much stock could be put in the correctness of feelings and instincts?

"So," Jack said. "Is there a moral insight to all this?"

"Modesty, good humor," Claire said. "We should all practice our powers of observation more."

"And spend less time trying to get others to see the world through our eyes."

"Exactly," Claire said. "Which brings us to the final concept."

"Part Three?"

"The *coup de grace*."

"Which is?"

"I could tell you but..."

"You'd have to kill me?"

"It's all there in your father's book," Claire said. "The one on the back seat of your car. If I told you, it wouldn't mean as much as if you found out for yourself."

Jack wasn't sure how to respond. There was no denying that Claire had aroused his interest, both in his father's philosophy and in her flirtation while explaining it. But the alcohol was making it hard to understand what she was saying.

They raised their martinis and drained them. Jack signaled the bartender for another round. Over the next half hour they each had two more, enough to wash away any guilt Jack still felt about falling off the wagon. They talked about everything except what they were both thinking about and how wrong it would be to act on it, which made it all the more tempting. Finally Claire brushed a wisp of hair behind her ear and stole a tipsy glance at Jack.

"I don't know if it would help," she said, "But I have a copy of Constantius's book in my room. Want to come up and get it?"

It was awkward and obvious and teenage-sweet, especially coming from a brainy Yale grad student.

"Okay," Jack said.

"I mean, only if you..."

"No," he said, "Sure. That would be great."

They paid the bill. It wasn't until Jack rose from his stool that he realized how hammered he was. So was Claire. Somehow they made it across the lobby and rode the elevator in silence.

They exited on the sixth floor. Claire led Jack down the hall to her door. She opened her purse and fumbled out her key card but had trouble getting it in the slot. Jack steadied her hand and the door clicked open.

They entered. As the door closed behind them, Claire lost her balance with a laugh. Jack caught her. She was trembling. Her skin was burning hot. She kissed Jack hungrily, desperately, and they slammed together hard and tight. Jack turned Claire around, holding her close, and buried his face in the back of her neck, letting her scent wash over him. Claire arched her back, moaning.

"Yes, yes..."

Urgently she pulled Jack to the floor and guided his hand under her skirt to show him how wet she was. Jack tore off her panties. Like prisoners starved of human intimacy, they ravaged each other. Jack closed his eyes and suddenly he was somewhere else, in that second-floor apartment in Santa Monica, with Becky, not just having sex but making love the way they used to, the way Jack imagined they might again until everything changed at the courthouse. Then all too soon Becky cried out in passion but it wasn't her voice and Jack opened his eyes to see Claire in tears as she came.

It was more than Jack's martini-fueled mind could handle. As he rolled off Claire, she curled up in a fetal position next to him and murmured something.

"What?" Jack asked.

"I love you," she said.

She took his hand and pressed it to her lips. A wave of remorse hit Jack, the full impact of what he had done. Untangling himself, he lurched to the bathroom where he shut the door and threw up in the sink. He splashed water on his face and looked at himself in the mirror before turning away in disgust.

When Jack came back out Claire was standing there anxiously, trying not to look as inebriated as she was.

"Are you alright?"

"Yeah," Jack said. "Had a little too much, I guess."

"Vodka? Or me?"

"Don't be silly."

As Jack gave her an evasive hug, Claire melted into him.

"My flight doesn't leave until ten forty-five," she said. "That means we still have plenty of time together."

"I should go," Jack said.

Claire shrunk back.

"No, Jack."

"Yeah, I think it's probably best."

"Please stay."

"Don't worry," Jack said. "We'll see each other again."

Claire could tell it wasn't the truth. Her face turned a violent shade of red.

"Why? I'm not smart enough, is that it? I can be smarter. Or pretty enough? I can be beautiful for you."

"Claire..."

"I'll be anything you want," she said. "Give me a chance."

Her tone was shrill.

"Claire, take it easy."

She tugged at the silver locket on her throat.

"Please," she said. "Don't make me do something horrible again."

Jack froze.

"What are you talking about?"

"I'm sorry, I'm sorry, I'm sorry..."

"Claire, for God's sake."

Jack reached out to steady her but Claire jerked away.

"Don't touch me!" she said.

"What's wrong?"

"Get out! Get out!"

Claire looked crazed, inconsolable. Before Jack could reason with her, she pushed him out the door and slammed it in his face.

42

JACK

t had been a year since Jack had talked to his sponsor. Jack called him. Where to start? His father, Claire—there was so much to say but words seemed inadequate. Nor did they bring any relief. After a few failed attempts to describe the hole in his heart, Jack cut the conversation short, then found a coffee place a few blocks over and drowned himself in espresso.

While the caffeine did its job Jack composed a fantasy inscription in his head:

To Dad. Thanks for the memories. Jack.

Hell, why hold back?

Dear Dad. Screw you.

Too much id, Jack decided.

What did he really want to say?

For Dad. Without whose unwanted phone call and vanishing act I never would have shed what last few crumbs of self-control and decency I had left. Thank you for robbing me of the comfort of blaming you for the past. And thanks for the irony: that now I know about the importance of change and unset Jell-O and even about your affection for the brothers of the Sahel (whoever the hell they are) yet I still have no idea why you left me that goddamned inscription. Your loving son, Jack.

Not bad, Jack thought. Now all he had to do was write a book and come up with some deep, clever title.

His head was throbbing. It felt like the percussion section of a madhouse orchestra was in there drumming and clanging full blast. Trying to focus felt like squeezing cold honey through an eye dropper. But he had to, Jack told himself. One unsolved mystery, the one that had resulted in that kid losing his life three years ago, was enough for Jack. He needed to know what had happened to his father.

Jack ordered another coffee for the road and walked back to UCLA where he found one of those pale green programs posted on a bulletin board. It showed that Constantius had given a talk earlier in the afternoon, his last of the conference. The only other event the Berkeley philosopher was scheduled for was his debate with Joseph Pearl on Saturday. That was tomorrow. McGurk, however, was listed for a panel discussion at six o'clock in the main lecture hall of the Humanities Building. Jack checked his watch. He had forty-five minutes to get over there.

Directions from a passing student led Jack across campus. It was still warm outside, a perfect late summer afternoon, but halfway to the venue Jack felt a tingly coolness on the back of his neck. It was the same sensation that had been triggered by that shadowy figure at the Getty and later by the sedan with the missing headlight. Jack glanced around. A few students were coming and going, others were playing Frisbee across the lawn. None of them seemed to be interested in him. Then Jack looked at a nearby building and caught a glimpse of a man standing at a third floor window, shrouded behind the reflection of the glass. The man appeared to be staring down at Jack. At first Jack thought it might be Trigwell, as insane as that was. Then he realized the man was about the same height and build as Singh. Jack stepped toward the building to get a better view but when he looked again the man had vanished.

Dark thoughts filled Jack's head. Why would Singh be following him? How was that even possible? Or could it have been Constantius? The more Jack thought about it, the pumped-up posture of the man in the window matched that of his father's archrival. There was a third possibility: it was neither of the philosophers but rather some innocent nobody who merely stepped to the window for the view. Jack wasn't sure which was worse: that there might be some dangerous aspect to his father's disappearance that he wasn't aware of yet, or that the part of his mind still thinking like a cop was playing tricks on him. The implications of both weighed heavily on Jack as he walked the rest of the way to the Humanities Building.

A gaggle of philosophiles were mingling out front. Among them, Jack spotted a portly gentleman who matched Claire's description of McGurk. He was feasting on a cupcake while conversing with students. Jack headed over.

"Excuse me, Professor McGurk? I need to talk to you."

McGurk raised a finger for Jack to wait until he finished some point he was making. Jack wasn't in a waiting mood.

"It's about my father," he said. "Joseph Pearl."

Hearing the name made McGurk stop in mid-bite. He quickly excused himself from the students and ushered Jack aside.

"So you're Joseph's son?" McGurk said. "Ah yes, I can see the resemblance. Are you in philosophy too?"

"God, no," Jack said.

"A wise decision. Big shoes to fill. Your father is a *beast*. When it comes to his output, that is."

McGurk was being too polite, Jack observed. If they were sitting at a poker table, Jack would have read it as an effort to conceal a weak hand.

"I'm glad you found me," McGurk said. "I've been wondering where the devil Joseph ran off to. May I assume that's what this is about?"

"Correct," Jack said. "So where is he?"

"Pardon?"

"According to another philosopher attending the conference, you claimed my father was laying low somewhere to rest up before his debate tomorrow."

McGurk looked flustered.

"I said that? I don't remember. But if I did, it was to cover for Joseph as a fellow faculty member. It wouldn't look right for such an important guest to miss so many conference events."

"When was the last time you saw him?" Jack said.

"Two days ago," McGurk said. "After his opening lecture."

"But you were concerned about him. Or should I say, about why he was avoiding you."

"What do you mean?"

"The message you left for him at his hotel: 'What happened to forgive and forget?' Does that ring a bell?"

McGurk's jowls sagged.

"How could you know about that? Unless your father mentioned it to you. How embarrassing. I assume he also told you about my transgression."

Jack had no idea what he meant but it sounded important.

"As a matter of fact, he did," Jack said. "In confidence, of course. But why don't you tell me again in your own words."

McGurk considered the half-eaten cupcake in his hand. He flicked it to some pigeons nearby.

"I don't know why I did it," McGurk said. "I'm still working that out with my therapist. All I can tell you is the door to Joseph's office was open and I saw it lying there and something possessed me to take it."

Jack frowned.

"By 'it', you're referring to...?"

"The sword," McGurk said.

"The, uh, *sword,*" Jack said. "Right, of course."

"The ceremonial saber that was presented to Joseph when he received an honorary doctorate last year from Cambridge University. We all have our sins. It seems mine is envy. After all, Cambridge is the birthplace of analytic philosophy, where the greatest philosophers who ever lived worked and studied. Everyone from Erasmus and Bacon to Russell and Wittgenstein."

A philosopher with a sword. You couldn't make that up, Jack mused. The only thing nuttier was the idea of another philosopher stealing it.

"And my father, as you said, found out about this."

"You can imagine how ashamed I was," McGurk said. "I expected him to be furious but he wasn't. That was worse somehow. In his usual gracious way, Joseph allowed me to return the sword without involving the authorities or the university. Still, he grew distant. I needed to talk to him about it."

Jack pressed him.

"And did you?"

"Yes," McGurk said. "While I drove him to an appointment he had made, at some odd little place in Hollywood."

Jack stared.

"Not a pawn shop?"

"Yes," McGurk said. "So he told you about that too?"

"Wait. You said you last saw him after his lecture."

"Driving him *was* after the lecture."

"Why didn't you mention that before?"

"You didn't ask," McGurk said. "Why all these questions? Is Joseph alright?"

"He's missing," Jack said.

"What do you mean missing?"

"Gone, unaccounted for."

McGurk looked aghast.

"I knew it," he said. "I told him to be careful."

"What do you mean?" Jack asked.

"While we were driving to the shop, Joseph mentioned seeing someone in a car in front of the lecture hall. It was the same person he had noticed parked outside his hotel the day before. He joked about it, that maybe a rival philosopher named Constantius was keeping an eye on him in anticipation of their upcoming debate. But apparently it troubled him enough to jot down the car's license plate."

Jack caught his breath.

"He told you he wrote down the number?"

"After it happened the first time."

"Did he write it on an envelope?"

"I have no idea," McGurk said.

"The person in the car," Jack said, "Did my father give you a description?"

"No, I'm sorry."

"What about the vehicle?"

"I seem to remember Joseph saying something about it being impressive or an 'impresser'. That's all I can recall."

Jack flashed on Franco telling him about the two license plates that matched the notation on his dad's envelope. One belonged to a Camry, the other to a Subaru Impreza.

"Back to the pawn shop," Jack said. "Did you go inside with my father?"

"I didn't want to impose."

"But you waited for him?"

"I offered but Joseph insisted on taking a cab back. That was the last time I saw him."

"And everything else you've told me is true?" Jack said.

"As God is my witness," McGurk said. "May I be struck dead by lightning and live in eternal damnation."

McGurk made the sign of the cross and kissed his fingers. It wouldn't have satisfied Joseph Pearl, being a card-carrying atheist, but it was good enough for Jack. Before McGurk could ask any more questions, Jack scribbled down his cell phone number and shoved it into the philosopher's meaty hand.

"In case you hear anything else," Jack said.

"Yes, of course. But—"

McGurk was talking to air. Jack had already hurried away.

43

JOSEPH PEARL

nch by painful inch, Pearl continued to drag himself down the lightless tunnel. For how long? He couldn't tell. All sense of space and time had disappeared. Now, nothing existed but the primal imperative to keep moving, to resist the urge to succumb to exhaustion. To stop. To die.

As a way to keep himself going, Pearl counted each time he pulled himself forward. When his mind became restless he switched to thinking of a philosopher for each letter of the alphabet—first by periods, then philosophical fields, then traditions and theories—until there was nothing else to think, nothing left to distract him from the unbearable physical and mental strain of hanging onto life, literally by his fingernails.

And then it happened. He thought of Ann. He remembered the Greek pillow prayer she would recite softly and lovingly each night when Jack was young, to soothe him and to help him fall asleep. It was the same prayer Pearl would sometimes hear Ann whisper to herself, both in Greek and English, toward the end when her life had begun to unravel:

Lord Christ, Son of God, have mercy on me, a sinner.

Why, Pearl wondered. Why in the name of logic and reason had his thoughts gone there? The more he tried to push the idea away, the more it lingered.

He dragged himself on through the sewer water. He could feel himself waning. With a rasp, the words escaped his desiccated lips.

"Lord Christ..."

Absurd.

"...Son of God..."

Hypocrisy.

"...Have mercy on me..."

An affront to everything he stood for.

"...A sinner..."

To his shock, Pearl felt something, a tiny surge of energy. It was enough to get him through one more attempt to pull himself forward, and to fill his mind with more questions. Could it be that he was having a religious experience? Or was he merely using his aversion to religion to taunt himself into not giving up?

Too weak to be sure, Pearl relented.

"Lord Christ...of God...mercy on me...sinner..."

Another surge. Another crawl. Pearl pushed on in the oppressive darkness.

44

JACK

The second Jack left McGurk, he called Franco about what he had learned. Franco passed the phone to Kevin, who had done some checking on Carmen Ortiz, the owner of the Subaru Impreza.

"She's squeaky clean, by all appearances," Kevin said. "Kindergarten teacher, got laid off last year. Just a single mom with a two-year-old, trying to make ends meet."

"What about the car's title and insurance," Jack said. "Anyone else listed on them?"

"Nope. Same with her house. But hey, check this out. According to the kid's birth certificate, the father is a gangbanger named Raoul Lugo. Known on the street as Reaper. Rap sheet a mile long."

Jack perked up.

"What kind of offenses?"

"Drugs, burglary, extortion," Kevin said. "Anything where money's to be made."

"Nice work, Kev. Thanks."

"Happy to help."

Franco got back on the phone.

"My hunch, Jack? This Lugo guy used his baby mama's wheels to tail your old man, figuring the car wouldn't be traced back to him."

"But why target my dad? Why kidnap a philosopher?"

"Guess that's the million dollar question."

"This Reaper," Jack said. "I need to find him."

"Easier said than done."

"It might help to contact the Ortiz woman."

"Already tried her home number," Franco said. "No answer. But I've alerted the Gang Unit to give it highest priority. They're shaking the bushes as we speak."

"Great," Jack said. "Wonderful."

"I told you, Jack, don't worry."

"Who's worried? I'm not worried."

"And in that world where rhinoceroses fly, they speak what language?"

Jack hung up. Were he still a detective, he would be out there shaking the bushes himself until he smoked out this grim Reaper, whatever his sick story, and made him confess what he had done to his father. But Jack wasn't a cop anymore, which meant through no one's fault but his own he was forced to sit on the sidelines and hope Franco came through.

Jack returned to his car. Before driving away, he looked at the passenger seat. Lying there was the manila envelope, the one containing the I.A. report, which he had brought with him from the loft. Why? Jack wasn't exactly sure. Could it be to remind himself to be careful in searching for his father? Or was there something in the pages, something Jack had overlooked, that might finally explain the unsolved mystery of three years ago?

For the second time that day, Jack withdrew the report from the envelope and flipped through the interview transcript. As he read, his throat tightened, reliving the memory:

```
PEARL: It took some digging but I finally
got a lead. Another location where El
Otro might be hiding. Only this time I
didn't tell anyone.
```

Jack skipped ahead several pages and stopped again:

```
PEARL: The house was gated with a fenced
perimeter but there was no one patrolling
the grounds. I cut the wires to the alarm
system, then broke in through a back
window.

IA: When did you know something was
wrong?

PEARL: Not until I got to the kitchen.
That was where I found the first body.

IA: Shot?

PEARL: Execution style. There were three
more in the living room. Two Hispanic
males, their machine guns nearby, and
```

a black guy with his Sig P-226 still holstered.

IA: Special Agent Simms.

PEARL: I had no way of knowing he was DEA. Or that there was another undercover operation going on. He was lying by an open wall safe that had been cleaned out. Only things left inside were some papers and an empty box for a Patek Philippe.

IA: Pardon?

PEARL: One of those high-end wrist-watches, the kind that cost as much as a car.

IA: What was going through your mind?

PEARL: That I had been set up. And that I was seriously screwed. That's when I heard a sound from the second floor.

IA: Why didn't you call for backup?

PEARL: I told you, I couldn't involve Franco. And there was no one else I could trust.

IA: Or get the hell out of there?

PEARL: Yeah, I should have. If only I had.

IA: So you made your way up the stairs.

PEARL: In the dark. Room to room. Gun up, hands shaking. I won't lie, I was scared out of my mind. Then I saw something glint through a doorway. I didn't think. I fired. Everything I had. It wasn't until my clip was empty that I saw him.

IA: The kid.

PEARL: He was slumped over the body of a woman who had been executed like the others. Holding her hand.

IA: His mother, it turns out.

PEARL: No words. There are no words for how I felt.

IA: So you ran?

PEARL: And ran. To the first bar I found open.

IA: Was that before or after you hid the money?

PEARL: Hey, fuck you too.

IA: Before he died, Agent Simms sent a message to one of our men assigned to the DEA case. A detective Trigwell. According to Trigwell, Simms reported the safe contained ten million dollars in unmarked bills.

PEARL: The watch box. There was nothing else.

IA: So what happened to the money?

PEARL: How the hell should I know? Ask Trigwell.

Jack slammed the report shut and threw it back on the seat. What had he missed? Simms, Trigwell, the watch box, the papers. He had been over it all a thousand times in his mind. Nothing had changed. It was still as opaque as ever, a riddle wrapped in a mystery inside an enigma.

As Jack pulled out his car keys to leave, something else fell out of his pocket: the key card from the W Hotel. Maybe he should check his father's room again, Jack thought. At least it would keep his mind occupied until Franco called back.

45

JACK

t was exactly ten past six when Jack arrived at the W. Once more he retraced his steps to Room 811 and let himself in with the key card.

Nothing had changed.

The white shirt was still draped over the chair. The beds were still made. In the bathroom, the straight razor and shaving brush remained untouched. It all had that staged look of a museum diorama replicating a place where someone famous had lived, or died.

Third time lucky, Jack hoped. He dug into every pocket. He flipped through every book. He even took the lid off the toilet to check inside. Not until he was confident that nothing could have escaped his notice did he turn his attention to the phone.

The red light was blinking again. Jack punched up voicemail and listened to seven new messages. Four were from unknown people attending the conference.

Two were from housekeeping. One was an automated reminder that check-out was noon tomorrow. There were no red flags. Jack recalled the message Claire left, the one his father had saved, and accessed the inbox to hear it again. To his surprise, there was now a second message saved there as well. It was that odd hang-up Jack had recorded to his old cell phone, the one he thought he had lost. Unconsciously, it seemed, Jack had pressed the save key on the hotel phone to make sure it would be preserved.

Jack sat on the bed and listened to it again, those electronic tones followed by the exhale and the click of the line going dead. He played it once more to concentrate exclusively on the tones. There were five of them, the first five digits of a phone number. By playing the message over and over and comparing each tone to those on his cell phone, Jack was able to figure out what the five numbers were.

The first was a 1, standard phone prefix. The next three were 6, 5 and 7, an area code. The last was a 2, the first digit of a local number.

Jack recognized 657 as Esma's area code. The number he had for her also began with a two. A fluke? Unlikely. Whoever had called Joseph Pearl without leaving a message had then called Esma. Why? It raised questions about Esma's distant vibe when Jack had last spoken to her, and why she hadn't mentioned being in touch with someone who also knew Jack's father when Jack grilled her about Henry. There might be a good reason that had nothing to do with finding his old man, Jack conceded, but his inner voice told him there was something there, something important enough to warrant a return trip to Anaheim Hills to question Esma in person.

In no time, Jack was back behind the wheel speeding toward Orange County. He considered calling ahead to make sure Esma was home. But if she had secrets to hide, Jack didn't want to give her the chance to make up an excuse not to meet with him. In poker, hitting an opponent with an unexpected raise was often the best way to learn what cards that player was holding, especially in a clutch situation. Jack decided to trust his gambling sense and take his chances.

The traffic was light, allowing Jack to arrive at Glastonbury Oval in record time. He parked in the cul-de-sac and took the path to the house where he pressed the bell. It chimed. After a moment, the door was opened by a young guy in a striped shirt and paisley tie talking on his Bluetooth.

"—The fifth of next month. Perfect! And please tell the Ambassador that Ms. Kaya deeply appreciates his support for the event."

Jack recognized the laid-back tone of Esma's assistant. The guy clicked off his earpiece with the swagger of a Hollywood agent who had just closed a three-picture deal.

"Another one of her charities," the assistant said. "God knows how she does it all. Wait here, I'll go get Aldo."

"Pardon?"

"Aren't you the dog walker? From Majestic Mutt?"

"I'm Jack Pearl. We talked the other day."

"Pearl? Oh, right. The son, not the father."

"I came to see Esma. Is she here?"

"Yes," the assistant said. "However, I'm afraid—"

"Tell her it's urgent. It can't wait."

"I'm sorry, she's unavailable."

"Never mind," Jack said. "I'll tell her myself."

Jack shoved past him and headed inside.

"Hey, wait," the assistant said. "You can't just—"

As Jack marched across the foyer, he spotted Esma in the palatial living room, every bit as striking and colorful as the first time he had seen her. Esma looked up from signing papers being handed to her by a well-dressed businessman.

"Jack? What are you doing here?"

The assistant rushed up behind.

"I tried to stop him but—"

"No, it's fine," Esma said. "Thank you, Bryce."

The assistant retreated.

"Sorry to barge in like this," Jack said.

"No need to apologize. We were just finishing up here."

Esma handed the signed documents back to the businessman who slipped them into his briefcase.

"I hope this takes care of it," Esma said to the man. "But should there be any more problems—"

"I'll call you immediately, of course."

As the man walked out, Esma shrugged to Jack.

"That difficult family matter I mentioned when we last spoke. Though, needless to say, not as serious as yours."

"Have you seen the news?" Jack said.

"About the stabbing at the pawn shop. Was it Henry?"

Jack nodded. Esma shook her head gravely.

"That poor, dear man. I pray he recovers quickly."

"I'm afraid it's too late for that," Jack said. "He died shortly after being taken to the hospital."

Esma touched her hand to her throat.

"My God," she said. "Who would do such a thing?"

"The police are on it."

"And how is Joseph involved? You said he was missing. Have you found him?"

Jack shook his head.

"It appears he was taken from the shop and that Henry either got in the way or was killed to prevent him from talking."

"What do you mean taken? Where? By whom?"

"I don't know yet," Jack said. "That's why I'm here, to ask for your help."

Esma looked a bit overwhelmed.

"Of course, Jack. Anything."

"I was hoping you could tell me about a phone call. Someone rang you early Wednesday morning, at seven forty-six to be exact. Who was it?"

"On Wednesday? Let me think."

"Whoever it was called my father right before. So it had to be a mutual acquaintance of yours, other than

Henry. I'm pretty sure he'd already been stabbed by then."

Esma shook her head.

"On Wednesday morning I was on my way to a breakfast meeting. I didn't receive any calls at that hour."

"Are you sure?" Jack said.

"Yes, quite."

"What about on your landline? Or another cell? Do you have any other phone numbers that start with a two?"

"None that I use myself."

"How's that?" Jack said.

"Well, Bryce's personal cell phone begins with a two, as does that of another of my employees. But no one trying to reach me would use those numbers."

"And there's no chance the call went straight to voicemail? Or that you had your calls forwarded to your assistant that morning?"

Again Esma shook her head.

"May I ask why it's so important?"

"I don't know yet," Jack said.

"What was the call concerning?"

"I don't know that either."

Jack was discouraged and drained and ready to give up. As he scanned the room in defeat, his eyes fell on the framed photographs on the Steinway grand piano, the ones he had disturbed with his wine glass at the party. One photo in front was a candid shot of Esma embracing an attractive young woman. It took

Jack a second to make sense of it and another second for the implication to sink in, but when it did Jack was thunderstruck.

Esma saw him transfixed by the photo and smiled.

"That's my daughter," she said. "Lovely, isn't she?"

"Your daughter..."

"It was taken last year, on her twenty-fifth birthday. As you can see, I'm very proud of her."

"Your daughter is...Claire Evans?"

Esma smiled and frowned with surprise.

"Why, yes," she said. "How do you know Claire?"

"But your last name is Kaya," Jack said.

"Kaya is my maiden name. I kept it when I married Claire's father. His surname was Evans."

Somehow that had escaped Jack's notice when he had researched Esma. He also had failed to pick up on the family resemblance between Esma and Claire, the similar cadence in their voices. It made Jack wonder what else he had missed.

"Oh, but of course," Esma said. "Joseph must have mentioned Claire. Did he also tell you he was the one who first sparked her interest in philosophy? In fact, I remember exactly when it happened. It was right after Claire's father passed away. She was heartbroken, we both were, and so I took her with me to a conference in Turkey. And Joseph was there, charming and brilliant as ever. After hearing him lecture, all Claire would read was philosophy. And now, wouldn't you know, she's at Yale working on her doctorate."

Jack's head was swimming. He struggled to connect the dots.

"So then it must have been Claire who made that phone call," he said. "Was it about her affair with my father? Was that the family problem you were referring to?"

All the color drained from Esma's face.

"What on earth are you talking about?"

"Wait," Jack said. "You don't know?"

"How dare you imply..."

"Then it must have been something else," Jack said. "Something important enough for Claire to be calling so early in the morning."

Esma struggled to contain her composure.

"I think it's time for you to leave."

Jack stood his ground.

"That man who was here. Who is he?"

"That's none of your business."

"What were those papers you were signing?"

"It has nothing to do with—"

"Either you tell me," Jack said. "Or the police."

Esma placed one hand on the piano to steady herself. The skin around her jaw tightened as she clenched her teeth. Then she bowed her head in submission.

"Claire...took some money."

"What do you mean?"

"From a trust account her father had set up for her," Esma said. "An annuity intended to provide a comfortable income and pay her school expenses. Several days ago, I'm told, Claire forged my signature and with-drew a large amount of the principal."

"How much?"

Esma shook her head.

"How much, Esma? Tell me."

"Five hundred thousand dollars."

Jack's eyes widened.

"Yes," Esma said. "That was my reaction too. It was so unlike Claire. I can't fathom why she would do such a thing. Then yesterday she attempted to withdraw the same amount again. Fortunately our banker, the man who just left, had already placed a freeze on the account."

"What did Claire say when you asked her about it?"

"I've been unable to reach her. She hasn't returned my messages. I've even called her friends at Yale, but no one seems to know where she is."

A million bucks. There was only one reason Jack could think of for someone to need that much cash in a hurry: to make a secret payment. If someone knew how much Joseph Pearl meant to Claire, and how rich she was, it would make the philosopher a prime target for a kidnapper like Reaper, and Claire the perfect ATM machine. But while it explained some things, Jack real-ized, it didn't square with others. Could Claire really have been trying to pull together a ransom without Jack having a clue? And how did a bottom feeder like Reaper come to know about Claire Evans and Joseph Pearl in the first place, not to mention acquire the inside knowledge necessary to execute his plan?

That's when it clicked.

Goatee.

Jack remembered the guy he had seen exiting the Palomar, the one who looked like the security man at Esma's party. It must really have been him, Jack realized, which meant he had to be in on the scam. Logic suggested he went to the hotel to talk to Claire about the ransom, maybe to warn her what would happen if she failed to come up with the second payment. That would explain why Jack had found Claire at the bar looking so upset. It also clarified her comment about not being safe and her sudden plans to leave town. It might even have been the reason she tried to kill herself.

And it provided a plausible explanation for that mystery voicemail with the electronic tones. After pouring her heart out in the phone message that led Jack to her, Claire rang back the next day to leave a second message for Joseph Pearl but changed her mind and hung up without saying a word. Then she started to make another call. It wasn't until she had punched in five digits that she realized the line was still live, the hotel voicemail still recording. Thus, the sharp inhale and the abrupt hang up: Claire killing the call before she said anything on tape she might regret.

And if she wasn't calling her mother, Esma—that number that started with 2 in the 657 area code—who had Claire been trying to reach at such an early hour?

Smart money was on Goatee, Jack felt sure. Something to do with the shakedown. Perhaps an appeal for more time to raise the additional cash.

It all fit.

Could Jack see Goatee and Reaper knowing each other? Without a doubt. And Goatee worked for Esma which gave him only one degree of separation from Claire. If this was about extorting money from her, Goatee had to be the missing link.

Jack returned his attention to Esma who had picked up the photo of Claire and was gazing at it tearfully.

"You mentioned another employee," Jack said. "The one with a phone number starting with two. Would that be your security man, the one with the short beard?"

Esma looked surprised but nodded.

"His name is Vincent," she said. "Vincent DeFreeze."

"How much do you know about him?"

"He was hired a year ago through an agency. Impeccable references. In the time he's worked here, he's been very reliable. That is, until he failed to show up for work yesterday. And today as well."

"Have you tried calling him?"

"Bryce did. But his number has been disconnected."

"What about his home phone, e-mail?"

"The ones we have for him don't seem to be working," Esma said. "Why? What does it mean, Jack? And what does it have to do with Claire?"

So he was right, Jack thought. There was no longer any doubt. His father had been taken. At last, after three days of going nowhere, Jack had an answer. He also had a new number to focus on: 67, the percentage of adult kidnap victims released unharmed. It gave Jack something to hang onto, something he had almost run out of. Hope.

"Jack."

Esma was still holding the photo in both hands, so tightly her fingers were white.

"Tell me everything," she said. "Tell me the truth."

"My father's been kidnapped. DeFreeze is involved. The money Claire took from her trust was to pay the ransom."

"Dear God in heaven..."

"I'll need everything you have on DeFreeze," Jack said. "Including those references you mentioned. It's probably all fabricated but at least it'll give me somewhere to start."

Esma drew in a shallow breath.

"First tell me about the affair," she said.

"There isn't time."

"Tell me about Joseph and Claire. I have to know."

"Look," Jack said. "My father is in serious danger. So is your daughter. Do you want to help them or not?"

"Of course, but..."

"Then please do as I ask," Jack said. "And do it *now*."

Esma heard him this time. There was no hesitation. In a blur of color she tore from the room.

46

SALAZAR

alazar took a seat on an empty bench in a quiet corner of MacArthur Park. It was a few minutes after seven and still bright outside. As children played nearby, Salazar checked his fingernails to make sure he had washed off all traces of blood. He knew Reaper would be horror-stricken when he learned about Carmen and little Raoul, even more so when the police arrested Reaper for the murders, based on the evidence that Salazar had planted at the house in Bell Gardens. And then Reaper would squeal. Oh, how he would squeal. With nothing left to live for, he would spill his guts to the cops about Salazar, everything he knew, every detail he could remember. But none of it would matter because Salazar did not exist. Salazar was merely a name that would be shed like so many others, nothing but smoke and mirrors. And by then Salazar, or Antonio Guzman Vargas as he had decided to call himself on Isla Margarita, would be long gone.

The children continued to play. Salazar watched them wistfully, remembering Ignacio, until the person he was waiting for arrived and joined him on the bench. It was DeFreeze. The big man removed his Raybans and stared at them.

"I let you down," DeFreeze said.

Salazar shook his head.

"You were the grease, not the engine."

"If I had known she wouldn't come through..."

"Her problem," Salazar said. "Not yours."

Salazar tossed a small brass key to DeFreeze.

"K-Town Boxing on Western. You train there, I believe."

"Yeah," DeFreeze said. "How'd you know?"

"In Locker 216, you will find a gym bag containing the amount we agreed on, plus a bonus. Hopefully enough to keep your mouth shut so I won't have to."

DeFreeze glanced uneasily at Salazar.

"Our years in the joint. I'm familiar with your work."

"Then we understand each other."

The two exchanged a handshake. As they parted ways, Salazar noticed the moon rising in the east, even as the sun was still shining low on the opposite horizon. The moon was full. According to police superstition, Salazar knew, it was the time each month when the tin foil hat brigade, the crazies of the world, came out to cause unexpected trouble. Salazar hoped it wouldn't interfere with his plans as he strode across the park on the way to his next destination. With Reaper and DeFreeze now behind him, there was only one more loose end to tie up.

47

JACK

Timing was everything. Two hours ago, Jack couldn't get away from Claire fast enough. Now he was desperate to talk to her. If Claire had failed to make a second ransom payment as Esma's account suggested, the situation could turn ugly fast, putting Joseph Pearl in increased jeopardy. Claire was Jack's best hope of finding his father in time. Maybe his only hope.

While Jack waited for Esma to return with employee records on DeFreeze, he called Claire's number. It rang through to voicemail. Jack hung up and phoned the Palomar to be connected to Claire's room but there was no answer there either. With a groan Jack realized why. After the way he had left things with Claire, she would want nothing to do with him. Rather than call her cell where she could see his number on her screen, Jack should have tried her hotel room first and might have gotten her. Now Claire would know it was Jack calling and, even if he phoned back on a different line, the chances were zero to none that she would pick up.

At least Jack knew that Claire hadn't checked out yet since the hotel operator had put him through. Once more he called Claire's room. When the voicemail beeped to leave a message, Jack spoke from the heart:

"Claire, it's me. Please don't hang up. Look, I know I'm the last person you want to talk to right now, and for good reason, but this is urgent. I know about DeFreeze and the ransom. We can still get him back... Joe, my father...but not without your help. Please, I'm begging you. For the sake of the man we both care about. Please call me the second you get this, before it's too late."

He clicked off. Esma still hadn't returned. Jack decided to call Franco to share the bombshell he had stumbled on. But when he tried Franco's number, there was no answer and it kept ringing without switching to voicemail.

Something was wrong.

Franco always answered his cell. *Always*. Had there been some new development, Jack wondered, or had one of Franco's other cases pulled him away? Whatever the reason, the timing couldn't be worse. Without Franco's access to police records, Jack knew, his lead on DeFreeze was worthless.

"Here it is."

Jack looked up as Esma swept back into the room carrying a folder full of papers. She held it out to Jack but he pressed it back into her hands and scribbled instructions on the folder.

"What are you doing?" Esma said.

"This is the personal e-mail of a police detective named Francis Russo. Make sure you scan everything you have here on DeFreeze and send it to Russo right away."

Esma looked bewildered.

"But aren't you even going to look at it?"

"No time," Jack said. "And don't breathe a word of this to anyone until Russo or I get back to you."

Jack raced out of the mansion.

48

SALAZAR

alazar was torn. Part of him, the simple man who longed to be on Playa El Agua with an umbrella drink in hand, wanted to let Claire go. But another part, the predator who left nothing to chance, refused to. Unlike Reaper or even Alice, Claire possessed information that could expose Salazar's true identity because of Claire's link to DeFreeze. Granted, the likelihood that anyone would learn of the prison connection between DeFreeze and Salazar was remote, but the possibility would always be there. Salazar knew himself well enough to recognize that it would nag at him, no matter how much he enjoyed his new life in the extradition-free safety of a Venezuelan island and no matter how many years passed. The idea would always linger in the back of his mind like water dripping from a leaky faucet. Better to err on the side of caution, Salazar decided, and put the matter to rest.

Unfortunately, the distraction of dealing with Reaper had made things more complicated. Had Salazar acted sooner, he could have lured Claire to a remote location and killed her with speedy efficiency. Now, he would have to go to her to do the job.

Having stolen a Honda Accord and switched out its plates, Salazar drove to the Palomar and found a parking spot around the corner. He checked his fake beard and wig in the rear view mirror. How amateurish, he thought. Yet the theatrical props were necessary for the sake of the hotel security cameras. So was the ULCA cap he wore to match the Bruins jacket he was wearing. In doing his homework, Salazar had learned there was a big football game at the university that weekend which meant many out-of-town fans would be staying at the hotel. It would be an easy way to blend in.

From the glove compartment Salazar pulled out his Kimber. Its blued steel glinted as he dry-fired it three times before sliding in the magazine. Then he attached a wet suppressor to the threaded barrel, pre-greased for maximum sound attenuation. He shoved the weapon under his jacket, donned a pair of glasses with enough tint to hide his eyes and climbed out of the car.

It was eight-fifteen, golden hour, that time before sunset when the sky bled and the shadows grew longer. Salazar walked up to the hotel. The front entrance was busy with people coming and going. Salazar noticed the doorman had left his post to help a valet unload luggage from a limo. That suited Salazar just fine. One of the things that made fashionable hotels so tricky was the way the staff fussed over guests and insisted on making eye contact. Salazar preferred anonymity. For his purposes, the less attention he attracted, the better.

He reached the doors to the lobby. As he pulled one open, he bumped into a young woman in a crimson coat hurrying out, wheeling a suitcase.

"Oh, excuse me," the woman said.

"No, sorry," Salazar said. "My fault."

A small carry-on bag fell from the woman's hand. Not until Salazar scooped it up and held it out politely did he realize the woman was Claire.

"Thank you," Claire said.

"My pleasure," Salazar said.

Their fingers touched as Claire took the carry-on. For a brief instant her gaze lingered on Salazar as if trying to place him, then she nodded goodbye and continued to the curb.

Salazar felt an emotion that was rare for him. Worry. His concern was not that Claire knew who he was. How could she? Their only physical proximity had been at the airport where Salazar had been very careful to make sure Claire didn't see him. Nor was Salazar troubled because his plans needed to be changed. Reworking tactics was something he had done a thousand times before. The source of Salazar's discomfort was that suitcase Claire was carrying. It meant she was headed for the airport. Of all places, the most heavily-guarded location in the city.

Salazar considered offering Claire a ride. Maybe he would tell her he was picking up his sweet, old grandmother at the airport. He might even show Claire her photo, the one of his *abuela* embracing him and Ignacio as kids, the single item he carried in his wallet that was real. But he knew it wouldn't work. It would only raise Claire's suspicions, now more than ever, given how nervous she had to be after reneging on their deal, plainly the reason she was fleeing town. Salazar might as well have ANGEL OF DEATH written on his forehead.

The doorman whistled to a yellow cab down the driveway which pulled up to Claire. As Salazar watched her get in, he realized he had only one option. It would require the kind of risk and improvisation he avoided like the plague but it was better than letting Claire get to LAX, a veritable fortress where she would be safe and free to fly away, out of his control. It was a simple plan. Salazar would intercept the cab on its way, quickly execute both Claire and the driver, then make a clean getaway.

There was no time to waste. Claire's cab was pulling away. Salazar noted the number 888 on its hire dome and sprinted back to the parked Accord. In seconds, he was speeding off in the direction the cab had taken.

It wasn't hard for Salazar to pick up Claire's cab again in traffic. Unlike other cities where taxis were plentiful, Los Angeles had relatively few. As expected, the cab traveled west on Wilshire, then ramped onto the San Diego Freeway heading south toward the airport.

Salazar followed a tactful distance behind, already plotting Claire's route to determine the optimal point of interception. Chances were, her cab would exit at La Tijera Boulevard, the favored shortcut of taxis, rather than continue down the freeway to the busier airport exit at Century. Then the cab would jag over to Airport Boulevard and bear right on 96th Street which fed into LAX. Once the cab got to 96th, it would be untouchable. The area was too congested and well-patrolled. That reduced the window of opportunity to the one mile stretch on La Tijera. It would be tight but not impossible. Salazar would pull up in the next lane, pretending to be a friendly motorist, and would signal the cabbie that his tailpipe was dragging. Then Salazar would stop to offer a hand, ideally on an unlit section of the shoulder between streetlights where the two muffled flashes from his Kimber would go unnoticed.

The La Tijera exit approached. As expected, the cab took it. So did Salazar. At the top of the ramp, the light turned yellow and the cab sped up to make a right turn, whooshing past a NO TURN ON RED sign. Salazar prepared to run the red when he saw a police cruiser staked out in the shadows across the intersection. He slammed on his brakes barely in time.

Trapped there, Salazar was forced to watch the cab's taillights getting smaller and smaller, becoming pinpoints of red. By the time the streetlight turned green again, the pinpoints were gone. With the police car still in view, Salazar had no choice but to drive away at the posted speed limit. Not until he was halfway to Airport Boulevard did he dare to accelerate.

Salazar searched for the cab but couldn't find it. He turned left on Airport, then right on 96th and continued to search in vain. As he passed the giant light sculptures marking the entrance to LAX, traffic thickened including many more taxis but none with 888 on the hire dome. Salazar forked off onto the DEPARTURES ramp and headed toward the terminals.

There were now police cars everywhere, along with others from an alphabet soup of law enforcement agencies, the highly visible security presence coordinated by Homeland Security to intimidate would-be terrorists. Salazar's well-trained eyes also detected CCTV cameras covering the airport from every possible angle. Undaunted, Salazar kept driving in search of the 888 cab until finally he spotted it swooping into the Delta Airlines drop-off area at Terminal 5.

A Hilton courtesy bus blasted its horn as Salazar cut in front of it to catch the T5 entrance lane. Rather than head for the busy white zone where the cab had gone, Salazar pulled over to the curb about thirty yards back, a quiet area that was free of traffic cops and offered a good view of the Delta check-in counters through the large terminal windows.

From his vantage point Salazar watched Claire emerge from the cab in her crimson coat. Expert marksman that he was, it would be easy for Salazar to take her out with two quick rounds, one to the chest and one to the head. Getting away was the problem. Before Claire even hit the ground, all routes to and from the airport would be sealed tight. That was the reason Salazar had to be so careful now. There could be no margin for error if he was to pull off the impromptu plan he had come up with. It helped that the windshield of the stolen Accord was tinted, which meant his face would not be recorded by any of the security cameras as long as he remained inside the vehicle.

Salazar pulled out his wallet and withdrew a crisp hundred dollar bill. In the glove compartment he found a scratch pad and a pen. He jotted down a message, tore the page off the pad and folded it twice. Then he shifted his attention back to Claire. She was inside the terminal now. Through the windows Salazar could see her stepping up to a self-check-in kiosk to get a boarding pass.

Salazar scanned the curb. All the traffic cops were still a distance away, patrolling the drop-off area. He estimated that he had five or six minutes before they would shoo him away. More than enough time. With a discerning eye, he studied people passing on the nearby sidewalk—flight attendants, passengers, airport staff—until he spotted the type he was looking for, a redcap who appeared to be not too bright. Salazar buzzed down his passenger window, careful to keep his head inside the car, and signaled the redcap.

"Excuse me, sir. Could you help me please?"

The redcap shuffled over.

"You don't wanna be parked here, boss," the red-cap said. "Them vultures give out tickets like candy."

"I know," Salazar said. "But I need to get a message to my sister. She went inside. I wonder if I could trouble you to take this to her."

Salazar held up the folded note with the hundred dollar bill. The redcap perked up as he saw the money.

"Your sister?"

Salazar pointed out Claire through the window.

"The one with the red coat," he said. "See her? All you have to do is give her this note. Please, I'd be so grateful."

"No problem, boss."

The redcap took the note and the money. As he shuffled off toward the terminal, Salazar leaned back and waited.

49

JACK

laire was all Jack could think of as he blew past traffic on the freeway. He had to know what she knew. Assuming he didn't kill himself first or get pulled over for doing twice the speed limit, Jack figured he could make it to the Palomar in half what it had taken him to get down to Orange County. But would Claire be there when he arrived? It was then that Jack recalled Claire saying she was booked on a red-eye to New York—departing at ten forty-five, she told Jack after their drunken sexual encounter. According to the clock on Jack's dashboard, that was in less than two hours which meant Claire would be leaving the Palomar for the airport soon, if she hadn't already.

Jack jammed his wheel to make a suicide exit off the Santa Ana Freeway and ramped onto the 105 heading west toward LAX.

Between glances at the road, Jack searched an airport information website on his cell. It showed there was no ten-forty-five to New York on the schedule. However, there were two flights with departure times close to that. One was on American at ten-forty, the other on Delta at ten-fifty.

The electric reds and purples of twilight had faded, yielding to darkness. As Jack sped past the light sculptures of the airport entrance, a jumbo jet passed low overhead, its earthquake roar rattling the taped-together side mirror on the Wagoneer. Jack followed signs for DEPARTURES and tried to calculate his poker odds. American or Delta. Which one was Claire flying out on? Terminal 4, American, was coming up first. Jack swooped into its white zone.

The place looked like one of those disaster movies where everyone was trying to escape before the end of the world. To add to the chaos, a female traffic officer was writing up a limo driver who was throwing a fit in her face. Jack took advantage of the distraction and jumped out of his car to scan the crowd for Claire.

There was no sign of her out front. Jack peered through the terminal windows. Claire wasn't there either. Was it possible, Jack wondered, that she arrived early and had already cleared security? If so, he was cooked.

"Move along, mister!"

The female traffic cop was striding over with her ticket pad.

"I'm dropping someone off," Jack said.

"Uh-huh."

With an exaggerated flourish the cop opened her pad and licked the tip of her pen. Jack took it as an omen and drove off for Terminal 5.

The Delta area was even more congested than American. Again, Jack double-parked and got out to search the throngs of passengers but Claire was nowhere to be seen. Jack felt his heart sink. On his way back to the car he threw one last look through the terminal windows and spotted a girl in a red coat.

It was her.

She was standing by a check-in kiosk with a suitcase and carry-on bag. Jack watched a redcap hand her a folded-up paper and walk away. As Claire opened the note and read it, her face turned white.

Jack kept watching, puzzled.

Claire threw a fear-slicked glance around. Then she collected her bags and walked with resistance toward the exit doors. Once outside, she crushed the note and dropped it in an overflowing trash container.

Jack was only ten yards away but the mob of people between them was too thick for Claire to see him. He felt the urge to rush over to her but something about the terror in her face and the way she was searching vehicles at the curb told Jack he needed to see that note first.

He left his car unattended, never taking his eyes off Claire, and pushed his way through the crowd to the trash can. The balled-up paper sat on top with discarded junk food and cigarette butts. Jack tore it open. Eight words stared back:

THE NAKED PHILOSOPHER

SILVER ACCORD OUTSIDE
OR YOUR MOTHER IS DEAD

An adrenal rush shot up Jack's spine. He looked over again to see Claire moving quickly toward a silver Honda Accord at the curb, its driver hidden by the tinted windshield. Claire threw her bags in the open trunk of the car, then slipped into the passenger seat and the Accord sped away.

Urgently, Jack shoved his way through the crowd, knocking people over, and dove into his car where another cop was writing him a ticket. The cop jumped out of the way, yelling and shaking his fist, as Jack tore off after the Accord.

Jack's mind raced. Who was driving the silver vehicle? Reaper? DeFreeze? And where was Claire being taken? Jack sped up and weaved through traffic. As he exited the airport, he caught a glimpse of the Accord thirty yards ahead, veering onto the southbound ramp for Sepulveda Boulevard.

Jack struggled to keep up. The Accord took the tunnel under the airport runways, then cruised south through a drab industrial wasteland, heading for El Segundo and the South Bay. A bad feeling came over Jack. Having been a cop, he could imagine several possible scenarios, none of them encouraging. And there was no telling where the Accord was headed. It could be driving for hours, to San Diego for all Jack knew. He didn't have hours. Neither did Claire, from the look of that note.

Jack glanced at his glove compartment. If ever there was a time he wished he still had his service weapon, it was now. Then he realized he had Claire's phone number. Calling her could be dangerous but so was doing nothing. Jack pulled out his cell and scrolled to recent calls, then hit the one for Claire.

It rang and kept ringing. Jack tried to see past the Accord's tinted back window but it was too dark. Why wasn't Claire picking up? Suddenly she did and she was breathless.

"Jack, help—!"

Right away she was cut off. Jack could almost feel the iPhone being ripped from her hand. Then a calm and courteous male voice came on the line, Hispanic accent, in control.

"You'll have to excuse Claire. She's not quite herself at the moment."

"If you hurt her," Jack said, "I'll kill you."

All trace of civility evaporated from the voice.

"Who is this?"

"Pull over," Jack said. "And let her go."

"What did you say?"

"Then you're going to tell me about Joseph Pearl. Where he is, what you did to him."

"You said to pull over," the voice replied. "How do you know we're in a car?"

Before Jack could answer, there was a sharp thud, as if Claire's phone had been flung against something, followed by a high-pitch squeal like feedback from a guitar. The Accord accelerated. So did Jack, his cell phone still glued to his ear.

"It's over," Jack said. "You can't get away!"

There was no response from the driver of the Accord, nothing but that feedback wailing over the line. Jack's blood ran cold as he realized it was Claire screaming and begging.

"Let her go, you sonofabitch!"

Then a new sound came over the phone: *pop, pop,* the unmistakable staccato of a suppressed handgun going off. A heartbeat later, the passenger door of the speeding Accord flew open and Claire tumbled out like a rag doll.

And then, like a bad dream, all hell broke loose.

As the Accord hurtled away, a Lexus behind it ran over Claire as if going over a speed bump too fast. The jolt made the Lexus brake hard and swerve into a truck in the next lane, sending it careening over the yellow line into oncoming traffic. With the sound of tearing metal, a wall of cars plowed into the truck head-on, causing it to burst into flame while other vehicles piled up in a nightmarish chain reaction. At the same time, Jack slammed on his brakes to avoid the fishtailing Lexus and was rear-ended by a bus with such force that it flipped the Wagoneer and wrapped it around a guard rail.

Jack blacked out. When he came to, he found himself hanging upside down, airbags deployed, bleeding from a deep gash on his temple. He could smell gasoline leaking. The force of the impact had driven the medallion of St. Michael into the dashboard like a knife. Somehow Jack dropped from his seatbelt and dragged himself out the shattered windshield.

He glanced around. The roadway looked like a war zone. People were moaning and screaming in the dark, limping away from their destroyed vehicles. Others were rushing over to help injured motorists. Through the smoke and wreckage Jack spotted Claire lying lifeless on the pavement, illuminated by the crisscross of broken headlights.

Jack limped over. Claire was face up. One leg was bent at an unnatural angle. Her crimson coat was splayed open to reveal two bullet holes in her chest, a pool of blood spreading under her like dye running from the coat's fabric.

Her eyes fluttered open. She was still alive. Jack dropped to his knees, afraid to move her. He pressed his bloodied hand to her face.

"Claire..."

A tear ran down Claire's cheek.

"What I deserve," she said. "For punishing Joe..."

Jack stared in shock as her meaning sank in, the devastating truth he had somehow been blind to. He jerked his hand away as if her face had burned it.

"Yes, it was me..." Claire said. "I paid to have him taken..."

"Claire, why?"

"To make him *feel*...feel the pain he caused me..."

"By having him killed?"

"Worse," Claire said. "Only thing more terrifying than death for a philosopher...strip away his conviction...make him doubt his most deeply held beliefs..."

She was delirious and dying. It wasn't the time for a philosophical debate. Yet Jack heard himself defend his father.

"No," he said. "That's not what you did. You can make anyone think anything if you torture him long enough. But it doesn't mean he abandoned his beliefs, only that he's human."

A sliver of uncertainty flickered in Claire's eyes.

"Doesn't matter anymore..."

Jack wanted to finish her off with his bare hands, both for what she had done and because he hadn't figured it out sooner. But he also felt overwhelming sadness for Claire. Jack wiped away her tears and touched her face again tenderly.

"Do you know where he is?" Jack asked.

"Tell your father..."

"Please. If you ever loved him. Before it's too late."

"Tell him I'm sorry, I'm sorry, I'm sorry..."

Her eyes went opaque.

"*Claire.*"

Jack shook her.

She was gone.

In the distance a siren wailed, then two and then a chorus, shattering the night.

50

JACK

L ike other victims of the crash, Jack was taken by ambulance to the closest hospital where he received stitches for his head wound. Then he was escorted to a doctors' lounge where two uniformed police officers questioned him about Claire. Since she was the victim of a shooting, they wanted to know Jack's relationship to her and if he had any information that might shed light on what had happened. Jack knew the drill. He had conducted enough of these interviews himself to know it was a routine death investigation at this point. The case hadn't been ruled a homicide yet or assigned to detectives. If he told the truth, it would open a huge can of worms. So Jack played dumb. He claimed to be just another driver caught in the pile-up who had seen an injured girl and tried to help.

Jack knew there was a problem when one of the uniforms got a phone call and stepped out of the room to take it. When the uniform came back, his politeness was gone.

"You're being detained," he said.

"For what?"

"You can take that up with the C.O. We have orders to bring you to Hollywood Station for more questioning."

Hollywood. That was Trigwell's turf. And C.O. meant custody officer, initials a civilian wouldn't know. In case Jack hadn't caught his contemptuous look, the uniform was telling him he knew Jack was one of his former brethren who had tarnished the shield.

It was an unpleasant trip to Hollywood, Jack's first time riding in the back of a squad car facing the business side of the grated partition. Being detained, Jack knew, meant he could be held without the usual rights associated with arrest. For how long was a gray area. A few hours maybe. But why? Jack wondered if it had anything to do with being unable to reach Franco. All he knew for sure was that if Trigwell was involved, it couldn't be good.

Upon arrival at the precinct station, Jack was escorted through the busy dispatch area to a window-less interrogation room consisting of a metal table and two armless chairs—'the box', Jack called it back in his detective days or, as Franco preferred, 'the room for the honesty impaired.' Jack heard the hum-click of the automatic lock as the door closed behind him. Some-time later, a friendly female duty officer brought him a coffee and asked if he needed to use the restroom or have his head bandage changed. Jack said no to both. The duty officer nodded politely and left him alone again.

Jack flashed on Claire. That aborted phone call she had started to make, its electronic tones captured by the hotel voicemail. A call to Goatee. Jack had been right about that. But despite his usually sharp instincts, it had never occurred to Jack that Claire would be calling as the person who had paid to have his father kidnapped, not to pay for his release.

Claire had hidden her hand brilliantly.

And Jack had been played.

With his back to the one-way mirror, Jack pulled out his cell phone. Since he wasn't under arrest, his personal effects hadn't been confiscated. Jack scrolled to the last number he had called, Claire's. Emotion, not logic, made him press the send button. The number rang and rang, then Jack heard Claire's voice from beyond the grave, eerily cheerful:

"Hi, it's Claire Evans. Your call is very important to me so...well, you know what to do."

Jack hung up before the beep. Had he really thought the driver of the Accord would pick up? Whoever the mystery man was, he was too smart for that. Anyone clever enough to have lured Claire out of the airport wouldn't have held onto her iPhone, knowing it could be tracked, nor would he have risked using his own car, which meant the license plate Jack had memorized during the chase wouldn't lead anywhere. The Accord was sure to be stolen. It would be found

torched somewhere, purged of prints and other trace-
able evidence.

Yet Jack had learned something new, something
important. There was a third player involved in Claire's
plan to punish his father. The cordial Hispanic voice
Jack had heard didn't belong to DeFreeze and sounded
too intelligent to be Reaper, based on Kevin's profile of
the gangbanger. It was pretty obvious that the driver
of the Accord was running the show, the brains behind
the abduction. And he had gotten away.

With Claire gone, the kidnappers no longer had
an incentive to keep their hostage alive which put
the situation in stark relief: even if Jack was released
immediately, even if he knew his father's whereabouts,
even if Franco got the entire LAPD to drop everything
and make a cavalry charge to the rescue, Joseph Pearl
would be found dead.

It was over. The time had come to admit defeat
and to let it go. Jack didn't believe in God. It was probably the only thing, besides his crooked nose, that he
had in common with his old man. Nevertheless, Jack
bowed his head. He prayed that his dad had not suffered before his death and had been spared pain and
anguish, in particular the psychological kind that Claire
had gone to such extreme lengths to make him feel.

The silent prayer was interrupted by the hum-click
of the door opening. Jack looked up to see Trigwell
walk in.

51

JOSEPH PEARL

Death tempted Pearl like a lover. It beckoned, it coaxed, it wrapped its seductive arms around him. Surrender, it whispered, surrender. Pearl resisted the siren song and fought his way back to consciousness. Then he stared in wonder down the pitch-black tunnel.

There in the distance, radiating down from the ceiling of the cement passageway, was a razor-thin shaft of light.

In his sixty years, Pearl had seen some arresting sights: the great wildebeest migration on the Serengeti plain, the ancient bust of Nefertiti in the Berlin Museum, the Aurora Borealis ablaze above Jasper, Alberta. Yet none was as exquisite as that fragile thread of illumination.

Let there be light.

More than the alphabetical recitation of philosophers, more even than Ann's prayer, the shaft of light offered Pearl a mental rope with which to pull himself forward. Yet he was unable to. Try as he might, he could not move a muscle. It appeared he had reached a new stage in the dying process, the point of no return, the critical juncture at which his mind and body were beginning to separate. Pearl could feel the symphony of pain ebbing as his corporal self prepared to be shed. Then he became aware of something feather-soft brushing the back of his neck, the whiskers of a rat. Pearl shuddered. Scared off, the rat vanished into the darkness.

The encounter yanked Pearl back into his body. His heart raced, his eyes shifted. Here was a new nightmare, more horrible than all the others. It was only a matter of time before the rat came back, and not alone. What could he do? The light. The light was his one chance.

Pearl steeled his nerves and commanded his crippled fingers to move. By some miracle they clawed a hold under the rivulet of sewer water and pulled his dead weight forward a few inches. The effort was so exhausting that Pearl wanted to give up. To force himself not to, he imagined rats swarming over him in a feeding frenzy, hundreds, thousands, eating him alive. The fear moved his cuffed hands another few inches.

52

JACK

Trigwell dropped a case file on the table and placed a microcassette recorder beside it. Then he took a seat opposite Jack and clicked on the recording device.

"This interview is being taped," Trigwell said. "And may be used as evidence should you be arrested and brought to trial. The time is twenty-three fifty-one on Friday, September third, and this interview is taking place at Hollywood Community Police Station."

Jack rolled his eyes.

"I'm familiar with the script. Can we cut the crap?"

He might as well have been talking to the wall.

"My name is Detective Trigwell. I'm here with Jack Pearl, who is being held as a person of interest in several homicides. Four, to be exact. Committed in three separate locations in the last forty-eight hours."

That stopped Jack cold.

"Four? What are you talking about?"

Trigwell saw that he had Jack's attention. He recited his rights, then told him to state his full name and date of birth. When Jack relented, Trigwell opened the folder and pulled out a quartet of crime scene photos. He placed them in front of Jack, lining up the edges as if they were panes of glass in a window.

"You recognize these people? Let me help you remember. This one is Claire Evans. You were with her at the car crash tonight. And this here is Henry Yates. He owns the pawn shop you showed up at yesterday."

Jack wasn't looking where Trigwell was pointing. His eyes were glued to the other two photos, the most grisly crime scene images he had ever seen.

"What in God's name..."

"Her name is Carmen Ortiz," Trigwell said. "Yeah, that's a woman. Hard to tell from all the butchering. And that decapitated doll in her arms? That isn't a doll, it's her kid. God rest both their souls."

Ortiz. The Reaper connection. Jack felt sick.

"I don't know them," Jack said.

Technically it was true.

"No, of course not," Trigwell said. "And I suppose it's a coincidence they ended up like this at the same time your ex-partner was making inquiries about them?"

Jack was alarmed to hear Franco brought up.

"Russo had nothing to do with this."

"Funny, he said the same thing about you," Trigwell said. "Like he did three years ago which, as all of us on the force remember only too well, helped you get off with nothing more than turning in your badge. But before you get all excited, you should know that Russo won't be bailing you out this time. At my request per an emergency directive, he's been placed on paid administrative leave, effective immediately, and ordered to have no contact with you until this matter is resolved."

So that was why he hadn't been able to reach Franco, Jack realized. Trigwell leaned forward and curled his lip.

"Your choice, Pearl. Either you start talking right now and tell me everything, and I mean the whole fucking tale, or I'll have you arrested and locked up."

"Very funny," Jack said.

"I'm not laughing."

"I didn't kill anyone and you know it."

"Okay, don't say I didn't warn you. You're under arrest on suspicion of first-degree murder."

Trigwell nodded to the one-way mirror. Instantly two more detectives walked in. Jack was handcuffed and Mirandized. Then, with Trigwell leading the parade, he was soldiered away to be booked.

All the cops in the station looked up from their work to give Jack dead-eyed stares, the kind reserved for outcast police officers. The flip side of the blue wall of silence. Jack kept his head down, letting Trigwell pull him along, until he heard a sharp female voice from somewhere behind.

"Let him go."

Jack turned to see Becky crossing the squad room, coming over. He thought he was hallucinating. Even crazier, Becky blocked Trigwell's path, forcing Jack and the two detectives to stop behind him.

"Who the hell are you?" Trigwell said.

"I'm Rebecca Knowles, Mr. Pearl's attorney."

Jack wasn't sure he had heard right. Neither was Trigwell.

"How did you know he was here?"

"That doesn't matter," Becky said. "Now please release my client. Don't make me ask you again."

"Look, hon," Trigwell said. "I don't think you quite understand..."

Jack could see Becky's button being pressed. Trigwell had no idea who he was dealing with.

"First of all, I am not your 'hon'," Becky said. "And second, unless you want the media all over this, doing stories about a certain detective with a history of making arrests without sufficient evidence—yeah, that would be you—then I suggest you put your hard-on back in your pants and take off those handcuffs immediately."

Trigwell looked like he had been spanked.

"You've got balls, lady."

"I'm waiting."

Trigwell turned to Jack, so angry Jack almost expected to see smoke come out of his ears.

"I'm not done with you," Trigwell said. "Don't leave town."

He signaled one of his men who removed Jack's cuffs. Becky gave them all a professional nod and led Jack away. He was too stunned to speak until they were out of the station.

"That wasn't fair," Jack said.

"Yeah, you're probably right," Becky said. "I should have called here first, had someone warn you I was coming."

"No, I meant what you did to Trigwell back there. You realize he'll go home later and beat his wife."

Becky let only a hint of smile escape.

"Trigwell," she said. "Wasn't he involved in that thing three years ago?"

"Good memory," Jack said. "He was the guy with the connection to the DEA agent, Simms, the one who was killed with those other people I found dead at the drug house that night."

"And for a while didn't you think it was him? The bad cop? The one who took the money and left that empty Rolex box in the safe?"

"Not Rolex. Patek Philippe. Patek Philippe Cala-trava, to be exact. And yeah, there were a bunch of things that pointed to Trigwell, but I could never prove it."

Becky saw Jack grimace and touch his head bandage.

"You okay?"

"Yeah. Thanks for coming."

"You can thank Franco."

Of course, Jack thought. Who else would have called Becky, knowing full well that Jack wouldn't approve?

"I'm surprised he would lift a finger for me," Jack said. "After the mess I dumped in his lap."

"C'mon, you guys are like family. You'd do the same for him. By the way, Franco said to tell you he hopes you understand he couldn't return your calls. And that he's sorry he wasn't more helpful in finding your dad."

Becky gave Jack a rueful look, obviously also feeling bad about having misunderstood at the courthouse when Jack told her his father was missing.

"Do you want to talk about it, Jack?"

"Not really."

"We could go get a coffee."

"No, that's okay."

Becky nodded, hiding disappointment. To Jack, she had never looked more beautiful.

"C'mon," she said. "I'll give you a ride home."

"No thanks," Jack said. "I'm good."

"You don't have a car anymore, remember?"

"I'll catch a cab."

"It's no trouble."

"Really, I'm fine."

Becky looked stung.

"Okay," she said. "You hate me. I get it. For moving on with my life. Not waiting for you. Letting myself care for someone else."

"No," Jack said. "You're wrong."

"Oh really? Then what? Tell me, Jack. It's just a ride. Why else would you say no?"

"Because I wouldn't want to let you go," Jack said. "I might even do something stupid like try to kiss you or guilt you into coming up for that coffee in a pathetic attempt to get you to stay. And then you would hate me. I would hate myself. But this way, there's still a chance after some time passes and I get over the self-pity thing, that we might actually be friends again someday."

Becky looked at him, disarmed.

"Wow," she said. "Thank you for being so honest."

"The least you deserve," Jack said. "After all I've put you through."

"Friends. I would really like that."

Becky opened her purse and pulled out a business card. Jack noticed her fingers were trembling ever so slightly as she handed it to him. Her fingers never trembled.

"Here," she said. "My home number and cell are on the back, in case Trigwell gives you any more trouble."

"Thanks again," Jack said.

"You're welcome."

"Okay. Well, goodnight, Becky."

"Goodnight, Jack."

Becky flashed a parting smile, conflicting emotions in her eyes. Then she turned and walked away. Jack watched her go and savored every last second of her being there, feeling lighter somehow. Then he got on his cell phone to call an Uber.

When Jack returned to Chinatown, he had to use a spare key he kept hidden behind a plant by his door, having abandoned his key ring in the ignition of his dearly departed Wagoneer.

He walked into the loft to find it dark and silent.

"Anybody home?"

A yelp of excitement came from the kitchen. Trouser bounded out to greet Jack, giving his face a slobbery tongue bath.

"Yeah, weirdo, I missed you too."

As they collapsed on the couch and wrestled affectionately, Jack thought about everything that had happened, the runaway rollercoaster he had been on for the last three days.

Jack closed his eyes.

Surrender came quickly.

He slept like the dead.

53

SALAZAR

"Traffic remains backed up for miles as Caltrans crews continue to work on the massive pileup that left three dead and more than twenty injured. According to police, the cause of the crash is still unknown."

With detached interest, Salazar watched the late-night newscast on a TV in the waiting hall at Union Station. Other people had also stopped to catch the breaking story including a pregnant woman with a pet ferret in her shoulder bag.

"Terrible thing," the woman said. "Probably a drunk driver."

"Or someone using a cell phone," Salazar said.

"As if our world isn't sick enough. Makes you wish you could give up everything and escape to some tropical island."

Salazar smiled to himself.

"I couldn't agree more," he said.

As the woman checked her train ticket and continued on her way, Salazar headed off in search of a restroom.

He found one and took a stall in the back that was empty. Once the door was locked, Salazar sat on the toilet and pulled out Claire's iPhone. Ordinarily, he would have disposed of it right away, as he had done with the Accord, but he was curious about the person who had tried to contact Claire.

'Jack', she had called him. With his number captured on the iPhone, it wouldn't be hard to find out who he was.

Salazar slipped on a pair of surgical gloves and used a chemically-treated lens cloth to wipe the iPhone clean of prints. He did the same with the phone's lithium battery, which he had removed earlier to make the unit untraceable. But now he wanted it to be tracked in order to throw off the police. It was the reason he had come here to the train station. Assuming the authorities were already searching for the phone, it would take them at least half an hour to triangulate its pings and get a location, more than enough time for Salazar to satisfy his curiosity before vanishing.

He returned the battery to its casing and powered up the iPhone. When its screen lit up, it showed something unexpected: a call had come in only eighteen minutes ago but no voicemail had been left. Salazar checked the number of the caller. To his surprise, it was the same one that Claire had answered before Salazar had ripped the phone from her hand, another call from the person named Jack.

Salazar considered its meaning. This Jack, whoever he was, clearly didn't intend to reach Claire since he had been there to witness her fate. Rather, it appeared his motive was to make contact with Salazar himself.

With growing interest, Salazar clicked online to a reverse phone number lookup site. When he entered the number, a name popped up:

JACK PEARL

Salazar was intrigued. The surname was the same as that of the philosopher he had kidnapped. That explained the desperation Salazar had detected in Jack's voice—a voice that sounded as if it belonged to someone in his late twenties or early thirties, which suggested that Jack Pearl was the son of the hostage.

To be certain, Salazar Googled JACK PEARL. He wasn't prepared for what came up. There were over fifty thousand hits, an avalanche of articles, all about a disgraced LAPD detective who was kicked off the force three years ago due to a case involving several unsolved murders and ten million dollars in missing drug money.

As Salazar scanned the first few articles, a recurring theme emerged: although Detective Pearl was never charged with any crime, it was widely believed that he had stolen the money and had gotten away with it.

Salazar checked the amount again.

Ten million dollars.

No, he told himself. Leave it alone. Tomorrow he would be on that plane. Temptation would only get him into trouble. But temptation was in his blood. Its pull reminded Salazar of the three rules he had lived by ever since he had committed his first kidnapping:

Rule Number One: Get the money.

Rule Number Two: Remember to get the money.

Rule Number Three: Don't forget to always remember to get the money.

Salazar consulted his watch. It was almost midnight. Nothing could be done until morning, when banks opened, in case he required Alice's assistance. He had time. Besides, more information was needed to weigh the pros and cons of what he was deliberating. Once he had considered all the variables, he would make an informed decision.

Salazar studied one of the internet photos of Jack, committing it to memory. He also burned Jack's phone number into his mind. Then he erased his web searches with some computer magic but left the iPhone on so it could be tracked.

When he returned to the waiting hall, Salazar spotted the pregnant woman again, still carrying her shoulder bag with the ferret inside toward a platform to board an announced train.

On his way out of the station, Salazar passed the woman and casually dropped Claire's iPhone into her bag.

No one noticed except the ferret.

54

JACK

Jack woke up with a pounding headache. It didn't feel like a Saturday morning. It felt more like the rainy Tuesday afternoon when, standing in numbed silence, Jack had watched his mother's casket being lowered into the ground.

Jack showered and changed the bandage on his temple, then he threw on some fresh clothes and headed down the street with Trouser to grab some breakfast. Along the way Jack noticed a washed-out blonde at a bus stop checking him out, apparently attracted to wounded-looking guys. Or maybe it was Trouser she was admiring. Either way, it made Jack feel better, hopeful about the future. With a little time, he thought, maybe he could put everything behind him, even the pain of losing his dad. Then he could do what he had been unable to these last three years: start living again.

When he reached an old-fashioned coffee shop on the corner, Jack tied Trouser's leash to an outside table. The Lab seemed oddly agitated.

"What's up with you, Trowze?"

Trouser returned a whiny bark.

"Hungry? Me too. Breakfast coming right up."

Jack walked into the cafe. He ordered a large coffee for himself and some food to share with Trouser: cheeseburger, eggs, pancakes. While he paid for his order, Jack noticed a newspaper on the counter. Its oversized headline screamed THREE DEAD IN MEGA-CRASH. Underneath were photos and details. In no mood to relive them, Jack turned his back on the paper and rejoined Trouser at the outside table. Together they scarfed down the food and drink until Jack's headache went away.

He was returning inside for a coffee refill when his cell phone rang. In hopes that it was Franco, Jack checked the screen but it read RESTRICTED. Disappointed, he answered it.

"Hello?"

"Hello, Jack."

Jack teetered to a halt. It was a voice he recognized. Cordial, confident, Hispanic accent. The driver of the Accord.

"Who is this?"

"You can call me Salazar. Where are you?"

"Why?"

"Answer my question."

"At a coffee shop."

"Alone?"

"Yes."

"Expecting anyone?"

"No."

"Good. Now listen carefully. If you talk to anyone else, the conversation is over. If you take another call, the conversation is over. If we get cut off for any reason, the conversation is over. Anything you say or do that does not pertain to our deal will be taken as an attempt to trace this call. Not that you could. Believe me, I have made quite sure of that. But if you try, you will never hear from me again."

Jack forgot about the refill, everything around him.

"Deal?" he said. "What deal?"

"A simple business transaction. I have something you want. And you have something I am willing to trade it for."

"What are you talking about?"

"Joseph Pearl, your father—yes, I know you are his son—in exchange for the money you stole three years ago."

Jack paled in shock. Last thing he expected to hear.

"What the hell?"

"All of it," the voice said. "Ten million dollars."

Jack heard himself laugh nervously.

"C'mon, this is a joke," he said. "You're kidding, right?"

"Do I sound as if I'm kidding?"

"I never stole any money."

"I think you did."

"Then you'd be wrong."

"In that case, I'm sorry to have wasted your time. Goodbye, Jack. Have a nice life."

"Wait!"

Jack didn't know what to say but he had to say something, for his father's sake. He had to keep this Salazar talking.

"Alright," Jack said. "You win."

A grim chuckle came over the line.

"Don't forget who you are dealing with. I have been doing this a long time."

Jack took a deep breath.

"One million," he said.

Jack knew he was walking a tightrope. If he agreed to Salazar's figure or anything close, the kidnapper would know something was wrong. By countering with such a low number, Jack hoped to sound as if he had it. Not that he did. He hadn't stolen that money. Ten million? Jack was lucky if he had a thousand bucks in the bank.

"This is not a negotiation," the voice said. "Again, the price is ten million dollars. To be wire transferred according to my explicit instructions."

"How do I know you have my father?"

"Because I am a businessman, not a thief. And because if I was not telling the truth, I wouldn't say what I am about to."

"What's that?"

"I cannot guarantee that your father is still alive. I have not seen him. I have no idea what his condition is. All I can give you is the location where he is being held. That is what your money would be buying."

Jack swallowed hard.

"God damn you," he said.

"So? Do we have a deal or not?"

Jack did his best to sound beaten.

"Okay, I'll make it two. Two million."

"You don't seem to be listening."

"An exchange," Jack said. "At an agreed upon location. I bring the cash, you bring my father alive and well."

Jack could hear anger rising in Salazar's voice.

"What do you take me for? Do you think I would be so foolish as to agree to that?"

"No," Jack said. "I think you're smart enough to know I'm not going to give you all that money to find a corpse."

"But suppose he is not dead? Your father, Jack. Your own flesh and blood. Suppose you could have saved him?"

"Two million. With proof of life."

"And if I say no?"

"You won't."

"Goodbye, Jack."

The line went dead.

Jack gawked at the phone in his hand and felt something die inside. As a cop he had won hostage negotiations. He had talked jumpers down from the ledge. He had even stopped a man from dropping a lit match on his three children after dousing them with gasoline. As a poker player, he had performed similar feats of magic. He had pulled off bluffs so convincing that even he himself was unsure what cards he was holding until he turned them face up. He knew how to walk right up to the edge of something without going over. Until now. Whatever it might be called—a gamble, a leap of faith, an act of madness—the thing Jack had just done was the greatest chance he had ever taken and also the biggest miscalculation, even bigger than the one he had made three years ago, an epic fail he would have to live with for the rest of his life.

There was no point calling back. RESTRICTED meant the number was blocked. But Jack tried anyway. That was how desperate he was. No surprise, the number wouldn't connect.

Devastated, Jack walked out of the coffee shop when his cell phone rang again. He couldn't answer it fast enough.

"You've had a moment to come to your senses," the voice said. "I'm going to give you one last chance. Six million dollars, to be wired without delay. Take it or leave it."

Salazar's words were music to Jack's ears. Just like that, everything had changed. Not only was Jack back in the game, the tables had turned. By calling back and dropping the price, Salazar had tipped his hand and telegraphed how hungry he was for the money. His threat was nothing more than an attempt to hide it. It was straight out of *Caro's Book of Poker Tells*. Strong means weak. Jack was now dictating play. But he had to be careful. He couldn't afford to get it wrong again.

"I'll split the difference," Jack said. "Three million, regardless of my father's condition, but only if you take me to him. The minute I see him, you get the access code to an offshore account holding that amount. Or I'll call my bank and arrange the transfer. Whatever you prefer."

Anger returned to Salazar's voice.

"Why do you insist that I bring you?"

"Because I don't trust you."

"It cuts both ways. At first you denied stealing the money. How do I know this isn't some desperate ploy on your part?"

"Because if it is, you'll kill me, probably after making me watch you kill my dad first if he's still alive."

"No, better than that," Salazar said. "I'll make you do it. Ever so slowly. I'll make your father watch you kill him."

The chilling serenity in his tone told Jack the threat was real this time, that Salazar was capable of making people do things they thought they could not be coerced to do. It reminded Jack of how Salazar had disposed of Claire, what kind of a monster he was dealing with.

"Very well," the voice said. "We have a deal."

Jack breathed a mental sigh of relief, while still having no idea how the hell he was going to pull this off. He thought of Franco again, the one person he could trust to help him. Somehow Jack had to find a way to contact his ex-partner on the way to wherever Salazar wanted to meet.

"Okay," Jack said. "So how do we do this?"

"Are you carrying a weapon?"

"Of course not."

"Another cell phone? Other electronics of any kind?"

"No."

"Good. Then turn toward the window."

Jack frowned.

"What?"

"Do as I say."

Jack turned.

"Okay," he said. "Now what?"

"See that black van across the street? I want you to walk over and get in the driver's side. But first, drop your phone in that trash can next to you so no one follows us."

Jack felt a stab of shock. Salazar was watching him and had been the whole time. The kidnapper must have found out where he lived, Jack realized, and followed him there to the coffee shop.

"Did you hear me, Jack? We don't want to keep your father waiting. And leave your four-legged friend where he is."

There was a click as the call disconnected. Jack's mind went into overdrive. He could still bolt to save himself or try calling Franco, but he knew both would be futile. Any deviation at this point would be a death sentence for his father and for Jack as well. Given how swiftly Salazar had tracked him down, it would only be a matter of time before he ended up like Claire. The cards were dealt. There was no going back now. Jack had to play out the hand for all the chips, win or die.

As instructed, Jack stepped to the trash receptacle and tossed in his cell phone, knowing he was giving up his only way to get help and of being found should he fail. The irony hit Jack. It was one more thing he now had in common with his father: both of them were under the control of the same ruthless killer and utterly defenseless.

Before walking away from the coffee shop, Jack stopped a busboy and handed him all the cash in his wallet. He pointed out Trouser.

"See that dog there?" he said. "That animal saved my life. He means everything to me. If I'm not back before your shift ends, please take him to the address on his collar."

The busboy looked at the money and nodded.

Jack stepped over to Trouser to pet him goodbye. From the time the homeless pup had first attached himself to Jack's pant leg, Jack had promised himself that he would never abandon his beloved companion under any circumstances. Yet he had no choice now. Jack smiled to hide his guilt and scratched Trouser in that special spot he loved, under his chin.

"Good boy," Jack said. "Stay here, kiddo."

As Trouser picked up on his tension and pulled at his leash with a moan, Jack tore himself away and crossed the street where he climbed into the black van.

Salazar was sitting in the passenger seat. He was taller than Jack expected but otherwise ordinary-looking, the kind of person who would go unnoticed on the street, which made him all the more scary.

"Beautiful dog," Salazar said. "Coincidentally, my brother always wanted a Labrador Retriever when we were growing up. Until life intervened."

Jack wasn't listening. His eyes were glued to the gun in Salazar's gloved hand, a Kimber .45 with a silencer attached, aimed at Jack's heart.

"A precaution," Salazar said. "As long as you hold up your end of the bargain, no harm will come to you. Or to your father, if he is still alive. You have my word."

Jack forced a nod.

"Where to?" he said.

"The rail yards south of Terminal Island. Not far from where you first stumbled on the drug operation that ended your career. Yes, I read all about it. Make sure you stay on the surface streets and obey the speed limit."

Jack reached for his seatbelt.

"No," Salazar said. "You won't be needing that."

Salazar's own belt was on, another safeguard in case Jack tried to crash the car. There was nothing he hadn't thought of.

Jack shifted into gear and drove away with the gun on him. For several blocks Salazar repeatedly glanced over his shoulder to make sure they weren't being tailed. Satisfied, he eased back in his seat.

As they cruised south through the city, Jack was tempted to ask Salazar all the unanswered questions he still had. How was he connected to Reaper? DeFreeze? Why had Carmen Ortiz and her child been slaughtered so viciously? And why had Salazar felt the need to kill Claire? But Jack decided to keep his mouth shut. Being too curious, he knew, could backfire, especially with a loaded gun pointed at him.

About half a mile from Terminal Island, Salazar gestured for Jack to take a deserted service road running parallel to the rail yards serving the Port. Then they turned onto another road, even more isolated, where a string of long-abandoned factories lined the tracks.

"There," Salazar said.

He pointed to a two-story building up ahead, a huge ugly structure with all its windows boarded up.

"There's a loading dock around back", Salazar said. "Pull up and turn off the van."

When Jack did, Salazar snatched the keys from his hand and nodded to a corroded metal door at the top of a freight ramp.

"Okay," he said. "You first."

Jack climbed out of the van and headed up the ramp. Salazar followed a cautious distance behind. Jack was almost to the door when he noticed a car parked at the far end of the building, a Subaru Impreza. Its meaning made Jack stop. Reaper was there. Jack glanced back to see Salazar had also noticed the car and seemed puzzled by it.

"Something wrong?" Jack said.

"No," Salazar said. "Everything is fine."

He was lying, Jack could tell. But why?

Salazar waved Jack on with his gun. They walked into the factory, the metal door clanging shut behind them. It took Jack's eyes a moment to adjust to the gloom of the hangar-like space, then gradually he made out endless rows of cobwebbed machines stretching off into the darkness.

It was too quiet. Where was Joseph Pearl? And why hadn't Reaper appeared? Jack looked at Salazar again who seemed to be thinking the same thing, his eyes darting all around.

"My father," Jack said. "Where is he?"

"Somewhere in the building," Salazar said. "I told you, that's all I know. You lead, I'll follow."

It wasn't what Jack wanted to hear but it gave him time to think of a plan. Whatever he came up with, Jack knew, it would have to be nothing short of brilliant to outplay Salazar.

Their footsteps echoed as they headed down a row of machines, into the bowels of the building. The only sign of life was a rat scurrying across a rafter above. They searched the next row to find nothing there either. About to start down a third row of machines, Jack stopped short. In the darkness up ahead he could make out a metal staircase leading to the second floor. At the foot of the stairs lay the body of a man, too still to be alive, his face hidden in shadows.

"There he is," Salazar said. "Your father."

It had been ten years since Jack had seen his old man but even in the murky light he could tell the person sprawled there wasn't Joseph Pearl. Common sense told Jack it had to be Reaper. While Jack wondered what that meant, Salazar circled to face him. The blued steel of his Kimber glinted in the shadows.

"Remember our agreement," Salazar said. "Dead or alive. The minute you see him, I get the money."

"It's too dark to make out his face," Jack said. "I need to be certain it's him."

"Who else would it be? Now it's time to pay up."

Salazar extracted a cell phone from his jacket.

"Press number one on the speed dial," he said. "A woman will answer, a banker. You will give her all the information she needs to make the transfer."

Instead of handing Jack the phone, Salazar tossed it over. Jack caught it and realized he was screwed. His last ditch plan, all he could come up with, was to try to wrestle away the gun from Salazar when he stepped over to give Jack the cell. But Salazar was too smart. From the moment Jack had answered the call, Salazar had controlled every step and made sure Jack never got close enough to put him at risk.

Jack stared at the phone in his hand but didn't press the button. As Salazar realized what it meant, his eyes burned with rage.

"You don't have the money," he said. "You never did."

"I'll get it. As much as you want, I swear."

"I warned you."

"Please," Jack said. "Let me find my father."

Calm as ever, Salazar stepped behind Jack and kissed his gun. Then he gently pressed it against the back of Jack's head.

"Goodbye, Jack."

Jack closed his eyes. As a shot rang out, Jack felt blood and brains splatter but realized he was still alive. He whirled to see Salazar collapsing in a heap, part of his cranium blown away. The unfired Kimber clattered across the floor.

Jack looked around in confusion.

From out of the darkness a figure emerged with a revolver pointed. It was the washed-out blonde Jack had noticed at the bus stop. Then others stepped out from behind machines and steam pipes, also with weapons drawn, wearing LAPD raid vests. As Jack stared in disbelief, the blonde raised a walkie-talkie.

"All clear," she said. "Tell Trigwell the shooter is down. We've got Pearl. He's safe."

55

JACK

The factory was crawling with CSI's by the time Trigwell arrived, flashlight in hand. Jack watched the detective stop by Salazar's body, now ringed with portable arc lights. The washed-out blonde briefed him and held up a wallet in an evidence baggie. Then Trigwell continued on to the staircase where Jack had been grilled by a couple homicide suits, not far from where Reaper still lay dead.

"Didn't I say I wasn't done with you?" Trigwell said. "Good thing or you'd be taking an eternal nap right now."

Jack gestured toward Salazar.

"Who was he?"

Trigwell shook his head.

"Not the person it says in his wallet. There was an old photo hidden in a back compartment, appears to be him as a kid with some old lady and another boy. Guess we'll have to wait until his prints come back."

"Did you check out his cell phone?" Jack asked.

Trigwell nodded.

"One of those prepaid throwaways that's hard to trace. But we managed to geotrack an incoming call placed yesterday from the only number on the speed-dial. Seems it originated from a four block radius in the commercial district of Beverly Hills."

"He mentioned a banker," Jack said. "Female."

"There are at least a dozen banks in that area," Trigwell said. "This being Saturday, most will be closed by now. But first thing Monday I'll get a team to go through all their surveillance videos. If either of these guys shows up on one, it might help us narrow things down."

Trigwell noticed Jack frowning at Reaper.

"Shitty way to die," Trigwell said. "Think he tripped?"

"Or was pushed by my father, trying to escape."

"Every inch of the building has been searched. Inside and out. No sign of anyone else around."

"He was here," Jack said. "Mind if I look for myself?"

Trigwell appeared irritated. He glanced at the suits who nodded that they were done with Jack.

"What the hell," Trigwell said. "Knock yourself out."

Jack started away.

"Pearl—"

Jack turned back.

"You'll be needing this."

Trigwell tossed over his flashlight. Jack caught it with a grateful nod and began searching.

If his father had fled down the stairs, Jack reasoned, it was likely he had continued moving in the same direction. That allowed Jack to concentrate on the part of the factory facing the spot where Reaper had gone down. Jack combed row after row of the cobwebbed machines. Nothing turned up. He doubled back and did it again and again. As the hours passed, cops came and went. Salazar and Reaper were taken out on gurneys.

Jack kept searching.

He was on his twenty-third pass when he caught something in the beam of his flashlight: a reddish-brown speck on the ground. Jack got down on his hands and knees to examine it. Could it be blood? If so, Jack told himself, it was too far away from where Reaper and Salazar had been killed to belong to either of them.

Encouraged, Jack crawled along on all fours, strafing the ground with the flashlight, until he found another speck. Then another. He followed the trail to an open drain hole behind one of the machines.

"Over here!" Jack shouted. "Hurry!"

Cops came running. So did Trigwell. Jack showed him a large dried smear on the edge of the drain hole. There was no need for a serologist or luminol spray to confirm it was blood.

"I'll need a rope," Jack said.

Moments later he was lowered into the drainage chute while Trigwell and his team held the other end of the rope. Jack dropped into the tunnel below. It was pitch black. The stench made him clamp his hand over his nose. He searched the area with the flashlight but there was no sign of his father and no more blood trail, nothing but a stream of sewer water trickling down the tunnel.

"Joe!"

Nothing.

"Joseph Pearl!"

Nothing.

"Dad!" Jack yelled. "Dad!"

It had been a long time since Jack had called him that. His voice echoed in the darkness.

No answer.

Jack set off in the direction the water was flowing.

At first he moved cautiously, shining his light in all directions while continuing to shout for his father. But soon a primal urgency took over and Jack broke into a run.

In the distance he saw a thread of light radiating down from the ceiling of the tunnel. At the base of the light shaft Jack could make out something lying in the shallow water, teeming with movement. When he shined his flashlight on it, dozens of red eyes glowed, a horde of rats feeding on the body of a man. The rats scattered as Jack tore down the tunnel to the man who was sprawled face down, handcuffed and covered in blood, his flesh ripped to shreds where the rats had gotten to him.

Jack turned the man over.

It was Joseph Pearl.

"Dad!"

Jack checked for a pulse but couldn't feel one.

"Dad, it's me..."

Pearl remained lifeless.

"No, please..."

Tears filled Jack's eyes.

"You can't...not now..."

He shook his father angrily.

"Don't you dare fucking die on me!"

Something moved ever so slightly.

One of Pearl's bloodied fingers.

Jack laughed and cried with relief. As he cradled his father in his arms, he heard voices echoing down the passageway and saw the crisscross of flashlights approaching.

Jack held his father close.

"It's over," he said. "Stay with me, Dad. You're going to be okay."

56

JACK

J oseph Pearl lay in a coma.

In addition to suffering from dehydration and hypo-
thermia, he had gone into hypovolaemic shock from
the countless rat bites. Jack also learned, when the
philosopher's medical history was checked, that he had
a rare but treatable cancer at the base of his spine for
which he had recently undergone surgery. Perhaps that
was the reason his old man had called out of the blue,
Jack thought, the matter he had wanted to discuss over
lunch. Jack wondered if he would ever know.

As the doctors came and went, they expressed cautious optimism. But Jack could hear what they weren't
saying. His father's condition was grave. There was a
good chance he wouldn't make it.

For two days and nights Jack sat by his side with
only occasional naps and trips to the hospital cafeteria
where he called Mrs. Woo. Thankfully, the busboy from

the coffee shop had brought Trouser to Jack's building as asked. Mrs. Woo reassured Jack that his faithful roommate was safe and sound in her care and getting along fine with Muffin and Fu.

On the third day a small package arrived at the hospital, a copy of Joseph Pearl's book that Jack had ordered to replace the one he had lost with his Wagoneer. There was only one thing missing, the hand-written inscription. One more reason why his father had to pull through. When he did, Jack would get him to write the words again: FOR JACK, LOVE DAD.

Jack considered the clay horse on the cover and the droll title. He cracked open the book. It was incomprehensible. For several hours Jack tried to find the mysterious Part Three that Claire had alluded to. He finally gave up. But as he closed the book, Jack realized the search had helped him get clear on something else: his own philosophy.

Part One: You don't have to forget to forgive.

Part Two: Every day above ground is a good day.

Part Three: When in doubt, bluff.

Sometime later Jack was drifting off when he heard a blip change on one of the monitors. He spun around to see his father stirring. Jack darted to his side.

"Dad..."

Pearl's eyes blinked open. For several seconds he appeared confused. Then his lips trembled with recognition.

"Jack..."

It was little more than a whisper.

"Don't talk," Jack said.

Clarity came to Pearl's eyes, an understanding of what must have happened for him to be there, alive. He nodded.

"Thank you..."

He took Jack's hand weakly in his.

"Thank you, son..."

That was all he said before his eyes closed again.

For Jack, that was more than enough.

57

JACK

The first person Jack called with the good news was Franco who was thrilled to hear that Joseph Pearl was going to be okay. When Franco suggested they grab some dinner to celebrate, Jack said he was beat and would have to take a rain check but Franco wouldn't hear of it. He sang the praises of a new steak joint in Los Feliz where he lived and told Jack to pick him up at eight.

The porch lights were on to greet Jack as he pulled up to Franco's place, a modest craftsman house with a well-tended yard. Jack climbed out of the Ford Focus he had rented until he could get around to buying another car. There were storm clouds in the distance. It had been awhile since the last good downpour. The city always looked better afterwards. Renewed. At least for a while.

Jack walked up to the front door. Hanging over the bell was a dog made of Legos which one of Franco's three daughters had given to him years ago for Father's Day. In the dog's mouth was a sign in the shape of a bone that read:

PEACE TO ALL WHO ENTER HERE

Jack rang the bell. Something about its jingle reminded him of the one at Henry's Pawn Shop. After a moment, the door opened to reveal Franco with a phone to his ear, wearing a ridiculously loud Hawaiian shirt.

"There he is," Franco said. "The man of the hour!"

Franco pointed to the phone with a comical, exaggerated 'it's the boss' gesture to Jack while he finished up his call.

"Babe, I want to hear about your geraniums, I really do, but Jack just got here. Yeah, I'll tell him. Kiss the girls. I love you too."

Franco hung up.

"Kate says to give you a big hug but I better not. You know how jealous she gets."

Jack grinned.

"Where is she?"

"Took the kids back east to Vermont, the family farm, to visit her mom."

"Nice," Jack said.

"She loves it there. So do I. Matter of fact, we've been discussing it a lot lately. Good schools. Fresh air. A place where you know your neighbors. And the best part? It's safe."

Jack gave Franco a second look.

"Wait. Don't tell me you're thinking of moving?"

"Actually, yeah, for a while now," Franco said. "Ever since Kate's dad passed away and left us a little money. 'Course I'd miss my friends like you. And the job. Chasing bad guys. But I'm sure I'll find something to do."

"So when is this happening?" Jack said.

"Pretty soon, we're hoping. Next few months. Soon as we can sell the house and tie things up here."

"Wow. That's great, Franco. Really. I'm happy for you! Gives us one more thing to celebrate."

"New beginnings," Franco said. "For both of us."

He gave Jack a friendly punch in the arm and grabbed his biker jacket. As Franco pulled out his keys to lock the front door, Jack caught a flash of gold on his wrist: a simple, elegant watch with a black leather strap.

"Haven't seen that before," Jack said. "Present from Kate?"

"What? Oh, this," Franco said. "Uh, yeah. Hey, I'm telling you, man, you're gonna love the steaks at this place."

Franco turned his wrist to pull down his sleeve, revealing the face of the watch before it disappeared from view.

It was a Patek Philippe Calatrava.

A chill went through Jack.

"Jack, you okay?"

Jack stared at Franco, speechless.

"You look pale," Franco said. "Something wrong?"

Jack forced a smile.

"No."

"You sure?"

"Yeah," Jack said. "Yeah, I'm fine."

Franco nodded.

"Okay," he said. "Good."

He locked the door.

As the storm clouds rolled in, they took the long walk back to Jack's car.

ABOUT THE AUTHOR

Paul Margolis is an award-winning screenwriter and producer who has worked extensively in both film and television. He lives in Los Angeles with his wife and three daughters.

Contact the author:
E-mail: paulmargolisauthor@gmail.com
Twitter: @PaulMargolis1
Facebook: Facebook.com/PaulMargolisAuthor
www.PaulMargolisauthor.com